In this book, you will find words of wisdom, sound guidance, motivation, and humor from more than 50 kind and generous people who agreed to be interviewed and quoted. They are, all of them, shining examples of how we can become successful, both professionally and personally. The advice they share throughout the book will give you an inspirational look at the endless possibilities of the human mind and spirit, and show you how to make the best of these possibilities work for you in real-life, practical situations. Some of those included in the book are:

- ◆ *Bill Bradley,* U.S. Senator, Olympic Gold Medalist, and two-time NBA Champion
- ◆ *Bruce Jenner,* Olympic Gold Medalist
- ◆ *Ann Compton,* ABC News White House Correspondent
- ◆ *Mary Matalin,* political consultant and television host
- ◆ *T. Boone Pickens, Jr.,* founder and chairman of Mesa Petroleum
- ◆ *Bill Clements, Jr.,* two-time governor of Texas and founder of SEDCO, Inc. (one of the world's largest drilling contractors)
- ◆ *Fred Plum, M.D.,* professor & chairman, department of neurology, New York Hospital Cornell Medical Center
- ◆ *Arthur Winter, M.D.,* neurosurgeon, director of New Jersey Neurological Institute and author of *Build Your Brain Power*
- ◆ *Dr. Frank Field,* CBS weathercaster and senior health and science editor

continued . . .

- ◆ ***Dominick Purpura, M.D.,*** head of Albert Einstein School of Medicine and president of the International Brain Research Organization
- ◆ ***Fred Epstein, M.D.,*** professor and director of the division of pediatric neurosurgery at New York University Medical Center
- ◆ ***Arthur Fry,*** inventor of the *Post-it* notes
- ◆ ***The Amazing Kreskin,*** dramatizes the unusual abilities of the human mind
- ◆ ***Lt. Colonel Dennis Krembel,*** command pilot with Operation Desert Storm
- ◆ ***Franco Harris,*** former Pittsburgh Steeler, 1990 Hall of Famer, and now with Super Bakery, Inc.
- ◆ ***Shannon Briggs,*** heavyweight boxer, with a record of 20–0
- ◆ ***Teddy Atlas,*** boxing trainer of Shannon Briggs, Mike Tyson, Michael Moore
- ◆ ***Mary Kay Ash,*** founder of Mary Kay Cosmetics
- ◆ ***Niall Mackenzie,*** top Grand Prix motorcycle racer
- ◆ ***Joe Montgomery,*** founder and president of Cannondale Corporation

"Successful people travel different roads to achieve success. This book illustrates those differences. It was not written about a single road or a single author's opinion. It is about a multitude of roads to success. And the question 'How did they do it?' is answered a hundred different ways.

"Barry Farber has achieved his own success with this publication. It is far beyond what we would call a 'diamond in the rough.' It's a polished gem."
—DEBRA J. SIECKMAN, director, Sales Development, Allied Van Lines

"Great reading! Anyone who has a desire to achieve something in this world should read this book . . . quick-reading and enjoyable."
—CHANDRAN RAJARATNAM, president and CEO, Gestetner Corporation

"Farber has masterfully woven the success factors of top producing people into chapter after chapter after chapter of his new book."
—PHILIP W. DEZAN, vice-president, Training and Education, Weichert Realtors

"This book gives its readers a pathway for life's journey, proving that there is a true leader within each of us. Whatever your occupation is, you can do better. Barry Farber has convinced me that everybody is a 'diamond in the rough.' "
—RICHARD J. LUISI, southeast area vice-president, Electrolux Corporation

"Seldom, if ever, has an author been able to reveal the keys to success in a manner that is so easily understood. . . . Every person who is concerned with achieving success in their business, or even their own personal lives, should read every page of this book."
—THOMAS B. WILLIAMS, vice-president, National Sales Manager, F. Schumacher and Co.

DIAMOND
in the
ROUGH

———◦•◦———

BARRY J. FARBER

BERKLEY BOOKS, NEW YORK

DIAMOND IN THE ROUGH

A Berkley Book / published by arrangement with
the author

PRINTING HISTORY
Berkley trade edition / May 1995

ISBN: 0-425-14733-9

PRINTED IN THE UNITED STATES OF AMERICA

10   9   8

DEDICATED TO:

Allison, Hallie and Jordan,
my true secrets to success and happiness

ACKNOWLEDGMENTS

Special thanks:

To Jeff Herman, the best agent in the biz. Nobody practices the art of "giving back" the way he does. He's truly one of a kind.

To Hillary Cige, for all her support and encouragement throughout this project.

To all of the people who so graciously agreed to be interviewed for this book, who gave their time and their ideas, who embody not only the reality, but the spirit, of success.

With extreme gratitude to all the people who helped arrange the logistics of all the interviews: Tom Armstrong, Ron Asinari, Patrick B. Ball, Matt Bell, Sally Buford, Paul M. Cohen, Robert Crowningshield, Don Franklin, Jeff Giniger, Susan Giniger, Anne Gooch, Eric Hauser, Stewart Hodson, Pat Jones, Barbara Kennedy, David Kessler, Harold Kwait, Jeffrey Lane, Robert Lefkon, John McLain, Dan Noyes, Harry Rhoads, Jay Roser, Dr. David Schneider, Bob Seigel, Adam Smallman, Bernard L. Swain, Sgt. Tammy VanDame, Don Wallace, Shirley Warren, and Robert Zimmerman.

And a grateful acknowledgment to Michael Roth, Sy Farber, and Ruth Gardner for their invaluable feedback.

And very special thanks to Sharyn Kolberg:

For all your help and passionate writing, which consistently exceeded every expectation. You're a valued friend, an expert listener, and your performance was flawless.

TO MY MENTORS, WHO HAVE MEANT SO MUCH TO ME

Mom and Dad, for their unconditional love, support, and guidance;

D.M. and D.P., for always being there to listen and share their love;

Marc Roberts, for mass doses of energy and inspiration and lessons on persistence that will never be forgotten;

Adolph J. Caprioli, for opening my mind to a thirst for learning;

Randy Gotthilf, for sharing his valuable knowledge and experience that has paid off down the road;

Steve Rauschkolb, for his demonstration of excellence in every endeavor;

Beverly Hyman, whose teachings live on forever; and

Earl Nightingale, for sharing "the strangest secret."

CONTENTS

Chapter Three
"BUFFETED STONES":
THOSE WHO KNOW FAILURE KNOW SUCCESS
51

Chapter Four
SHINING EXAMPLES:
SEEKING OUT POSITIVE ROLE MODELS
75

Chapter Five
DIAMOND MINDS:
THE INCREDIBLE POWERS OF THE HUMAN BRAIN
98

Chapter Six

THE CUTTING EDGE:
LEARNING HOW WE LEARN
116

Chapter Seven

CUTTING TO THE CORE OF THE MATTER:
FINDING THE PASSION FOR WHAT YOU DO
142

FOREWORD
BY CHARLES GARFIELD

For over twenty years now, I have been fascinated by, and have spent my life studying, peak performers—who they are and how they do what they do. What I've discovered over the years is that peak performers can be found everywhere, in every environment and every profession. They are not extraordinary people, although many have lived extraordinary lives. Many more have lived lives of quiet excellence.

All have particular qualities in common. These are not qualities you inherit through genes or social status; rather you develop them through education, through hard work, and through watching peak performers who have gone before you.

That's why *Diamond in the Rough* is such an effective encyclopedia of success. It not only contains the characteristics all peak performers cultivate and exhibit, but it also shows you how to put these qualities to work—with real-world, real-life practical applicability.

And then, of course, there are the models of success, the high achievers profiled in this book who exemplify America's best and brightest. I was pleased and delighted to read the information and insights this diverse group add to the book—people who are the very embodiment of the peak performers I have studied and admired all these years.

Reading this book should prove to be both an inspiration and a practical education for anyone who is interested in improving the quality of his or her life. It's definitely a jewel of a book.

INTRODUCTION

Looking for adventure? Want to go on a treasure hunt that, in the end, will reward you with the most valuable, precious jewel you'll ever find? If you do, turn the pages of this book. Read them carefully. Take notes. Fill in the blanks. Follow the MAPs. When you have finished, you'll find that the treasure has been in your own backyard all along. For that precious stone, that diamond in the rough waiting for its chance to shine, is you.

No matter where you are in life, whether you're a student or a CEO, there are probably some areas of your life with which you are unsatisfied. The purpose of this book is to help you discover and unlock your hidden potential, to get the most out of the one life you have to live, to love what you do and do what you love.

It is possible, you know. Nine out of ten people, when asked why they go to work every day, answer, "to pay the bills," "to earn the rent money," "to put food on the table." All important responsibilities, but nothing to get passionate about. I wanted to find out what makes that tenth person want to go to work. I know that there are people out there (myself included) who love what they do, who do much more than pay the rent and put food on the table—who live with energy, enthusiasm, and passion.

Therefore, this book contains interviews with highly successful people from all walks of life who have proven that ordinary people can develop their potential and achieve extraordinary success.

Who are these people? Did they start out as the "shining diamonds" we now see, or were they once unpolished stones hidden among the rubble? How have they been able to succeed where others have failed? Is it in their genes? Is it in their stars? Or is it in their attitudes, and their willingness to go that extra mile? And most importantly, is success possible for only a special few, or is it an attainable goal for anyone willing to try?

The answers in this book came directly from the people who ought to know: people who are high achievers in their chosen fields. Some have instantly recognizable names, some do not. Success and fame do not necessarily go hand in hand. The information is based on interviews I conducted with more than fifty men and women who, through their own efforts and energies, were able to tap into their potential and are living the lives they love.

I also wanted to find out where that potential originates—how the brain works, how we learn, how we process information, and how this knowledge can enhance our lives. So I interviewed top scientists and psychologists from such prestigious organizations as the Cornell University Department of Neurology and Neuroscience, the National Academy of Sciences Committee on Techniques for the Enhancement of Human Performance, the National Foundation for Brain Research, the National Institute of Mental Health, and the International Brain Research Organization.

This book is meant to be an encyclopedia of success. Reading through the chapters you will find fascinating information on the human mind and how it works, as well as how the real-world achievements of peak performers parallel the theories and techniques outlined by the expert scientists and psychologists. You'll learn about:

♦ The power of positive thinking. An old cliché that happens to be true: It's not what happens to you that counts as much as how you react to what happens. All successful people are realistic optimists.
♦ Effort. The only way to get something you want is to put in the effort required to get it. There are no easy answers, no get-rich-quick schemes or scams.

♦ Failure. One of the most common aspects of success is the ability—and the willingness—to accept the challenges failure presents.

♦ Mentors. Learning to ask for help and support, and finding resources for getting the help you need.

♦ Brain power. No matter who else we may find for love and support, in the end it's our own incredible mind that brings us through the good and the bad, the success and the failure.

♦ The learning process. Failure isn't failure as long as we learn from it. Learning how we learn, from infancy to adulthood, can teach us how to think in ways that foster success—how to learn new skills more effectively, how to improve our memory, and how to think creatively.

♦ The passionate pursuit. Finding the passion in our lives by using our past accomplishments and our dreams of the future to discover what it is we'd love to do.

♦ Setting goals. How to turn passion into practical reality.

♦ Giving back to others. There are many different viewpoints, opinions, and ideas gathered in this book. However, there was one thought, expressed in one way or another, by every single person interviewed: The most treasured aspect of being successful is that it enables you to help others achieve the same.

This book is the compilation and distillation of scientific research, real-life success stories, and interactive action plans. It is meant to be a workbook, not a theoretical treatise. Mark it up. Rewrite important points in your own words. Find the person (or persons) whose story you identify with, and follow his or her advice. This is your life, and the power to be the best lies within you.

Each of us is a diamond in the rough.

No matter where we come from, no matter how "unpolished," how imperfect, how deeply buried our potential may be, it is always possible to make that hidden beauty shine through. It takes work to make a diamond shine, and it takes care and effort to become the people we want to be. It is never too late or too soon to start that adventure, to take the first step on the road to success. *Diamond in the Rough* is designed to make that journey a little easier.

Chapter One

SHINING THROUGH WITH
A POSITIVE ATTITUDE:
THE BEAM TO SELF-ESTEEM

"Before you can define success, you need to look at the whole person and consider his personal life, his professional life and his spiritual life. Does the person apply himself one hundred percent? Does the person utilize the talents that God has given him to the best of his ability? If he uses his God-given talent as best he can, I would call him a very successful person."

—LT. COL. DENNIS KREMBEL, USAF

"Success means that you have maximized the potential that God gave you for excellence."

—SENATOR BILL BRADLEY

This book is about potential.

We all have it. We all start out as unformed, unpolished gems, diamonds in the rough. Those who are successful discover the gem within themselves, mine their own potential, and capitalize on their inner beauty and value.

It takes art, skill, and concentrated effort for a person to take a diamond, which comes from the remote depths of the earth, to recognize its potential, and to cut and shape it into a precious stone. It also takes art, skill, and concentrated effort to recognize your own potential, which comes from deep within your soul, and cut and shape it into its most rewarding and fulfilling form.

This book will show you how to discover your own potential, and how to use it to achieve success in your life and in your work. And it all begins with how you think about yourself, your life, and your work.

Why is it that two people of equal talent and ability don't always achieve equal success? How come people in such diverse areas as athletics, business, industrial supply, publishing, science, television news, and politics can rise above rejection, hardship, and failure? What is the common denominator that puts these people in the category called "successful"?

The strongest link between all these people is summed up in one word—attitude. Attitude is defined as the mental position you take regarding a fact or a state. Suppose you get cut from the basketball team, fired from your job, or turned down for a date. What is your mental position toward these facts? Are you devastated? Destroyed? Or determined to learn whatever you can from it and move on?

You're entitled to your emotions. Emotions are neither positive nor negative. It isn't "bad" to feel fear, anger, or depression. Emotions make us human, but they can have a negative influence if we let them deter us from moving forward. No one expects that mistakes and disappointments will not have an effect on you. You may be sad, hurt, or depressed. It's what happens to your attitude when you experience these emotions that counts. It's your mental position, your attitude toward any incident, that determines whether it will scar you for life or serve as a lesson and a pathway to other opportunities.

The most successful people are able to maintain a positive mental position even when adversity strikes. They allow themselves to experience their emotions, work through them, and then go on with their lives; they know that it's necessary to jump the hurdles to finish the course.

"Your living is determined not so much by what life brings to you as by the attitude you bring to life; not so much by what happens as by the way your mind looks at what happens."

—JOHN HOMER MILLER

THE ATTITUDE OF SUCCESS

There are some people—ordinary people—who have harnessed the incredible power of a positive mental attitude to help them achieve extraordinary success. More than fifty of these people were interviewed for this book. Not all of them are famous. Not all of them are wealthy. Not all of them have clout, status, or live in the fast lane; yet they all have attained success.

As you continue to read this book, you will come across stories of people who were able to successfully discover and develop their own passion, talents, and gifts, sometimes despite tremendous obstacles. These stories, and these high achievers' insights, advice, and suggestions are meant to show that anyone who sets his or her mind to it can be successful.

You'll also find information from some of the top scientists in the country—neurologists, neuroscientists, psychologists—who are not only top achievers themselves, but who are on the cutting edge of research into how the mind works and how we can help it work more effectively. There are also experts in the fields of motivation, self-esteem, and peak performance. All of these people have based their research on studies of hundreds of other successful people. The coming chapters, then, are filled with the cumulative knowledge of thousands of people interviewed by the experts who were interviewed for this book.

This was my dream when I started out to write this book. I've been involved in sales training and personal development for almost twenty years. All during that time, I have looked up to those who have attained success before me, admired and emulated their techniques, and tried to apply these techniques to my own career—and life.

A few years ago I interviewed over one hundred of the most successful salespeople, sales managers, sales trainers, and top management in the country and put their ideas and techniques together in a book called *State of the Art Selling*. It became obvious while talking with these sales superstars that the concepts they espoused—setting goals, developing a positive attitude, dealing with failure and rejection—had a much more universal application than selling the most vacuum cleaners or closing the biggest sales.

These people were talking about success. Their ideas were not abstract theories developed through years of psychological analysis. These were insights and practical tools developed from years of experience living in the real world.

So my dream became to interview successful people in all walks of life to get their insights and suggestions. You will find many different viewpoints in this book. That's because there is no one way to success. If you read one person's story and don't think his or her ideas will work for you, read on. You'll find someone else's ideas will give you the inspiration and motivation you're looking for.

COMMON THREADS

You won't find any magical answers. There is no wizard to grant your wishes, no clearly demarcated yellow-brick road you can follow that will lead you and all others who walk along it directly to the land of Oz, to fame and fortune. Not one of the high achievers interviewed took the same path as any other. They did, however, have several traits in common:

♦ **They have healthy positive attitudes.** They believe that the right attitude can often mean the difference between success and failure. They expect things to turn out well and have confidence in their own abilities to make that happen.

♦ **They take action.** If high achievers desire a particular outcome, they will put everything they have into its realization. They don't expect to be handed anything on a silver platter; they don't even begin a project unless they know they're willing to put in the effort it will take to make it successful. They work hard because they know that nothing worthwhile is ever achieved without effort.

♦ **They learn from failure and disappointment.** They welcome problems as opportunities to use their creative energies, and they look upon even the largest of obstacles as challenges to be met and savored. They are not defeated by rejection. They get discouraged and depressed like everyone else, but they quickly bounce back and redouble their effort and resolve. No one wants to fail, but high achievers accept failure as a part of life, and know that there is a lesson to be learned in every setback.

♦ **They surround themselves with positive ideas and role models.** High achievers are constantly looking to improve themselves. They never assume that just because they have reached a certain level of success they can stop learning. They might not have a college education or even a high school diploma, but they place a high value on continuing their education. They study their craft, their industry, their skills, their hobbies. They read constantly, share ideas with others in their industry, and seek out mentors whose wisdom and experience can help them achieve their goals and desires.

♦ **They are passionate about what they do.** It's possible to become famous and/or wealthy doing something you hate. But does that equal success? No one in this book thinks so. Asked ''What is the secret to your success?'', every person interviewed answered that they had found something they loved to do.

Some people found their passion very early in life; others wandered around from here to there until they discovered their life's work. But all of them eventually found vocations they truly loved. And because of that, all of them have gone through life with the enthusiasm and energy that passion produces. Once each person discovered his or her passion in life, it became like a magnet, drawing them inevitably closer to success.

◆ **They set goals.** They focus on what they want to achieve, establish priorities, and know what they have to do in order to keep moving forward. Their plans are flexible enough to allow for the unexpected, but they always have a specific destination in mind. Goals provide them with purpose and allow them to wake up each morning energized and looking forward to the tasks they know must be accomplished that day.

◆ **They feel a joyful obligation to give back to others.** They are grateful for what they have been able to achieve, and are happy to help others do the same. They know that by elevating someone else's success, they elevate their own. They are competitive but not cutthroat. They have integrity and compassion and a desire to make a meaningful contribution to their profession, their community and their world. They agree with William H. Danforth who more than seventy years ago wrote in his inspirational book *I Dare You!* "Catch a passion for helping others and a richer life will come back to you."

You will find many books and magazine articles that tell you how high achievers are different from the rest of us. This book, however, is a study of how much these people are just like everyone else. The differences we see in them can be duplicated by anyone willing to study what they have to say, follow their examples, and apply their advice and suggestions to their own lives.

The chapters that follow are deeper explorations of each of these facets of success. One is not more important than any other; it's the combination of all these elements that is the recipe for peak performance. It's a recipe anyone can follow.

Complete the action plans at the end of each chapter to help you get started. They're not difficult, but they can't be completed simply by thinking about them. They require that you take action. Dare yourself to "just do it." Your rewards will be greater than you'll ever imagine.

ENTHUSIASM: THE GREAT EQUALIZER

How are high achievers able to maintain positive mental attitudes? How do they keep their enthusiasm for life going day after day?

Enthusiasm comes from the Greek word "entheos," which means "the god within." Isn't that an apt description? Think back to times when you've been enthusiastic about something. Didn't it make you feel good? Empowered? Spirited? As if the "god within" was giving your life a lift and a shine?

Enthusiasm is the outward manifestation of our inner passion. It's an ardor, a zeal for living that buoys our spirit and gives us energy. Enthusiasm can often carry us far beyond any skill or talent we may have. In many instances, we can supersede our deficiencies by turning on an engine of enthusiasm, either physical or mental.

Two elements are essential to foster enthusiasm:

♦ Learning. The thirst for knowledge should never be quenched; rather, it should build as you move toward your goals. Children have a natural enthusiasm for learning, which can atrophy during years in an uninspiring educational environment. Rekindling that innate curiosity can remind us that the more we know about something we love, the more enthusiastic we become about knowing more.

♦ Accomplishment. Keeping our goals in sight, literally and figuratively, is like coal to the fire of enthusiasm. Enthusiasm builds with the accomplishment of every task; seeing the results of our efforts builds up a reserve of enthusiasm, which can be applied to the next task in line. Any proof of our accomplishment—something written, something built, an award, a simple thank you—all motivate us to move on.

A POSITIVE ATTITUDE: GETTING OUT
FROM UNDER THE OLD CLICHÉ

It's sometimes difficult to talk about a positive attitude because it has become so much of a cliché in our society. We commonly hold that people who espouse positive attitudes are obnoxiously perky, and possibly oblivious to the tribulations of the real world. We don't really believe that "positive thinking" contributes to success; we believe that those people who achieve are somehow different from us—smarter, richer, luckier.

Many people feel they're not successful because they don't have a God-given talent in a certain area. What they don't realize is that talent is meaningless without the proper attitude behind it. They also fail to recognize that a positive attitude can take many forms and has many names, including the "three D's": discipline, desire, and dedication.

Ask boxing trainer Teddy Atlas about the D for discipline. Atlas, who's trained top fighters including Mike Tyson, looks for more than talent when he's evaluating young fighters.

"If somebody asks me which quality or asset I would choose for a fighter, most people would think that it's physical talent like speed or power," he says. "The most important quality that a fighter can have, if I have to pick one, is discipline. We can always develop talent. But you have to understand that talent won't make for anything more than a good show on the heavy bag if the fighter doesn't have the discipline and the emotional control to execute it under pressure. Otherwise, the talent means nothing."

The second D stands for desire—the attitude that says, "I'm committed to doing and being my best at all times." This is the attitude that is sought out by people in leadership positions, such as Lt. Col. Dennis Krembel of the United States Air Force. In order to be an effective leader, Krembel must, of course, maintain his own positive attitude. But as a squadron commander and flight instructor, he must also seek out the "best of the best" for the defense of our country.

When asked what he looks for in a future "top gun," Krembel answered, ". . . one thing I always look for is desire. In many cases, I'll even take desire over talent. I'm looking for a person who wants to do the best he can with the talent he has. If he or she puts forth one hundred percent effort, that's what I want.

"All of the people I work with are committed and patriotic; they've chosen to make great sacrifices to be in the military. But if I look at one person who's got the talent, and at another person who's got the desire . . . I'll take the person who's willing to go that extra measure. . . . I'll probably invest more time with that person, because I know he's going to go longer and farther in all the things that we need to make a fighter squadron successful."

Discipline and desire are two examples of how a positive attitude can manifest itself, and are just part of what makes a champion boxer or a successful squadron. The third *D* represents dedication: a willingness to do whatever it takes to get the job done. There is a saying, Successful people do the things that unsuccessful people don't like to do. This could be the motto of Mary Matalin, television commentator and deputy campaign manager for President George Bush during the 1992 campaign. Matalin is always willing to do whatever is necessary to make her campaign successful and her candidate a winner. She is energetic, opinionated, sharp-tongued, and quick-witted, and she has a definite "let's-do-it-now" attitude towards life. She has been active in campaign and party politics since college, starting at the grass-roots level in local and statewide campaigns in her native Illinois. In her earliest campaigns, she brought people lunches, made copies, did all the typing, ran errands—even when those weren't her jobs. But for her, it was the only way to learn the business.

"A lot of kids resent answering the phone; they think it is a meaningless task," she says. "But the only way that you understand how the game of politics is played, who the players are, how fast-paced it is, and how to coordinate fifty spinning plates is to answer the phone. And it's not just, 'Hi. This is Mary Matalin's office, can I take a message.' During the campaign, there were days where I got four hundred calls. The person on the phone has to be able to take care of 50 or 60 percent of those calls and not bother me with them. It amazes me that nobody wants to do that.''

Matalin, who is not shy about voicing her opinion, is not afraid to take a controversial stand. One of those is that women are often too sensitive about things that go on in the workplace. ''I say to women specifically, don't think that every man is out to subjugate you, humiliate you, denigrate you, or harass you. Men . . . are being tempered by our increasing presence in the workforce, but they sort of speak a different language. I've always found it better for my successes to learn the system and learn the language. If I see things a different way, I try to say it in their language first. Men and women communicate differently. . . . My point is, don't think that if they don't respond favorably to your first idea, that there's something sexist about it.''

But Matalin doesn't think women are the only ones who need a change in attitude. She says that most recent college graduates ''. . . have been infused with the notion that they can start at mid or top management, that they can go in and be cocky and ask for the moon. It doesn't work that way in politics. The cliché notion that you start out licking envelopes is true.

''Grunt work is not demeaning. Start out by being the person who always jumps up to get the coffee, or says 'I'll run down to the White House to pick up that package.' People on the campaign respond to staffers and volunteers who just want to get the job done. And they start giving them more jobs. . . . You've got to put in your time.

''People feel so unnecessarily, inadvertently slighted or cut out . . . Who goes to what meeting, which office is where, who's going to get what kind of nameplate—all these things are irrelevant. It's just *effort and attitude* that count.''

''Men differ less in their abilities than in the degree to which they use them.''

—CHARLES DARWIN

ACCEPTING THE POWER OF OUR SELF-IMAGE

Effort and attitude—it is for the apparent lack of these two traits that many a kingdom is lost. Perhaps that is because these traits are not very effective unless they are built upon a strong foundation—one that starts with a belief in yourself and your ability to be the best that you can be in any circumstance.

Our minds, our thoughts, our attitudes, are the power centers of our lives. In many ways this is a simple concept, yet its awesome truth is sometimes difficult to grasp. It can be summed up in a phrase I heard on an audio tape by an inspirational man named Earl Nightingale, who read it in a book by Napoleon Hill, who probably got it from someone else. This phrase has changed people's lives, and it has had more influence on the way I think about success than any other quote I've ever heard: *You become what you think about.* Each of us is our own self-fulfilling prophecy.

"Sometime in our life we have to assume responsibility for ourselves," says internationally known management consultant Beverly Hyman. "I have a pet phrase that I use, which is 'you become the author of yourself.' If you can look at your whole life, what you were given and what you added to it, then you take it into your own hands and say, 'this is the genetic endowment I have been given, but at this point I own my own life. I author my life. I'm writing the chapters.' So often I hear people say, 'this person did this to me, that person did that to me.' We do it to ourselves. As Shakespeare said, 'Things are not as they are, but as *we* are.' "

If you believe you're a "winner," you are. If you believe you're a "loser," you are (until you change your belief). It's your belief that makes the difference. Even the best of our scientists today cannot explain exactly how this works—but it does. All of the people interviewed for this book can attest to that. They don't go around saying (or thinking) "I'm so wonderful. I can do anything I want, just because I'm the great, great me." But they believe in their ability to achieve. They're infused with desire, discipline, and dedication, and appreciate the values of these attributes.

Our society often makes it difficult to accept the good things about ourselves. We've been taught that thinking well of ourselves will turn us into conceited egomaniacs. Most of us have a difficult time accepting the praise from others that could help us build our self-esteem.

"A long time ago someone taught me that when I get a compliment I shouldn't deny it, I should say thank you—and try to feel it," says Bev Hyman. "I also think that praise strikes to the core, in terms of self-esteem, of our own values. When someone is praising us, what's coming into play is what is of value. I know for myself I want desperately to be praised for certain specific things that I hold dear, that I value. You could praise me all day long about the things that I don't value and it would be meaningless.

"I remember a moment I had when praise was particularly sweet. Clearly what I value is the intellect. When I started my doctoral program it wasn't so much to study a discipline as it was to find a teacher. I selected this particular program because the man I wanted to be my teacher headed it up. I studied with him for four years and he had a huge impact on the way in which I think. But at first, he was suspicious of me because I "was too good looking." He was prejudiced against good-looking women, he didn't think they were very smart. When I went in to have my evaluation on my doctoral candidacy exam, I sat down and he said 'I read your exam and I owe you an apology. You're not a student. You're a scholar.' I almost fell off my chair. He was giving me praise in the area which I valued most."

We often use praise from others to confirm our worth. We must be careful, however, not to empower people to disconfirm us. Just as we need to learn to accept praise, we need to reject criticism that is not constructive or is destructive to our self-esteem. Sometimes that criticism comes from the worst possible source—ourselves.

"We all have within us an inner critic, an inner voice, negative self-talk," says Hyman. "When someone gives you a compliment, stop, listen to what they say, take a deep breath, just like you're inhaling the aroma of a fine wine or soup cooking, and inhale all the way down to your feet. Repeat what they said to you in your own voice. Then and only then say thank you.''

THE CHEMISTRY OF CONFIDENCE

I once heard a sports trainer talk about what makes an athlete great and he used the phrase ''the chemistry of confidence.'' I'm sure that this chemistry actually exists, that by believing in ourselves we create a positive chemical-neurological reaction, which in turn creates and attracts other positive reactions, which creates further reactions. When this chain of positive reactions is strong enough, even mistakes, failures, and disappointments cannot break it.

To forge the first links in this chain of self-belief, we must be willing to accept who we really are. We need to give ourselves credit for and capitalize on the strengths we already possess. At the same time, we can acknowledge our weaknesses, or shortcomings, and our hang-ups and work to get beyond them. We can learn to love ourselves as interesting, imperfect human beings.

I know this isn't the first time you've heard that. You probably think that the only people who go around telling people to love themselves are gurus and new-agers. You might be surprised to hear these words coming from the mouth of a stocky, feisty former Israeli army officer who became the founder and president of Remarkable Products, this country's largest supplier of laminated calendars and related office products. Jack Lehav, ''born the day Israel was born as a country,'' grew up with the emotions of ''a small country surrounded for many years by hostile countries.'' Even growing up in that uncertain atmosphere, Lehav learned to maintain a positive attitude.

''You learn from old people the good things,'' says Lehav. ''My grandmother told me you always have to like the face you see in the mirror. Fall in love with yourself. . . . Be convinced that you are the best. Every morning when I stand in front of the mirror I look at my face, I wink, and I go out for the day. . . . I deliver a message to myself. 'Today you are going to make it.'

"You have to believe in what you do. I would paraphrase it in the most simple and beautiful way: Some people are born to be a fifty-gallon barrel and some are born to be a ten-gallon barrel. If you are one of those born to be a ten-gallon barrel, make sure you fill up those ten gallons. Don't be ten gallons in a fifty-gallon barrel."

SURROUNDING YOURSELF WITH MARKERS OF SUCCESS

I have the word *attitude* taped right onto my bathroom mirror to remind me first thing in the morning that my own thoughts and beliefs can shape the whole day ahead of me. It always amazes me that my mood can shape the outcome of the entire day, but it's true. I don't expect that having a positive attitude will always make things turn out right. Or even that I will like myself one hundred percent of the time. There is never a straight line between where we are now and where we want to be. But a mistake, a failure, or a negative thought is just another bend in the road. Go beyond that bend and you're that much closer to your destination. Give up when you hit a rocky patch and you'll never reach your goal.

A study conducted by the Harvard Business School determined that four factors are critical to success in business: information, intelligence, skill, and attitude. When these factors were ranked in importance, this particular study found that information, intelligence, and skill combined amounted to seven percent of business success and attitude amounted to ninety-three percent! What is true for business is also true for our lives—our attitude is overwhelmingly the most important factor to our success. It's often been said that it's our attitude that determines our altitude.

Mistakes, failures, and negative thoughts usually hit us strongly and make a painful emotional impact, so they are easy to remember. Because of this, our achievements and successes often go by unnoticed. It's time to pay attention! Try surrounding yourself with tangible, visual reminders of things you have accomplished in the past and things you hope to achieve in the future.

My office is one example of how this works. The walls are literally plastered with reminders of positive achievements. On one wall I've pasted the cover of my book *Breakthrough Selling,* publicity that's been received on the book, letters of praise, anything that reminds me of how well the book has done. I've also hung letters I've received from people who have participated in my training programs, telling me how their lives have changed and how they've achieved success by putting my ideas into practice. Another wall holds the covers of magazines in which articles I've written have appeared. On a third wall hangs my goal board, on which I write down all my short-term goals, my long-term goals, and my daily, weekly, and monthly to-do lists.

The last wall holds my MAP board (discussed in chapter 8). This is what keeps my business going. With this board I can tell at a glance the status of all my accounts. The key to my whole system of office decor is that at any given moment I can look around me and see where I've been, where I am, and where I'm going.

What I'm doing is developing a portfolio of accomplishments. We all keep scrapbooks and reminders of the good times in our personal lives. Why not do the same for our professional lives?

Sometimes in the day-to-day running of my business I might not get through to someone important; I might not get a client to use my training services; I might get turned down for an article I've proposed. But I can turn around in my chair, look at all that I've accomplished, and know that these setbacks are only obstacles on the way to opportunity.

When I run into one of these "failures," I can look up at

my walls and remind myself of all the successes. They did not all come quickly and easily; many obstacles were in their way. But I can literally see that in each case, I was eventually able to reach my goal.

I know that if I concentrate on the negative I will not be able to go on. I also know that if I remind myself of my successes, I can take the actions necessary to succeed again.

Success breeds success: this is the "law of effect." We're at our best after we've experienced success. Having been a salesperson, I know that when a person has just closed a sale, her first instinct is to stop what she's doing and go out and celebrate. But in my training, I tell people they shouldn't go out and celebrate—they should go out and make another call! They will never be more primed for success than they are at that moment.

NEUTRALIZE THE NEGATIVE

The law of effect doesn't come with a hundred percent guarantee. You can't always change an unpleasant or disappointing situation. Human beings are often at the mercy of outside elements. We can never control all the circumstances that shape our lives. But these unforeseen events and negative influences are not usually what stop us from thriving and surviving. We don't need outside circumstances to discourage us from getting ahead. We don't need other people to tell us we can't achieve. We're too busy discouraging ourselves.

We actually get into the habit of thinking negatively, and this is difficult to break. We pick up on the fact that we have made a mistake or suffered a setback and use it as proof positive that we are indeed as stupid, lazy, inept (insert your own put-down here) as we thought we were. With this constant barrage of negative self-talk going on inside us, it's a wonder anyone achieves anything at all!

Luckily for us, wonders are achieved all the time, and it is possible for us to get out of our self-made traps and get on with our lives.

"If you do what you've always done, you'll get what you've always gotten."

—ANONYMOUS

You can't eliminate negative thoughts altogether. You can't wish them away or try to fool yourself out of them. Instead of concentrating on subtracting the negative, find ways to add in the positive until the negative thoughts are at the least neutralized, and at the most, overwhelmed.

How you respond to a negative thought or event is more important than the thought or event itself. In his book *The Seven Habits of Highly Effective People,* Stephen Covey talks about the difference between being reactive and being proactive.

Reactive means that you feel, and therefore act, as if you are always the victim of circumstance. No matter what happens to you, it's always something or somebody else's fault. If you've had a bad day, it's because your boss was nasty to you; if you didn't get much done it's because it was too hot (or too cold, or too noisy, or too quiet) in your apartment—there's always an excuse.

The most effective people, however, are proactive. This means that you take responsibility for things that happen to you; that you respond to a situation instead of allowing yourself to be victimized by it. You can't control your boss's behavior, but you can choose whether to let it affect your whole day. You may not be able to control the heat in your apartment, but you can control your response. If you're reactive you will simply say, "It's too hot, I can't work." If you're proactive, you will take steps to relieve the discomfort—open some windows, change your clothes, call the landlord—whatever it takes to change the situation.

High achievers know that a positive attitude can make all the difference between success and failure. They too have negative thoughts and emotions, but they know how to shift their focus away from the self-destructive and onto the strong, the healthy, and the positive.

If you have listened to the radio anytime since 1959, chances are you've heard the unforgettable voice of Radio Hall-of-Famer "Cousin Brucie" Morrow. Besides being a radio personality, an author, and an expert musicologist, Morrow serves on numerous boards of directors including *Variety,* the Children's Charity, the National Foundation for Facial Reconstruction, and the National Music Foundation. A shy kid who stuttered and stammered, he grew up to be an articulate man of great energy and an exuberant personality.

"Do I have bad days?" he says. "Of course I have bad days. But then I try to grab myself by the boots and say, 'Now what can I do to make this right?' The thing is to stay strong and keep bouncing back. . . . One of the great secrets in life I've learned . . . is the feeling and energy of positive action. I believe that worrying about the negative and things that are falling apart is a worthless effort and a destruction of energy. I believe in keeping a positive attitude and saying, 'That didn't work. Now I'm going to make it work and here's how I'm going to do it.' Too many people worry and waste their energy and their life. The flow must continue."

It's that kind of attitude that enables us to "make things happen." Stewing in our own negative juices is not the recipe for success. One of my favorite stories is about a guy who's laying on the ground, moaning and groaning. Somebody walks by and asks why he's moaning. The guy on the ground says, "I'm moaning because I'm laying on a nail." The passerby asks, "Why don't you get up off the nail?" And the guy on the ground says, "It doesn't hurt badly enough."

If you get tired enough of not being fulfilled, eventually you'll do something about it. You can't change your situation simply by complaining about it. If you want things to change you have to take the first step.

THE DARING ATTITUDE

It sometimes takes a lot of courage to take that first step. The laws of physics try to take over: A body at rest wants to stay at rest. It takes energy to overcome inertia. The only thing that will jump start that energy and get it going is attitude.

This is not a new discovery. Dr. Norman Vincent Peale's classic book *The Power of Positive Thinking* has been in print for many years. Many other books, before and since, have espoused the benefits of a positive attitude. One of my favorites, a book that continues to inspire me daily, is a simple tome written in 1931 by William H. Danforth, founder of the Ralston Purina Company and grandfather of Dr. William H. Danforth, chancellor of Washington University in St. Louis (who is quoted elsewhere in this book).

In this little book, *I Dare You!* Danforth lays down a continuing challenge. "I want you to start a crusade in your life— to dare to be your best. . . . Once you dare, once you stop drifting with the crowd and face life courageously, life takes on a new significance. New forces take shape within you. New powers harness themselves for your service."

These are the powers of positive thinking. It may be a cliché, it may sound corny, but it is the power of positive thought turned into positive action that will carry the day. You can't make a change by sitting around and thinking how bad your life is, or by telling yourself how lazy, stupid, or untalented you are. Your life won't change by sharing your misery with others or by listening to other people complain about the negatives in their lives.

We can't afford to spend our lives in the company of those who would drag us down. We all know unhappy, unsuccessful people, some with a lot of potential, who do nothing but complain. There are two ways of dealing with these kinds of people: get rid of them or try to help them. The first—getting such people out of your life—sounds harsh. But to stop seeing some people is often the only way to remove their negative influence, and it may be necessary for your own survival.

Joe Girard, the "World's Greatest Salesman" according to the *Guinness Book of Records,* is adamant about refusing to let others' negative attitudes influence him. "If my friends want to tell me about negative things, I tell them unless you have something that we both can benefit by, don't tell me, 'cause I don't want to hear it.' I don't hang around losers, cry babies or lazy people. I hang around people who can give me a jolt of positive energy."

It would be great if everyone we knew could give us a jolt of positive energy. However, some of the most negative people we know may be people to whom we are particularly close, people we care about, people we don't wish to simply push out of our lives.

Is it possible to keep these people in our lives without "catching" their negative energy? Yes, it is. The next time someone you care about starts complaining, don't commiserate. Think of ways you can help. Say, "I understand exactly how you feel. Now let's come up with some ideas to help you turn things around."

I have a friend who recently became a salesperson in the insurance industry. Starting a new job in an industry that was new to him was tough. He was feeling down one day because of the difficulties of starting from scratch. A few rejections had left him disappointed; he didn't know what to do next. He could have used a change in attitude, but my telling him to "think positive thoughts" was not what he wanted, or needed, to hear. What he needed was to take action. Almost any action would help. Everyone hates being stuck, feeling that there's no way out of their present situation. Taking a positive action, no matter how small, breaks the bind that negative thoughts create.

I suggested some actions that my friend might take, such as sending handwritten thank-you notes to all his prospects, even to those who didn't buy from him. I also suggested he send out flyers with a 'just wanted to keep in touch' greeting and some educational information relevant to his business. Both of these are great ways to get people to remember your name the next time they have a need for your product or service.

Two things happened as a result of our conversation. My friend took the actions, started working on weekends, reduced his depression, and increased his sales—so much so that he became his company's number-one new agent in the state, and number three in the country. And I was reminded of two excellent methods I had used to improve my own business. It's easier to be objective about someone else's problems than about your own; when you help someone else with their problems, you often wind up helping yourself as well.

POSITIVE IN, POSITIVE OUT

The guiding principle of a positive attitude, as in every area of life, is the Golden Rule. If you want positive results from people, you've got to take positive actions toward them. People naturally react according to the way they are treated. If you go out into the world with a positive outlook and are excited to see people, you'll usually get the same back from them. You can't simply sit back and wait for the world to bring excitement to you. As the late, great motivational speaker Earl Nightingale used to say, waiting for excitement to come to you is like sitting in front of a fireplace saying "give me heat" without putting any wood on the flames.

It's not difficult to generate the heat and excitement you need. Mary Kay Ash, founder of Mary Kay Cosmetics, says that her success, and that of the more than 300,000 salespeople in her organization, is based on enthusiasm and attitude. When I asked Mary Kay how she keeps her people motivated and excited, she replied, "Let's start with why I chose cosmetics. If you ask me for a common denominator among women, I would have to say it's a lack of belief in their own God-given ability. They don't believe in themselves. They say things like, 'If I can,' and 'I hope' and 'Maybe.' I had to choose a product that I felt women could be enthusiastic about, something they could believe in. They have to believe in what they're selling. So I chose cosmetics even though I didn't know a thing in the world about cosmetics. But I figured that I could learn. . . . Given a product that really did good things for them, I felt women could be enthusiastic about it. The result has been tremendous, because we have a wonderful line of cosmetics that can really change a woman and the way she looks and feels about herself. I often say I go to bed Elizabeth Taylor and wake up Charles DeGaulle every day. It's so wonderful that you can fix yourself up and make a difference in how you look and how you feel.''

Mary Kay has another tactic that she uses to keep all her employees enthusiastic. ''Whenever I meet anybody in the elevator or the hall, I say, 'Hi, how are you,' '' she says. ''If I haven't met them before, they'll say, 'Oh, I'm fine, I'm okay.' And I say, 'No, you're great. Remember that.' The next time I meet them and I say, 'Hi. How are you?' They say, 'I'm great!' That enthusiasm helps them to feel better about themselves, and it helps me to feel better as well. The result is that everybody goes around here with smiles on their faces and everybody *is* great.''

One of the most important lessons Mary Kay ever learned, she says, is to visualize every person you meet as having a sign on their chest that says, ''Make me feel important.'' Do your best to make that happen. Find out what's important to them, ask them questions, put yourself in their shoes. Doing research for this book, I wanted to find out how people could learn to be more in tune with each other, how to really know what someone else was thinking. So I went to an expert. For the last thirty years, ''The Amazing Kreskin'' has intrigued audiences around the world by dramatizing the unusual abilities of the human mind. Kreskin doesn't call himself a mind reader, as that would imply that he could totally penetrate the processes of the human brain. He can, however, occasionally perceive a single thought or a series of simple thoughts. ''Basically, I apply the power of positive thinking,'' he says, ''which may be mankind's ultimate mental tool.''

Kreskin believes that the road to success is paved with empathy—learning to think the way other people think.

"Listen to the way someone talks," he says. "Watch the way they walk. When you're conversing with them, move the way they do. . . . When you finish your meeting, your conversation, your confrontation, walk away and get by yourself. Think about what they said. Put yourself in their shoes even if you hate them. . . . If you do that you may start to think, 'Now I understand why they feel this way. Maybe next time I'm with them I'll approach them differently.' That's the way you learn to deal with people."

When Kreskin was a youngster he idolized Arthur Godfrey, whom he heard on the radio. According to Kreskin, Godfrey had a way of making you feel as if he were speaking right to you. He infused his sales pitches with an empathy that made you want to buy. Kreskin feels we could all learn a lot from this style.

"Feel the way other people feel," he advises. "If you—in whatever your lifestyle—can learn to do that, you'll sell twenty times more, make more contacts, make greater negotiations, because the dividing line and the separation between people begins to fade away. . . ."

It is Kreskin's belief that there's something you can learn, something of interest in everyone you meet. "When you pick up a book, it doesn't frighten you. It doesn't threaten you. You want to find out what in that book interests you. So when you meet someone, don't be uptight about it; consider it an investigative adventure. And the way to find the answers is to listen to what they have to say."

Listening well requires concentration. It's been proven that we think at least four times faster than we speak. Therefore, our minds are always racing ahead. To be a good listener, you must slow yourself down, really look at the other person, and concentrate on what is being said. Mentally review and summarize what you've heard. If there's something you don't understand, ask for clarification.

"If you want to read someone's thoughts," says Kreskin, "just listen. Forget about what you intend to say to them. . . . Don't worry about how you're going to react to what they say. . . . The other thing is, people talk to us often when they're not speaking . . . by how they are acting and nodding, or how they respond when you touch them. . . . In our society, we turn our sound so loud . . . we're not learning to pick up the intricacies, the shadows, the shadings. . . . I don't care if it's a business meeting, a love affair, or a bond with friends. You've got to learn to tune in. You don't have to take a course in music appreciation to sufficiently tune in to someone else. You can do that without any score at all.''

"No one can make you feel inferior without your consent.''

—ELEANOR ROOSEVELT

READY, SET . . . ATTITUDE!

It doesn't take years of hard work or mystical experiences to develop a positive attitude. It takes practice.

People react to the way you approach them. If you are annoyed and upset with the world, you'll surely find people who are annoyed and upset with you. If you're warm and open, you'll find people will be that way with you. When I went to Kreskin's house to interview him, I had never met him before. He immediately took my hand and started pumping my arm so vigorously I thought it was going to fall off! But he made me feel he was interested in me, that he couldn't wait to see how our conversation was going to turn out. I couldn't help but feel the same way toward him.

However, you can't sit around and wait for a Kreskin to come along and make you feel good. Even if people don't react the way we'd like them to, it's our responsibility to maintain a good attitude.

I've heard a story about a man who walked by the same newsstand every morning and bought a paper from the same vendor. Every morning he gave the vendor a huge smile and a friendly hello, and every morning the vendor ignored him. A friend asked the man, "Why do you continue to give this vendor such a friendly greeting? He never even talks to you." The man replied, "I'm not going to let that individual determine the way I'm going to be all day." This was a man who was being proactive to his environment, not reactive.

You, too, can be proactive and positive with practice. Think about how you start your day. Perhaps you wake up to a clock radio just when the news is coming on. Then you turn on the television to the morning news show. Or you grab the newspaper and read it over breakfast and on the train to work. While it is absolutely necessary to keep up with current affairs, is it absolutely necessary to *start the day* with visions of a troubled economy, businesses going down the tubes, and the imminent end of the world as we know it? How do you think you're going to perform on a day that starts like that?

Imagine instead setting your clock radio fifteen minutes earlier to a station that plays more music and less talk. Imagine that you don't turn on the television, but instead use the time to create your own personal images of success and accomplishment. And imagine that rather than picking up a newspaper, you spend just fifteen minutes reading something that will give you positive input—whether it's research for a project that means a lot to you, words of spiritual encouragement, or motivational material. How do you think you'll perform on a day that starts like that?

Sometimes when I wake up in the morning, I put on a headset and listen to Earl Nightingale or other motivational tapes for twenty minutes or so. It automatically focuses me on the positive and starts my day off with a jump.

The Amazing Kreskin uses other techniques to get him through the day and the night. He says that our parents had the right idea when they didn't let us read a scary story or see a horror movie late at night because we might have nightmares. For that same reason, we shouldn't use our pre-sleep hours to focus on all the bad things that have happened to us—it may not produce nightmares, but it will certainly have a negative effect. Instead, he says, before we go to bed we should "reflect on some of the really constructive gains that were made during the day. Even if it was a really terrible day, reflect on the one gesture, the one comment someone made to you that added a little bit of light to a dark day. You are now programming your unconscious to focus on the positive. . . .

"In the morning, use rehearsal techniques. See the direction you want to go. . . . Suppose you have a date or a meeting with someone you don't know very well. Think about what is positive about that person, what makes you comfortable. . . . Think about how valuable it is to leave them with a positive thought. There is always the possibility that you may never see that person again. Wouldn't it be nice if the scene they have in their mind about you is a positive one? If you impress someone with a positive thought, it will usually germinate a positive end."

A positive attitude isn't something we're born with. We develop a variety of attitudes as we grow up, some positive, some negative, depending on our environment, our education, and the circumstances of our lives. Sometimes it's difficult for us, as "jaded" adults, to imagine making changes in how we view the world. But often making a change in attitude is like staring at an ink blot. At first glance, you may see nothing more than a dark black blob on a page. Then you look again, shifting your viewing angle, clearing your vision. Suddenly you see a beautiful butterfly. Once you've seen it, the blot on the page, which has remained the same, will never again seem a shapeless mass.

So it is with a change in attitude. Your circumstances may not immediately change along with your attitude, but once you look at your life from a positive angle and a clearer vision, you cannot help but see the butterfly. In the words of Oliver Wendell Holmes, "Man's mind, stretched to a new idea, never goes back to its original dimension."

"The longer I live, the more I realize the impact of attitude on life. Attitude, to me, is more important than facts. It is more important than the past, than education, than money, than circumstances, than

failures, than successes, than what other people think or say or do. It is more important than appearance, giftedness, or skill. It will make or break a company . . . a church . . . a home. The remarkable thing is, we have a choice everyday regarding the attitude we will embrace for that day. We cannot change our past . . . we cannot change the inevitable. The only thing we can do is play on the one string we have, and that is our attitude. . . . I am convinced that life is ten percent what happens to me and ninety percent how I react to it. And so it is with you. . . . We are in charge of attitudes.''

—CHARLES SWINDOLL

Five Essential Facets of Chapter 1

1. Enthusiasm is the great equalizer. It can help us over obstacles, and can often make up for deficiencies or lack of skill in a given area.
2. Two steps are necessary to keep enthusiasm going: learning as much as possible before we take action; and reviewing our accomplishments and successes.
3. Remember the three *D*'s of a positive attitude: discipline, desire, and dedication.
4. Focus on the positive. In any negative situation, failure, or setback, look for the good that has come out of it and the lessons that can be learned. Whether you are born to be a ''fifty-gallon barrel'' or a ''ten-gallon barrel,'' be sure you fill it up to capacity.
5. Surround yourself with markers of success, key achievements or goals, or anything that can focus you on the positive when things are tough.

Think about actions you can take from these five ideas or others discussed in this chapter.

Thirty-Day Action Plan For Chapter 1

For the next thirty days, focus on the following:

Avoid tabloid newspapers, magazines, and television programs that focus on bad news and sensational headlines. Be particular about the kinds of information you're absorbing every day.

Start every morning on a positive note. For fifteen minutes, read or listen to a positive message from the self-help area or from educational material appropriate to your profession.

Tape the word *attitude* to your bathroom mirror, in your car, wherever you can look at it every single day. Realize that your success is determined more by your attitude than anything else. Take a proactive approach to the day's events and to others around you.

Avoid gossip for thirty days. If people around you are gossiping or focusing on the negative, change the subject or walk away. If you have nothing good to say, don't say anything.

Take a positive physical approach as well. Clean out your system for thirty days: exercise regularly, stay away from excess caffeine, alcohol, tobacco, fatty foods.

Keep a diary of all the positive events that happen every day. What did you do well today? What did you accomplish? Write down any compliments or praise you might have received. Nothing is too small or trivial to be included. Review the diary at the end of each week.

Look for the good in each individual. Try to compliment at least three people every day.

Make everyone you meet glad he met you. Picture everyone you meet with the words "make me feel important" on their chest.

Evaluate your efforts. What was this month like?_____

_____

_____

How was it different than times past? _____

_____

_____

How did my attitude make a difference in my job or in my relationships with others? _____

_____

_____

_____

Now that you have a strong positive attitude, the next step on the road to success is to take action, to make the effort. The purpose of the following chapter is to let you know there are no easy answers, there is no shortcut, no promise you will "make a million dollars in ten minutes without even trying."

We get out of life what we put into it. Taking action lifts us out of complacency and depression. Putting in effort allows us the chance to make our dreams come true, and to show ourselves at our very best. When we know what it means to really work, we know what it means to really live.

Chapter Two

IT TAKES MILLIONS OF YEARS TO MAKE A DIAMOND:
DEBUNKING THE MYTH OF THE OVERNIGHT SUCCESS

"Success means that whatever you're doing, you feel that you've accomplished something. I wonder if you can ever say you've accomplished as much as you expected? It's not whether you made $10 or $10,000. That has nothing to do with success. Accomplish as much as you can, and do the best you can."

—VINCENT SARDI, RESTAURATEUR

"True success would be accomplishing something that is extremely difficult, at times almost impossible, and in the end, being successful."

—DAVID LUBETKIN, PRESIDENT,
INDUSTRIAL EDGE USA

The recent film "A League of Their Own" tells the story of the first professional women's baseball league, formed during World War II. The outstanding athletes in this league endured hardships and even ridicule as they traveled across the country from one baseball diamond to the next. In the movie, one of the league's star players is about to quit the team just before the big play-offs. Her coach, naturally upset, says, "But I thought you loved baseball!"

"I do," says the player tearfully. "But it just got too hard."

"Of course it's hard," the coach answers. "If it wasn't hard, everybody would do it!"

Being successful is hard in many ways. If it wasn't hard, everybody would do it. When we look at successful people, we see the *results* of their blood, sweat and tears—we don't usually see the effort that went before. We look at a successful doctor and don't think about the many years of schooling, internship, and residency before he even started to practice. We read about a successful businesswoman and never realize the considerable work she put in to earn her position. We watch the Olympics and see athletes in peak performance—we don't see the hundreds of hours of training and preparation for those few golden moments.

That's why we often give up when we hit rocky patches on our own roads to success. We think, "It looked so easy when they did it. I must be doing something wrong." And we give up.

Successful people are much more tenacious than that. They know that hard work is part of the bargain. As a matter of fact, they're often suspicious when things come too easily. High achievers are willing to give 110 percent, to put in an uncommon effort to see their dreams become reality.

The purpose of this chapter is to debunk the myth of the overnight success, and to show that ordinary people, expending extraordinary effort, can be whatever they want to be. You can think about wanting to be successful all you want. You can listen to audio tapes and read books like this one. They point the way, they pump you up, they provide tips, tools, and techniques. But they can only go so far. After that, it's up to you.

Not so long ago, every American's dream was to work hard and eventually become an athlete, a lawyer, a doctor, an artist, a business owner, an entrepreneur. Now every American's dream is to win the lottery. The odds of attaining success in the first dream are high; the odds for success in the second are a million to one. Yet many of us continue to play against the odds, hoping that luck, magic, or miracles will suddenly transform our lives, solve all our problems, and relieve us of despair and depression.

One thing has become abundantly clear from all the people interviewed for this book: There is only one sure-fire antidote for depression and that is action. Faced with many obstacles, including depression, each high achiever profiled here increased his or her effort and met challenges head-on.

In the sales training industry, this phenomenon is well known. Salespeople get depressed when they aren't generating enough activity. As soon as they renew their efforts at making contacts, pursuing leads, and establishing follow-up procedures, their depression begins to lift and their productivity begins to climb.

Why is that? Because when we put in the effort, we know that further along there will be a pay-off. It gives us something to look forward to. Effort is the tool with which we build our future.

> *"The dictionary is the only place where success comes before work."*
>
> —Arthur Brisbane

IT ALL BEGINS WITH THE HUSTLE

On a hot, humid summer night, my friend Frank and I decided to go down to the courts and play a little one-on-one. We started playing basketball, and I was going for the shots. I was making a few; I was missing a few. We were just playing our usual game.

Then two guys we didn't know showed up, wanting to use the court. We decided to play two-on-two. Turned out those guys were really good. Suddenly I realized that if I wanted to keep up—if I wanted to *beat* those guys—then I had to really hustle, to focus and concentrate and then add that jolt of extra energy that would take me over the edge.

I thought of something Bill Clements, former governor of Texas, had told me. "Energy is the secret to this whole situation," he said. "You can be a person of great integrity, character, and all these other wonderful things, but if you don't have the energy, and if you don't really put your shoulder to the wheel, so to speak, and start pushin', you're not going to get to first base."

I started making more shots. That gave me confidence, made me feel better about my ability to play the game. Then I had to keep it up. I had to analyze what I was doing to make the shots so that I could make them again. The more we played, the better I got, and I was making shots I couldn't come close to making when we started.

This was no NBA tournament. Shaquille O'Neill and Charles Barkley have nothing to fear from me. But I improved *my* game by increasing the amount of effort I put into it. Driving home afterward, Frank and I started talking about the game. I told him about my "hustle" experience, and how that extra energy increased my confidence, which increased my competence. But I felt like there was something missing, some step I had forgotten. Frank said, "Consistency" and I knew he was right. I yelled out, "That's it! I'm putting this in the book!" Frank looked at me like I was from another planet (my enthusiasm is sometimes a little loud). But this basketball game was, for me, a perfect demonstration of the four-step formula to success:

Hustle → Confidence → Consistency → Competence = Success

♦ **Hustle:** To hustle means to adopt the positive attitudes of discipline, desire, and dedication discussed in chapter 1, and to give that extra ten percent; to go beyond what is expected of you. This is not the negative connotation of hustle which implies underhanded activity, but the positive sense of the word, which implies a spark of energy, which ignites . . .

♦ **Confidence:** Each time you give yourself that jolt of extra energy, it produces results. You're moving inch by inch toward your goal. The closer you get to your goal, the better you feel about yourself. The better you feel about yourself, the stronger your ability to repeat your successes, which leads to . . .

♦ **Consistency:** Once your confidence starts to build, you can keep it going through practice and repeated performance. The hustle is good for a shot of energy, but is difficult to maintain. Practice and repetition produce a consistency of performance that distinguishes a champion from a "flash in the pan." Maintaining a consistent level of performance is also known as . . .

♦ **Competence:** Confidence and consistency often lead to the "discovery" of abilities we didn't know we had or weren't sure we could develop. Building competence in one area frequently contributes to competence in other areas, and dramatically increases the overall probability of success.

Another *C* word—though one to avoid, not embrace—is complacency. The dictionary defines complacency as satisfaction accompanied by unawareness of dangers or deficiencies. We're satisfied with what we've got and unaware of how much more we could have. It's easier to stay wherever we are, even if it's not really where we want to be, than to dare make a change. This reduces our confidence, keeps us from perceiving and receiving opportunities, and stops us from achieving our goals. If that's the way you're feeling, then you definitely need a little hustle in your life.

"Success is not the result of spontaneous combustion. You must set yourself on fire."

—REGGIE LEACH

WHATEVER HAPPENED TO THE OVERNIGHT SUCCESS?

The "hustle" and the "three *C*'s" of the formula are the foundations of the road to success. We do not see them in any highlight films or "photo ops" of a successful person. What we see is the end result, the seasoned professional.

Senator Bill Bradley of New Jersey, for instance, has known the meaning of effort ever since he was a young child. Even in high school he practiced his basketball moves relentlessly. He had the key to the high school gym (the only student to do so) and he practiced by himself on weekends and holidays. One drill he repeated over and over again. From five spots on the court he'd shoot twenty-five times. If he didn't hit twenty-two baskets out of twenty-five shots, he'd start over again. He was determined to stay there until it was done—and done right.

When the roaring crowds watched Bradley play basketball for the New York Knicks, they saw a champion who displayed ease and grace on the court. They had no idea of the practice, discipline, and effort that went into making the winning player.

Sometimes, however, we witness a "one-hit wonder." This term is generally used in the music business to refer to someone who comes out of nowhere, rises to immediate fame with one spectacular hit record—then quickly disappears from the music scene forever.

Most of the time, the reason this kind of success cannot be sustained is that it happens too quickly. The formula for success is sidestepped, and there's no technique to fall back on when the luck runs out.

"You only live once in this world, and you just have to go for it. But it's hard work," says writer Robert Shook. "When you see somebody on stage performing and you say, 'Gee, how can I ever do anything that good?' you have to remember that guy probably practiced ten hours a day, for five, six, eight, ten, twenty years to get that good."

After thirty-six books, Shook sometimes looks back at his first attempts and wonders how they ever got published! According to him, his writing skills at that time were not exactly up to par. "But," he adds, "one of my all-time favorite quotes is from Benjamin Disraeli, who said, 'The secret of success is consistency of purpose.' "

Shook has three children—all of whom are published authors. "I taught them that writing is a discipline," he says. "If you write one or two hours a day, that can be very good. But if you do it eight, ten . . . hours every day? Just think about that. . . . If you just write one page every single day, in a year's time you can have a book done. If you write three pages a day, you can have three books done!"

Writing is not the only area in which Shook employs discipline. He also includes physical exercise in his daily regimen. A writer's work is so sedentary, he feels, that if he didn't exercise he'd be "in the worst condition of any human being in the world." Physical fitness is not that unusual, except that Shook hates to exercise.

"It's painful. It hurts. It's like torture," he says. "But that's part of the discipline. . . . Fighters have their fighting weight— I have my writing weight. And why am I so disciplined? Because if you just do something over and over again, it's amazing how good you can get. And the more you do it, the more competent you become."

Shook is not the only high achiever concerned with the physical side of life. Although it does not seem to be a prerequisite, many of the people interviewed for this book come from athletic backgrounds, are currently involved in fitness programs, or at the very least, use sports analogies to explain their success. One person who believes strongly in the value of physical fitness is the renowned and sometimes controversial chairman and CEO of MESA Inc., Boone Pickens. Pickens calls his company "the most physically fit company in America." He constructed a first-class, two-million-dollar athletic facility for the company, and company benefits include use of the gym and participation in the corporate Wellness program. It is Pickens's contention that fit employees are "more productive, more creative, and more competitive."

Pickens expects extra effort from his employees (as he does

from himself) from day one of any project right through to its conclusion. To motivate people, he often uses sports metaphors when he speaks, whether it's to a meeting of his shareholders or to one of his employees. This is especially true when he talks about preparation, which is to him one of the cornerstones of any successful endeavor, and which requires just as much effort as any other part of a project.

"You could set up a booth right here on the corner in front of this building and interview people passing by," says Pickens. "You could ask them, 'Would you like to play for the Dallas Cowboys?' Probably one out of ten would say, 'You're darn right I would.' Then you would say, 'Let me put this meter on you to see if you would really like to play quarterback as much as Troy Aikman would.' I think you would actually have people on that meter who would score higher than Troy Aikman at *wanting* to play—not to take anything away from his commitment. But it won't work. And the reason it won't work is because those people are not prepared."

It is Pickens's belief that the lack of preparation causes a lack of confidence, whether it's "taking a girl out, taking a test, or having to stand up in front of a group." And to Pickens, the best preparation of all is "hands-on experience. You can read all you want to," he says, "but if you've never been there to fly the airplane, you better be a pretty good reader when they say, 'Okay, you're going to fly.' "

In a speech Pickens often gives to shareholders and to college students around the country, he offers several suggestions to help people who want to get ahead. Some of those suggestions are:

♦ Learn to analyze well. There's no substitute for good research.
♦ Don't be afraid to act. Someone once described the management of a major American corporation to Pickens by saying, "They analyze well, but then it's like, ready, aim, aim, aim, aim . . . they never can bring themselves to fire."
♦ Be a team player. As long as you work for someone, you owe them your allegiance and support. If you find that you

are constantly dissatisfied or frustrated, go somewhere else.
♦ Never cheat to win. Business has rules; there's no reason to break them.
♦ Don't let success go to your head. No matter how successful you are, don't ever get to where you can't go back to eating hamburgers.

Pickens summarized his formula for success this way: "Come early. Stay late. Work hard. Play by the rules. Stay physically fit."

"My own self, at my very best, all the time."

—MOTTO, AMERICAN YOUTH
FOUNDATION CAMP
(FOUNDED BY WILLIAM H. DANFORTH)

BUT I AM WORKING HARD . . . AREN'T I?

A basic truth of life is what you put into it is what you get back. The rewards you get out of any endeavor depend on the amount of effort you put into it.

Many people focus on the wrong end of the stick. They're constantly complaining about their job, their relationships, their lives. They feel they're not getting enough out of life. But do they ever ask themselves, "Am I putting enough in?" No, they don't. They're waiting for things to get better, for the economy to improve, for their ship to come in. They're waiting and waiting . . .

Sometimes we fool ourselves and think we're putting in the effort when we're really just going through the motions. Many people are out of work these days, and I've often heard them say, "I sent out one hundred resumes and I didn't get any response. I did everything I could." And they think they've put in one hundred percent effort!

One hundred percent effort means that you've exhausted every possible opportunity for reaching your goal. If you're looking for a job, one hundred percent effort would include researching individual companies you want to work for, sending these companies personalized letters, calling to follow up, calling other people in the industry, networking. One hundred percent effort means telling a potential boss you really want to work for, "I'm sure you've got a lot of applicants here. But I believe so strongly in my ability to meet your needs, I'll work for you for thirty days with no pay. Let me prove to you my enthusiasm, my integrity, and my ability. In thirty days, evaluate my performance. If it's not up to par, let me go. But when I prove myself to you, I expect to be given the job and paid for those thirty days of work." Now that's putting in one hundred percent effort!

> *"Don't mistake activity for achievement. Just because you're moving fast doesn't mean you're going somewhere."*
>
> —ANONYMOUS

A STREETCAR NAMED OPPORTUNITY

Don't be discouraged if the rewards of your efforts are not immediately forthcoming. One other piece of advice Boone Pickens offers to anyone who wants to succeed in life is to have the courage to stick with your goals and ideas, even if they don't always pan out. "Remember, there are plenty of opportunities around," he said. "As I look back I can honestly say I've had an 'opportunity of a lifetime' every week. You don't have to ride every streetcar. There's one coming by every fifteen minutes."

We often look back at a missed opportunity and think, "I really blew it. I'll never get another chance like that one." And we give up trying. Most people who don't achieve as much as they want to in life don't fall short because of a lack of ability, but because they gave up too soon. Those who do achieve know that it is only concentrated, concerted effort that will produce results.

Bruce Jenner, the great Olympic athlete, played sports for many years before he got "serious." When he was a sophomore in college, he discovered the decathlon. At that point, he made a "commitment to running" not knowing how far he could go, but willing to put in the effort. He devoted every possible moment to his training, and then some.

"There was always a clock ticking in my head," he says. "Every second that goes by is gone. It's lost. It's my enemy. There was a burning question down deep inside . . . 'If I really focus on this, how far can I go with it? What is my maximum?'"

"Since I made this commitment to myself, I didn't want to say these words once the games were over . . . 'I could have done it if . . .' I wanted to know on that day . . . I will have done everything you can possibly do. If I don't win, it's going to hurt, it's going to be tough. But I'm a real good human being. I can survive. I will go on with life. It may take me a day, it may take me a week, who knows, it may take me ten years of my life to recuperate. But I can. I'm smart enough, I've got good enough friends, I have a good enough family— I will survive if I lose. But what I have to do right now is prepare myself to win. . . . Every night I was satisfied that I'd done everything I could do on that day. What's amazing is if you do that, how many mountains you climb."

There is an incredible satisfaction that comes from knowing that your effort—not luck or magic—made you a winner. People often envy high achievers, not for the effort they put in, but for their "luck" and their "golden opportunities."

"People always say, 'Oh, you've been lucky,'" says Jenner. "I always believed that the harder I trained, the luckier I got. . . . Luck is part of the game, but when I prepare for something, I don't prepare to be lucky, I prepare to be good."

The dictionary defines luck as a force that brings good fortune. What is that force? In many circumstances, it comes from deep within us. It's the positive attitude that allows us to visualize a successful outcome of our efforts. It's the actual effort we expend, and the knowledge that this effort will move us closer to our goals. The result may not always be exactly what we've planned—we can't win every race. But those who ride the ups and downs and don't depend on luck to get them through have a much better chance of winning the next time.

Dr. Irene Kassorla, internationally known psychologist, lecturer, and author of bestsellers such as *Go For It!* and *Nice Girls Do,* knows, and appreciates, the value of putting in that extra effort. Dr. Kassorla first came to the attention of the medical community when she began research experiments with schizophrenic patients at the Institute of Psychiatry at the University of London. She was credited by the *London Times* as being a "miracle worker" when her patient, who was a mute and catatonic fifty-two-year-old man who hadn't spoken a word in thirty years, began to talk. When asked how this feat was accomplished, Dr. Kassorla replied, "It was a little drop in the bucket every day. A small drop—and some days the bucket emptied and we started all over again."

She credits her success in this case with her patience, her understanding and caring attitude, and most of all, with her hard work. There was no single moment when a miracle occurred, and Dr. Kassorla refuses to think in those terms because that might suggest that "... the violins will start playing, the trumpets will start blowing, the screen will part and there you will see your victory. That isn't the way it works. It's just tedious; and day-to-day, you just keep going."

"Lady Luck has nothing to do with it, absolutely nothing," she says of her success. "You're lucky if you're sitting in the library, learning and doing research. You're lucky if you're working late. You're lucky if you're trying harder than the next guy—and I've got news for you, when you rest—nothing happens."

"Opportunity is missed by most people because it is dressed in overalls and looks like work."

—THOMAS EDISON

SUCCESS COMES ONE DAY AT A TIME

If you want an example of who that "next guy" might be, you could find two of them in David Lubetkin and Steven Weintraub. For many years, the men had been actively involved in running the family business, Brick Church Appliance Company. The company had grossed over one hundred million dollars before it was sold in 1990. For a while, both Lubetkin and Weintraub were at a loss as to what they would do when the company was sold.

Finally, they decided that they would take over the management of another family-owned business, Apartment House Supply Company. At that time the company, which had been profitable for many years, was managed by "outsiders" and was "running in neutral." When they actually took over the company, they discovered that it was "far worse than neutral, it was in reverse."

"We found ourselves in a tough situation," says Lubetkin. "We had a business that had current customers, that had inventory, and all of a sudden we're thrown into this company that was experiencing all kinds of difficulties, including unhappy customers who kept getting the wrong products with the wrong prices. There was no computer system, no controls; it was a tough, tough situation. And what made it even worse was the fact that Steve and I knew nothing about the products we sold.

"Basically, from day one, we had to come in very early in the morning to begin to learn about the business, to study the better players in the industry . . . to try to understand what we did sell, and to get an overall basic plan of action."

Weintraub adds: "We had to learn about the products. We had to talk to manufacturers, read books, look at trade magazines." The two men devoted all their time to their new business; this meant seven days, and sometimes seven nights, a week.

"I'd say we worked twelve hours a day," says Lubetkin.

"We had to computerize the business, which was a major undertaking. . . . The initial loading in of data takes hours and hours, you've got to load in all the customers, all the inventory. You've got to make sure the inventory is divided in an intelligent manner. And for this particular system we had to load in all the accounting—it was about a year-and-a-half project."

It wasn't always easy for the two to keep going; it was tedious work with no guarantee of success. "I guess what kept us going was that dream that one day, if we worked hard enough, and had a game plan, that we could develop this business to a very serious level," says Lubetkin. "There were plenty of times—specifically I can remember being in the warehouse, sitting on the floor, and dividing parts that were just thrown in bins, taking them out one by one and trying to set them up in the warehouse. . . . It was an incredible undertaking. . . . We had to go through bin by bin, piece by piece, organize and set it up in the computer, and train people. . . . We had twenty construction workers there for six months. While all this was going on, we're just trying not to lose the customers we had."

But the two were determined to succeed. "I would say ninety-nine out of a hundred people definitely would have failed," says Weintraub, "because they would have come home depressed, and they would say to themselves, 'What we're doing is impossible.' But we always believed that if we could take it one day at a time, improve it little by little, plan ahead and dream ahead, that we'd succeed. Slowly but surely we got new customers. Our warehouse started being organized. We started to understand the computer system. We were beginning to understand the products we sold. We were beginning to attract some good employees. One day it all just started coming around."

It's true, most people would have given up in such a situation. But both Lubetkin and Weintraub had faith that with hard work, they could achieve their dream.

"Sometimes it was overwhelming," says Lubetkin. "Sitting there in the warehouse when you have eight thousand parts you have to count and you're able to do fifty or eighty a day.

You say to yourself, 'How are you ever going to do this?' But I think what kept us going was the never-say-die, never-quit attitude. We stayed motivated because we know nothing good is easy.''

> *"People who would never think of committing suicide or ending their lives would think nothing of dribbling their lives away in useless hours every day."*

—THOMAS CARLYLE

RESISTANCE TRAINING

Nothing good is easy. It all keeps coming back to that. It all comes back to one individual's persistent effort. There are dozens of stories, many of which we've all heard, about hard-working individuals who started at the bottom and rose to the top because of their willingness to do the work.

That is exactly what Paul Pavis did. He is now in the enviable position of director of entertainment for Harrah's Casino Hotel in Atlantic City, New Jersey. He initially learned his craft and "paid his dues" by working as a stage manager in small theaters across the country, and by teaching scenic and lighting design in colleges in Maryland and Rhode Island. He came to Harrah's in 1981 and within eight years attained his present position. He knows that it's the work he put in all those years before that allow him to enjoy his current career, and to be good at what he does.

Pavis gets hundreds of letters and resumes from people looking for work in the entertainment industry. He has strong opinions about people who start out thinking they can bypass some of the hard work and jump right into the spotlight. "I've met a lot of folks who come from college and they say, 'Now that I've got my degree, I want to be the manager,' " says Pavis. "In fact, when you have a degree, that just gets you up onto the playing field. Then you have to start playing. I went from being a college professor to shoving road boxes and moving tigers in magic shows because you have to be willing to do every job that the people you supervise have to do. And you have to know what that job is before you're ready to supervise other people who perform it.''

Of course, it's not only in business where effort makes the difference. Pavis's personal heroes are those people who struggle against incredible odds to achieve their goals. His motto is, ''If it doesn't kill you, it makes you stronger.''

''It's like resistance training in athletics,'' he says. ''Football players now run with a parachute tied to their backs. Evander Holyfield wears a vest that has elastic bungee chords tied to his boxing gloves so that there's resistance when he swings his fists. Then when you take them away his fists fly out at twice the speed. If it works physically, it works psychologically.''

He calls this ''working against the grain,'' and he knows whereof he speaks. A few years ago, Pavis was diagnosed with Stage Four Lymphoma, which is cancer of the immune system. Stage Five is death. He had immediate emergency surgery to remove his spleen, followed by nine months of chemotherapy and finally a bone marrow transplant.

''Through that whole two-year period, I kept getting stronger psychologically,'' Pavis relates. ''I said, 'This is not going to kill me. I'm going to come back.' I'm clean now, I have no cancer, through a combination of psychology and aggressive management by the medical care profession, family support and the motivation of wanting to be there to support my own family. Knowing I didn't want to leave my little kids. And my own ego. I've got things I want to do for me, I'm not leaving yet. . . .

''I try not to take things too seriously. I really concentrate when I find my brow furrowing or my jaw tensing up. I stop and say, 'Wait a minute, this is show business and a gambling hall. This is not world peace or brain surgery here. Let's take it easy. You can't have a bad day. I know what a bad day is, and this isn't one of them.' ''

ACTION IS ALWAYS THE KEY

Paul Pavis puts effort into everything he does, including his recovery from illness. This is not to say that everyone who dies from cancer does so because they haven't tried hard enough. That's absurd. But when you talk to people who have recovered, they often make remarks similar to Paul Pavis's: "I couldn't go yet, I had too much left to do." Not too much left to think about, or too much television left to watch, or even too many books to read. Too much left *to do*.

Survival is often dependent on action. In 1972, Danielle Kennedy (who is now one of the most sought-after speakers in the country) was twenty-seven years old and six months pregnant with her fifth child. Her family was strapped for money. There was really no choice for her but to go to work. It was a matter of survival, and Kennedy proved to be up to the challenge.

"I decided on real estate," she says, "because it was a wonderful time in southern California to get into real estate, and I loved looking at houses. I had a tough time finding anyone who would take me seriously with this big tummy when I would go out on interviews. I was rejected more than I was taken seriously. Finally someone said you can work here but you can't take floor time, meaning I couldn't get business from customers calling in on ads or off the street. So I said to my manager, 'Then how do I get my business?' She pretty much said, 'That's your problem, I guess you'll have to go out and knock on doors.'

"Can you imagine a woman six months pregnant going out there? I had absolutely no training. I started out just basically willing, as opposed to defiant, which I found out is a key issue with salespeople. Eighty percent of the ones who aren't doing anything are the ones who are defiant. They say, 'No, I don't do cold calls, I don't send out hand-written notes. I'm just sitting around waiting for the business to be handed to me.' I had a head start and I didn't even know it. I thought I had the biggest obstacle of all, being a mom with all those kids and not getting floor time and not getting free access to customers. . . . I had every objection in the book thrown before me and these other people, I thought, had it made. But the difference was, I put in the effort. . . . I put a twenty-five-foot cord on my kitchen phone and I just started telling everyone I knew. I wrote letters to everyone back to grade school with a very subtle approach, saying things like 'Guess who's gone into real estate!' and 'If you have any real estate needs count on me.' "

That was how Kennedy began to build her business. Slowly but surely, Kennedy moved from being a successful real estate agent to being a successful speaker and seminar leader. Like everyone else profiled here, her success came little by little, day by day. There are no shortcuts, no secrets, no speedways. Sometimes it's hard. If it wasn't hard everybody would do it. . . .

Shannon Briggs is twenty years old, six-foot-four, and weighs in around 210. He's a heavyweight contender from the tough Brownsville section of Brooklyn, New York, just like other boxers before him, Mike Tyson and Riddick Bowe. He even trains with Teddy Atlas, Tyson's first trainer. Listen to what fighter Shannon Briggs has to say on the subject of becoming a champion:

"It's hard. I'm twenty years old. A lot of my friends hang out, they go to clubs and things like that. I can't. It's not a one-day, two-day, three-day thing. And it's twenty-four hours. I can never slack off and say, 'Okay, I'm going to hang out for a couple of hours and forget boxing.' I sleep it, I eat it, I drink it. It's full time. When Sunday comes, if I'm not in the gym, that day is my rest day to prepare for Monday. . . . I'm human. I do want to do other things. I do want to hang with the girls and the guys. When I go into the gym a lot of days I feel like I can't even walk. But I have to trigger something in my brain that says no matter what, I've got to push."

This heavyweight contender's life has not been an easy one, and there were times when he was tempted to give up his dreams. But Shannon is willing to do whatever it takes, no matter how difficult, to win.

"The training is the hard part," he says. "The fighting is the easiest part. Because the training is every day. You've got to spar every day, you've got to run every day. The day of the fight, you relax, you don't run. The fight might only last two seconds. . . . But there's only one way to do it, and that's to do the work. There's no other way. Period."

"It is not the critic who counts, not the man who points out how the strong man stumbles or where the doer of deeds could have done them better. The credit belongs to the man who is actually in the arena, whose face is marred by dust and sweat and blood, who strives valiantly, who errs and comes short again and again because there is no effort without error and shortcomings, who knows the great devotion, who spends himself in a worthy cause, who at best knows in the end the high achievement of triumph and who at worst, if he fails while daring greatly, knows his place shall never be with those timid and cold souls who know neither victory nor defeat."

—THEODORE ROOSEVELT

Five Essential Facets of Chapter 2

1. The major antidote for depression is action.
2. The key to "coming back" when you're slowing down is all in the hustle. Give that extra effort that leads to the three *C*'s—confidence, consistency, and competence—which together equal success.
3. Give one hundred percent all the time. Ask yourself after every endeavor, Did I give it my best? Remember William H. Danforth's motto: to be our own selves at our very best all the time. Knowing you put in your best at work allows

you the guilt-free pleasure of enjoying your leisure time.
4. Remember that luck is when you're learning, when you're doing the research, when you're working late, when you're working harder than the next person, when you're putting in that extra effort. Other people see luck in the wrong place; they see it in the positive outcome. We know where it really is—in the hard work and the effort.
5. Practice resistance training for the brain. Whenever you're doing something that's tough and painful, but must be done, remember that what we resist most is what builds us the most. That's what builds character. That's what helps us when we're suddenly hit by an obstacle. We build our substance and stamina through the resistance training. It's getting through the tough little steps and stages that build character, not going over the finish line.

Think about actions you can take from these five ideas or others discussed in this chapter.

Thirty-Day Action Plan for Chapter 2

Be yourself—at your very best in everything you do. After every task, ask yourself, "Can I do it better?" Do all the little extras you'd rather not do. There's one thing everyone has in common: there's always room for improvement.

Most people don't succeed because they don't think. Sit down with a notepad and write down your goals and ideas. Come up with ways that you can improve the things you're doing now, and ways you can work more efficiently in the future.

Are you at your physical best? Do you get enough exercise?

Are you balancing your life with leisure and social activities as well as work? Being your best includes more than just work, you know.

Practice the "and one more . . ." principle. Do this action plan, and one more. Whenever you're about to stop selling, studying, exercising, practicing—whatever it is—do one more. One more hour, one more push-up, one more phone call. You'll be surprised at how rewarding it is.

You are the only one who can change your attitude, who can put in the effort. They are the foundation upon which success is built. However, before you begin to understand success, you must begin to understand failure. More than likely, you'll experience failure before you ever reach success. If you understand it, you'll know that failure is one of the most effective methods through which human beings learn and grow—all human beings, no matter who they are or what their occupations.

Some of life's greatest lessons are taught through hardships, failure, fear, and mistakes. The next chapter will show you how you, like many of the most successful people around, can learn to overcome obstacles, to confront fear and turn it into a motivating force, and to take action in the face of adversity.

Chapter Three

"BUFFETED STONES":
THOSE WHO KNOW FAILURE KNOW SUCCESS

"Right now, success to me means becoming heavyweight champion of the world. It also means letting people understand that I came from a bad place, but I used my head and made my way out. I want to show others they can do it too. That's success."

—SHANNON BRIGGS, HEAVYWEIGHT TITLE
CONTENDER

"Success means figuring out who you are, not who other people think you are or who you think you should be. It's being able to say, 'This is what I am. It may not be enough for some, but it's enough for me to be able to make a difference.' Think about the power one person has to make a difference—Martin Luther King, Jr., Albert Schweitzer, Eleanor Roosevelt. One person can make a difference in a short period of time if they do what's really true to them—and that takes courage."

—JOHN JAMES, PSYCHOTHERAPIST, COAUTHOR OF
PASSION FOR LIFE

There's a stone at the bottom of a river. It's misshapen and cloudy. It has no elegance, it contains no romance. Carried by natural means for hundreds, perhaps thousands of miles from its original source, it now lies hidden from view, almost out of reach.

It is a diamond.

Diamonds found in gravel at the bottom of rivers are usually water-worn and rough in appearance. However, these diamonds—the ones that have withstood the water's buffeting and come out whole and strong—frequently yield the best cut stones.

We sometimes feel as if we have suffered the ravages of water buffeting. Throughout our lives, we are hit by storms of rejection and disappointment. Yet deep inside ourselves lies hidden potential that needs to be shaken out of us. This potential is often released by the very storms that seem so devastating and destructive.

Life is a grindstone—it either grinds you down or polishes you up, an old saying tells us. Each time we experience a setback or disappointment we also gain new information. If we use that information and learn from it, we actually become like the buffeted stone—stronger and more resilient. Failure leads to success as long as we're learning its lessons.

We learn more from failure than we ever learn from our successes. We build inner strength and character when things are most devastating. Each time we run into obstacles or experience adversity, we can get through it if we look for the lessons they provide.

The purpose of this chapter is not only to show you how to change obstacles into opportunities, but also to let you know that many of the most successful people have had to deal with physical and mental handicaps. They've known and overcome failure, rejection, and disappointment. They've had to learn how to treat failure as a teacher and adversity as an ally.

Most of us, upon experiencing failure, immediately begin to

put ourselves down. We think we somehow deserve it; that failure means we're bad people. We confuse the failure of our undertakings with failure of ourselves as people. High achievers know how to separate the two, because when you start taking failure personally, you get depressed, discouraged, and dispirited. The stories you'll read in this chapter will show you not only that successful people manage to go on after experiencing failure, but also how they do it.

> *"Adversity is the diamond dust heaven polishes its jewels with."*

> —ROBERT LEIGHTON

WITHOUT FAILURE, WE'D HAVE A POORER WORLD

When Thomas Edison was inventing the electric light, he failed 1,200 times before he finally got it to work. A journalist asked him, "How did you deal with 1,200 failures?" Edison replied, "I did not fail 1,200 times. I was successful in finding 1,200 ways the light bulb didn't work."

What some people call failure, others call feedback. Corny as it may sound, those who are successful in coping with failure learn to pick themselves up, dust themselves off, and start all over again. As they say, fall down seven times, get up eight.

When we look at any incoming data as a positive source of feedback, no matter how negative it seems, we are polishing our own inner resources. Each time we confront our own failures, go beyond them and take another action, we have, in fact, succeeded.

Everyone is frustrated when things don't go as planned. But inventors expect failure; every time an experiment "fails" they can eliminate materials or processes that stand in the way of the solution.

Arthur Fry, scientist and inventor, has been dealing with "failure" ever since he was a child. He'd often bring appliances and machinery home from the city dump and take them apart. Sometimes he could put them back together—and sometimes he couldn't. But that never stopped him. He was (and is) always curious about how things work. His sister once said, "Ask Art what time it is and he tells you how to build a watch."

Perhaps the most famous result of Fry's curiosity is the ever-popular, always-handy Post-it Note. When Fry presented his idea to manufacturers and engineering researchers, what seemed to be an uncomplicated product turned out to have many difficult technical problems.

"The engineers said, 'We don't know how to do these things—they're tough,'" says Fry. "But I said, 'I know I'm asking you to do things that are not easy. But everyone else can do the easy stuff. The difficult things—where you get knocked down two or three times and you keep getting up and fighting your way around the barriers—are the ones that are rewarding in the end. I'm asking you for help because you're the ones who can solve these difficult problems.' Guess what happened? Everybody really worked hard and found they were capable of solving those problems."

What would happen if scientists and engineers gave up after one so-called failure? We wouldn't have the Post-it Note, the electric light, the automobile, penicillin, or thousands of other inventions and discoveries. And we wouldn't have people who have reaped the rewards of repeated effort, knowing that they didn't let one step backward keep them from going forward.

"If you ask any old-timer what they did in their life," says Fry, "they won't tell you about the easy things that everybody else can do. They'll tell you about the things that challenged them, things that they were able to accomplish and that they were proudest of."

Failure is actually an important part of the scientific process. Dr. Edmund J. Sybertz, Distinguished Research Fellow of Cardiovascular Pharmacology at Schering-Plough, is well acquainted with failure. He and his staff of fifty scientists often work for years developing drugs that never make it to the marketplace.

"Maybe two drugs might go to market over a scientist's lifetime," says Dr. Sybertz. "Many products die along the wayside. It's frustrating, but the process is so important, as is the acquisition of knowledge along the way. . . . You go into this knowing what the odds are. If you're successful, that's great; it's very gratifying. If you're not, then frequently you've contributed something that has increased scientists' overall knowledge and can be applied to understanding disease or discovering other drugs."

Dr. Mortimer Mishkin, chief of the laboratory of neuropsychology at the National Institute of Mental Health, concurs. "More often than not, it's a failure to support an idea that leads to the greatest discovery—because then you have to go back to your initial assumption, and look at why you expected what you expected. When you start questioning your assumptions, you end up changing them. . . . You may end up with totally different ideas than the one you went in with. From that standpoint, failure is the most important part of discovery."

THE UNKINDEST CUT OF ALL: DEALING WITH REJECTION

My first book, *Breakthrough Selling,* was turned down by twenty-six publishers before one finally bought it. Talk about rejection! Now I know why so many talented writers don't get their work published. When they're constantly exposed to that type of rejection, their confidence and their perseverance get worn down. Sure, after the first rejection I was disturbed, but not devastated. Five or six rejections later, however, I was starting to get very concerned.

Then I called my agent and asked what the problem was.

He said that there were just so many other books out there on sales, publishers were hesitant to take on another one. But I knew I had a fresh approach and important ideas to add to an admittedly crowded field. So after the next rejection, I called the publisher and asked what I could do to improve my chances. What was missing from my book? What did it need to make it stand out and invite acceptance?

I followed the next rejection with a similar phone call, and the next and the next. Suggested changes were made. Now I was looking forward to each rejection. Without even knowing it, these publishers were helping me write my book!

The valuable lesson I learned was not to equate rejection with failure. When the twenty-seventh publisher bought my book, he was not getting a manuscript that had failed twenty-six times. He was getting a manuscript that had benefited from the advice of twenty-six talented, knowledgeable professionals. Rejection is just one person's opinion. You cannot take it personally, or it will destroy your confidence and keep you from moving on.

Of course, I'm not the only writer who's ever had to deal with rejection. Robert Shook was an insurance agent for seventeen years before he became an author. His first book was rejected twenty-two times. But he believed in the work and didn't give up on it. Thirty-six books later, Shook has interviewed and written about some of the most successful people in our country, and has come to some conclusions about their success.

"Successful people are able to accept failure and not be defeated by it," he says. "They can go from failure to failure and still not fail. I know many people with so much ability—but as soon as they get knocked down once or twice, they get discouraged and give up.

"I remember when I was in college, I had a friend who was handsome and popular; he was president of the class and everyone thought he would be president of the United States. He had so much going for him. But he had a flaw. . . . He couldn't stand to fail, and he couldn't take it when he did. He didn't do well in his first job out of college, then he went to another job and another job. He quit whenever he experienced a small failure or bumped into the tiniest obstacle. Although he had far more ability than I had, I'm far more successful. He had so much natural talent, but he's failed all his life because he quit too easily.''

"Never let the fear of striking out get in your way."

—BABE RUTH (WHO HIT 714 HOME RUNS—AND
STRUCK OUT 1,330 TIMES)

USING LOSING: WHEN FAILURE MAKES YOU WANT TO COME BACK STRONG

Athletes know a lot about winning and losing, about failure and success. Pros play hundreds of games during their careers, and they know they can't win them all. They can't afford to let one loss affect the way they play for the rest of the game or the season.

Although Senator Bill Bradley was an Olympic gold medalist and NBA champion, he lost his share of games. It was his philosophy about failure that helped him get through the rough times.

"The taste of defeat has a richness of experience all its own,'' the senator told me during our interview. "Life is a series of small defeats and small victories. If you're totally thrown by the defeats, it's unlikely that you will have as full a life or experience as many of the victories—because your ability to gain a victory is directly related to your ability to come back from a defeat.

"In basketball, you can't afford to think about the game you lost last night, because you're playing again tonight. . . . If you can't find a way to shake the defeat and go on to the next game, you're in trouble. Once a game is lost, it's gone. . . . The richness of the experience is in understanding the pain of defeat, putting it in perspective, living through it, and moving on.''

The pain of defeat is shared by every athlete, including boxer Shannon Briggs. Briggs is intelligent, polite, and ambitious. He's got a distinctive hair style and a powerful left hook, and he knows that boxing is his ticket out of the 'hood. He's well on the road to a glorious career. But he's had his share of failure along the way.

In 1991, Briggs was clobbered in the first round of his fight in the Pan-American Games by Cuban fighter Felix Savon. Then, in June of 1992, Briggs suffered a wrist injury that kept him out of the Olympic trials. Two tough blows, even for a tough kid from the streets of New York.

But Briggs was not willing to give up, even though some of his friends and colleagues gave up on him. He uses his "failures" as motivation to go on, and to go on stronger than before.

"After losing, I went back to Olympic training camp, and no one had anything to say to me," says Briggs. "People who were my friends before wouldn't even speak to me. That motivated me. I came back, I trained hard. Now I had to show them. There are people who don't even know me, who prejudge me, who say 'I don't like this guy. He thinks he's this, he thinks he's that, look at his hair.' Those are the people that I'm fighting for, those are the people that I have to show."

Sometimes it's just that passion for proving other people wrong that keeps us going. When I left the corporate world to start a business of my own, some people were very supportive. But there were also many people who said, "You'll never make it," "You're crazy," "The economy is just too bad," "You're bound to fail." Those comments were like a whip at my back, keeping me moving forward. Every time I worked late into the evening so I could reach people on the West Coast, every time I made one more phone call instead of quitting for the day, I was one step closer to proving those people wrong. If everyone around you is being negative, you can use that as a positive force.

The people who motivate Shannon Briggs the most are those who, for reasons of their own, want to see him fail. People who tell him he "can't do it" make him want to prove them wrong.

"There are fighters out there saying, 'He's not really that good.' I'm proving it to them. I'm mentally psyched. I loved it when a friend of mine said, 'This guy said you didn't want to go to the Olympics because you didn't want to fight Savon again.' I'm doing it for him."

But Briggs also knows he can't make it on his own. His desire to prove himself isn't his only fuel for fighting. Briggs is surrounded by a team that pumps him up and keeps him going. His manager and his trainer both contribute greatly to his success.

"What makes me get up and want to run that extra mile is because I know that if I fail, I'm carrying these guys with me. . . . I go down, we all go down. They do their job to help me be successful, and when it's time to fight, it's payback time. I know I've got a good team. I can't let them down."

WHEN OTHER PEOPLE'S STANDARDS STAND IN YOUR WAY

You may not have a manager and a trainer to keep you going. But you have friends and family, and you have yourself. *You* are the challenger, the one who dares you to go on. *You* are the team that must not be let down.

Sometimes it is the very people around us that keep us from moving ahead. We find ourselves reluctant to take a risk, to try something new because of what others around us are saying or doing. We're not only afraid to fail, we're afraid we'll look foolish, or that we won't measure up to what we think other people want us to be. We judge ourselves against what others own, wear, look like, or have accomplished.

The best way to compete with others is to create for yourself. You want *others* to compete with *you* because you're the creator, the innovator. You don't want to be the follower or the copycat. The most important question is not "What can I do better than everyone else?'' It is ''What am *I* best at doing, and how can I use it to help me succeed?''

Time and energy are the fuel for creativity. If we spend all our time and energy being concerned with others' performance, or how others see our own performance, we give up those precious resources. We can't control what other people do. If we let others define failure for us, we lose our ability to succeed.

People in the public eye are particularly susceptible to this kind of pressure. Football Hall-of-Famer Franco Harris is now a successful businessman and president of Super Bakery, a company that manufactures and distributes nutritional doughnuts (that's right—nutritional doughnuts!). But when he left football, he had no idea what he wanted to do. He is now a great exponent of, and spokesperson for, people who are starting second careers.

''I had one wonderful career,'' he says. ''It was great, I loved it. Then I had to find a second one. . . . When I left football, I really didn't have any plans. When I was let go, I sat down for about twenty minutes with all kinds of thoughts running through my head. And then I said, 'Enough of this. I'm going to get up off the couch, go downtown, and get on with my life.' Luckily I didn't sit there with visions of past and future football going through my head to keep me down. I got them out of my mind and said, 'Hey, I'm going to go get busy.' And I went and got busy and I never looked back.''

Like millions of other people, Harris had to deal with the myriad problems of starting a new career. For a high-profile person, however, those problems can be exaggerated.

''When I first started my business, it was just me,'' Harris explains. ''One day I got a call from a store wanting me to bring some boxes of my product over to them. It was a Saturday, an hour drive one way, but I said to myself, 'you have to do this, you're starting a business.' So I went to make the delivery. As I was carrying the product into the store an older couple was backing up out of the parking lot. And this older guy goes, 'That's Franco Harris!' And the wife says, 'That's not Franco Harris. He wouldn't be carrying boxes into a store!'

"It made me think. Is that what people think about me carrying boxes? Does she think that because of where I was before, carrying boxes into the store makes me a failure? If it was anybody else in business people would say, 'Wow, he'll do whatever it takes to make his business work.' "

Harris didn't let other people's opinions stop him from pitching in and doing whatever was necessary to make his business a success. He uses his own strengths and abilities, and the tenacity and persistence he learned as a Steeler, to keep him going. He never sees himself as a failure, but as someone who has succeeded more than once.

"With what's happening in this country today, you really have to look at a second career as the second part of your life," he says, "and it's very important that you approach it with the same enthusiasm. Don't be afraid and don't think that it means that you're a failure. Don't think that starting at the bottom again is something to look down at. Because if you use what you've learned from your other profession you're going to move along a lot quicker. . . . Starting a new business, starting all over again . . . to some people that's scary. But to me, it's very exciting."

WHAT TO DO WHEN THE PRESSURE IS ON

If Franco Harris had let himself be influenced by other people's opinions, he never would have been able to keep himself going. But he did not give up under pressure.

We usually think of pressure as a destructive force. But there are times when pressure can produce amazing results.

Diamonds are formed through pressure. Both soot—which is soft, black, and virtually worthless—and diamonds—which are harder than any other natural substance, transparent, and sometimes priceless—are made of carbon. The difference is that soot forms at ordinary temperature and pressure. Diamonds form at a temperature and pressure equivalent to that existing 150 miles below the earth's surface. Anything that can withstand that kind of physical pressure has got to be special.

Humans can't withstand that amount of physical pressure, but they can withstand great amounts of emotional pressure. This kind of pressure is probably felt most vividly by athletes—especially Olympic athletes.

As Bruce Jenner tells it: "There is no bigger pressure cooker in the world than the Olympics. I don't care what you do, how much money you've got on the line—the games are the ultimate pressure cooker. They happen just once every four years, and every human being in the whole world is invited to be there.

"It's like a piano player who spends twelve years of his life learning to play music. After twelve years of isolation, he'll go out in front of the world one time, play one great song, and that's it. Once the concert's over, he puts his hands in his pockets and never touches the piano again. And the world applauds and says that was the greatest music we've ever heard."

For some people, just the thought of that kind of pressure would be enough to make them give up. But not Jenner.

"People have to realize that it's all part of the game: pressure, anxiety, fear, doubt. If you feel a lot of pressure and fear, it's because what you're doing means something to you. If you don't feel those things you're probably in the wrong business. You should go do something else."

Jenner uses fear as a motivating force. He thinks of fear as always being three feet behind him. "That's where I want it to be," he says. "And I'm never going to run slow enough to let it catch me. When you're coming up to that last turn and you're pumping, use that fear to your advantage."

Shannon Briggs has also learned to use fear as a great motivator. "I had a lot of fear when I was growing up, tons of fear," he says. "I don't think fear is something I should be ashamed of. I lived in bad neighborhoods all my life. I had fear growing up in those neighborhoods. But I wanted to deal with it. That's what I think is the good part, using that fear and not letting fear take over. I learn from it. So now, I put all my experiences together, and I channel my fear into my boxing.''

He didn't learn to channel that fear by himself. He had help from his trainer, Teddy Atlas. Atlas, who started out as well-known trainer Cus Damato's right-hand man, deals with fear every day. He's had to teach many young boxers to acknowledge and accept their own fears in the ring.

He tells them: ''Nature gave us fear before people were writing books, before we started defining all these things so philosophically. Fear was put there to help you survive as long as you can. A fighter has to learn to accept that fear.''

People think a fighter must never be afraid. Atlas knows that the first thing a fighter thinks when he feels that fear is ''There is something wrong. I'm not cut out for this, I'm yellow. I'm not made for this.''

''When a kid first sees a fighter,'' says Atlas, ''he says 'That's guy's a Spartan, he's a warrior. That guy's not afraid of anything.' Then the kid starts fighting, and he's just as scared as anybody should be. If he's normal. If he's not, he better find a doctor, 'cause nature short-circuited, a wire fell off.

''Without fear, without the simplest form of fear, we couldn't survive a day. The simplest thing, like crossing the street, would kill you, because you'd just be thinking about where you want to go. You wouldn't be thinking about the danger of getting hit.

''I explain to fighters they have to learn to understand fear, that it doesn't make them inferior. Fear is the biggest problem for people achieving any goal. But in boxing it's worse, because the intention is to hurt you. Fighters are the same as other people. They've got layers and layers of fear formed from thoughts and beliefs they got from their mother, their father, their uncle, their brother, their sister—before they ever get to me in the gym. I've got to take those layers and peel them off. I know it sounds corny, but I've got to peel them off before I ever teach them how to throw a jab. I've got to open their eyes to what's real, to what can affect them and what can't affect them.

"Fear is like fire. When it's controlled, it'll cook for you, it will heat your home, it will do a lot of good things. When it's not controlled it will burn up everything around you, consume everything.

"Same with fear. When it's controlled, it will make you better. It will make you prepare. . . . It will make you do what you have to do to survive. And if it's not controlled it will consume you just like fire; it will destroy you. You have to understand fear is an ally, not an enemy."

"Studies show that the number-one fear people have, the thing they're more afraid of than anything else, is speaking in public. The number two fear is death. That means that most people would rather be in the casket than giving the eulogy."

—JERRY SEINFELD

FALSE EVIDENCE APPEARING REAL

Someone once told me that *fear* is an acronym for the phrase "false evidence appearing real." Therefore, the first step in dealing with any fear is to face it head on and analyze it to find out what is real and what is not. As every horror fan knows, it's not the monsters we can see that are so scary—it's the unexplained sounds in the night, or the shadowy figure cloaked in darkness. When we don't know what's real and what's not, our imagination begins to work overtime. It's the unknown that frightens us.

Taking any kind of a risk means stepping into that unknown. There is no way to guarantee the consequences. But there are ways of dealing with the fear of failure. In their book *Beyond Fear,* Robert Handly and Pauline Neff describe "anticipatory anxiety," or the expectation of failure. We think about all the bad things that can possibly happen, and our fear grows larger and larger. But, the authors say, "In reality, the surge of adrenalin that causes you to shake and tremble has a very short half-life. If you can stop the fear thoughts that reinforce your anxiety for only a few moments, you will be calm enough to perform well.''

When *Breakthrough Selling* was published, I worked hard to get the book publicized. The first time I was scheduled to be interviewed on a live radio program, I was nervous. My hands were sweating. I didn't know what to expect. I had no idea what the experience would be like, but I was sure it would be nerve-wracking. I was afraid that my nervousness would interfere with my ability to recall or relate the ideas I wanted to get across. I was relying on false evidence: information supplied to me by my imagination.

I got through the experience. When it was over, I spoke to the producer. "This was my first time," I confessed. "I was nervous, and I'm sure I didn't do very well."

"What do you mean?" she said. "You were great!"

Still, I asked her how I could improve for my next radio show. She gave me some helpful tips. Now, after doing over two hundred radio shows, I still ask for advice to help me improve. I know there's always room for improvement.

I still get nervous—and I'm glad I do. The butterflies I feel keep me energized and intense. I use that adrenalin buzz to keep me on my toes.

PREPARATION IS THE KEY

If you think about the times in your life when you were most afraid, they are probably the times when you were least prepared. We've all had nightmares about being back in school and running into a classmate who says, "Well, you ready for the big exam?" You look at him in wonder and say, "What exam?" Of course, you haven't studied, you're totally unprepared, and you're paralyzed with fear!

Although there are some "pop quizzes" in real life, most of the time we are given a fair amount of warning before we must face potentially scary circumstances. We can either spend that time nurturing our fear or we can spend it preparing for the task ahead. When you study for an exam, when you know the material, you may still be nervous, but you will not be paralyzed.

When facing a frightening situation, you can reduce your fear by increasing your knowledge and focusing your nervous energy on your preparation instead of on your imagination. Get to know your subject inside out; study all about it. In this way you conquer your fear by confronting it and outsmarting it.

As difficult as it may be for most of us to confront our fears, consider the difficulties for those whose failures are exposed to the public. Political consultant Mary Matalin explains that failure is ''. . . particularly hard in campaigns because when you fail everybody sees you. It's a public humiliation. Your candidate loses and it changes the course of history. As painful as it is, you are obliged in this career to know what failed and painstakingly dissect it so that you don't repeat it. . . . A real failure is to repeat the same mistake twice.''

Often, the activity involved in preparing for a frightening event takes so much time, there's no time left to be scared. Ann Compton is an ABC News White House Correspondent now covering her fourth president.

''My job is to keep people informed about what's going on in the White House,'' she says. ''One of my great shortcomings is that I have no fear. I'm not a fearless person—I just don't have time to sit down and worry about fear. I was one of the questioners in the final presidential debate in the 1988 campaign. I was faced with the prospect of sitting there, not only in front of sixty million people on television, but in front of the political press, my peers, asking two men, one of whom will be president of the United States, questions for ninety minutes.

''They called me a day and a half before the event to say you've been chosen for the debate panel, get to Los Angeles. After it was all over, somebody said, 'God, weren't you scared?' Only then did I realize what I'd just been through. I just didn't have time to be scared.''

There is perhaps no greater demonstration of the "no time to be scared" phenomenon than when you are in a life-threatening situation. Nowhere is fear more prominent and failure more devastating than flying a fighter plane in a wartime situation. The following is a dramatic sequence of events, described by Desert Storm fighter pilot and squadron commander Lt. Col. Dennis Krembel, about what happens when a pilot engages unidentified aircraft flying over enemy territory. Imagine the fear of losing your life or failing when life and death are at stake. Imagine the amount of training and preparation necessary to combat this fear. . . .

"The first time you see your name on the flying schedule, you're glad because now you're going to participate and contribute to the overall effort," says Lt. Col. Krembel. "But at the same time, you experience some anxiety. As the hour draws near, that anxiety grows—and you deal with it. You do everything within your power to ensure you and your flight members are prepared. Once you step up to the airplane, once things start happening, you don't have time to be scared.

"Imagine you're leading a flight of four and you detect unidentified aircraft at a range of forty miles. Typically, you close at a rate of one mile every three seconds. At long range, a flight leader uses his radar, and the radar of other flight members, along with AWACS (Airborne Warning and Control System) to determine the overall tactical picture. So he has a lot of informational sources.

"The flight leader is trying to determine the number of airplanes, their identification (friend or foe), and their intent. He needs to communicate with the AWACS controller and his other flight members. As he approaches thirty to twenty-five nautical miles, he has to assign groups of targets to certain flight members. Eventually the flight leader wants to target the greatest threats. This process requires precise communication. In a short time, unidentified aircraft have to be confirmed as hostile and then engaged. Additionally, the pilot utilizes information from other sources, such as the Radar Warning Receiver, which is a radar detector. It tells the pilot if an adversary might attack. This information is communicated to the flight leader and he must decide if the flight is offensive, defensive, or unknown.

"The flight leader must then elect to engage or withdraw. His decision is based on his situational awareness, provided by critical information from a multitude of sources. He has to correlate and integrate this information and then decide: stay and fight, or leave."

A pretty amazing scenario so far. But here's the most amazing thing of all: These planes started forty miles apart. By the time they are fifteen miles apart, the pilot must decide whether he's going to engage or withdraw. How long does it take him to travel that distance? *Seventy-five seconds!* Within seventy-five seconds he must make an unbelievable number of critical assessments and decisions—and deal with his fear as well.

The number of times a pilot actually finds himself in this situation is minuscule compared to the amount of training and preparation that has come before it. It's because of that preparation he is able to deal with the fear at all.

Not every fearful situation is going to be this extreme, giving you no time to think about how to do the task at hand. Whatever the situation, however, preparation is the key. It's only when we realize we don't know how to do something, when we feel insecure and out of control, that fear takes control of us. We can let that happen, we can let fear inhibit and even paralyze us. Or we can decide that fear is our servant, not our master, and keep on taking life's risks and challenges.

Lt. Col. Krembel was fortunate enough to return safely from Desert Storm. Early in his career, though, he had a very personal, potentially career-ending brush with tragedy that forced him to boldly confront his fears.

"When I went through initial training," he says, "a good friend of mine was killed in a midair collision. I was about one hundred feet from his aircraft when the incident occurred. It was quite frightening, and it had a big impact on me.

"I was young at the time, and it scared me a lot. I had vivid pictures of the impact, and of what actually took place. For several days, I couldn't put it out of my mind. I considered the following: Death is an inherent risk in this type of flying.

What am I going to do? Am I going to give up my profession because of that? You reflect and look at your life, and you evaluate what are you trying to do in your life, and ask yourself, what is your life all about?

"It boils down to faith. The bottom-line decision was to keep flying. I'm going to be damn careful about how I do it, but I need to press on. The country needs top qualified fighter pilots. . . . But the anxiety has always been with me. You just realize it's always going to be there and set it aside. It's a human reaction. You keep a healthy respect for the fact that you can't put two airplanes within the same piece of sky, and you do everything within your power to eliminate the potential for that, but you can't throw in the towel just because it might happen."

> *"Courage is not the absence of fear, it is the conquest of it. Not until you dare to attack will you master your fears."*
>
> —FROM *I DARE YOU!* BY WILLIAM H. DANFORTH

KEEPING FEAR IN ITS PLACE

Franklin Roosevelt said, "We have nothing to fear but fear itself." If you let the fear take you down, it will. If you acknowledge it, stand up to it, and go on anyway, it will get smaller and smaller.

When Teddy Atlas trains his fighters, the first thing he has to do is get them to be honest with themselves—to admit when they are afraid, and to know when they are looking for excuses.

"First thing I do when I get a fighter," says Atlas, "is get him in real good physical shape. I put him in the ring. The guy he's fighting keeps coming, keeps coming. Two rounds go by, which is a very short amount of time, and my guy's dead tired. I take him—this is the honesty—and I say, 'You know why you're tired?' ''

The fighter usually answers with ''Yeah, 'cause I'm boxing.''

Then Atlas tells him, ''No, you're tired because you want to be tired. Because what you're doing is tough. Fear, your little pal that nature put on top of your shoulder, only cares about one thing, your survival. He doesn't care if you're a winner. He doesn't care if you're successful or rich. His job is to make sure you live to see another day.''

Atlas tells his fighter that when some big guy keeps coming at him, the body's natural response is to find a way to get out of the ring.

He says, ''This guy is a relentless, unstoppable force—in your mind. But it's just your imagination. Because sitting outside the ring, people are saying, 'Look how slow this guy is, he walks into every punch.' But your imagination is making this guy King Kong.

''So you find a way to survive. The easiest way is to get tired. Because that's acceptable. Because all the people watching will say, 'If you were in better shape and you trained more, you would have beat the guy.' And you say, 'Hey, you're right. I'll beat him next time.' ''

But Atlas knows this is an excuse. This is False Evidence Appearing Real. He shows his fighter movies of other boxers in the ring. He shows him a fight in the ninth round where the champ is dead tired, and he's losing the fight. Suddenly he lands a punch against the challenger; then before you know it he's throwing punch after punch, and he's not tired anymore. He looks like it's the first round and he just got shot out of the cannon.

''He was never tired,'' says Atlas. ''He was mentally tired, he was discouraged. His will was broken. He was looking to get out. But when he sees the other guy's knees buckle, when he sees there is a chance to win, all of a sudden he isn't tired anymore.''

Atlas knows it's not real fatigue that gets in his fighters' way—it's fear. He tells his fighters to talk to their fear, to put it in its place:

"You can take that fear and put it aside. You can say, 'Excuse me fear, I'm going to take you and put you right there. Stay there, hang out for a while, I'm going to go fight. I'm going to put you in your place. Now hang on and *watch me perform.*'"

"One who fears, limits his activities. Failure is only the opportunity to more intelligently begin again."

—HENRY FORD

Five Essential Facets of Chapter 3

1. Failure is the ultimate learning tool. Every disappointment teaches a positive lesson—you just have to look for it. It's only when we make the same mistakes over and over again that we have failed. It is in times of adversity that we grow the most.
2. Success is our greatest revenge. When people are discouraging or critical, use your "I'll prove them wrong" energy as a motivator to push you into action.
3. Once you perceive a problem or an obstacle, learn from it as quickly as you can and then move on. Don't bathe in defeat. If you've made a mistake, understand that you'll do it differently next time. Dwelling on previous failures causes you to fail in the future.
4. *Fear* is the acronym for false evidence appearing real. Therefore, the first step in taming any fear is to analyze what is real and what is not. It is the unknown that frightens us, and our imaginations fuel our fear.
5. Preparation and action are the greatest combators of fear. The only way to conquer any fear is to study all you can, and to prepare in every possible way. You can reduce your fear by increasing your knowledge and focusing your nerv-

ous energy on the preparation instead of on your imagination.

Think about actions you can take from these five ideas or others discussed in this chapter.

Thirty-Day Action Plan for Chapter 3

If a challenging situation produces fear that inhibits you from taking action, you can relieve a portion of that fear by writing a list of "do-able" steps. Making a specific plan often eliminates much of the fear.

What goal would I like to accomplish where fear is blocking

me from taking action?_____

_____

What books, tapes, magazines are available as resource materials on the subject?_____

_____

Do I know anyone who has accomplished the goal I'm seeking? How can I contact that person and/or find out how they did it? What was their biggest fear and how did they deal with it?_____

_____

_____

What's the worst thing that could happen to me if I try and fail?

_____

What could I learn in the process?_____

_____

What benefits could I receive if I try and succeed?_____

_____

By what date am I going to accomplish this goal?_____

(Write this date in your calendar where you can see it daily.)

Follow up your action plan:
Did I achieve my goal?_____

What did I learn from diving in and confronting my fear?

_____

_____

If I didn't accomplish my goal, what can I do differently or more effectively next time?

_____

_____

_____

Now you've seen that it's possible for anyone to overcome the most difficult obstacles, and to conquer debilitating fear. You know that failure isn't failure as long as you learn from it. What you don't know is that you don't have to fight all your fears and insecurities alone. The road to success doesn't have to be barren and lonely. There are people everywhere who are willing to help if we are willing to ask. We can use a variety of resources, such as books and tapes, for inspiration and examples. The following chapter will give you an idea of what a mentor really is, how to find one (or several), and how to become one yourself.

Chapter Four

SHINING EXAMPLES: SEEKING OUT POSITIVE ROLE MODELS

"To me there is only one definition of success, and that's what makes you happy. To some people it's money, to some people it's respect, to some it's power. For me, it's working with people who are funny and work hard and are committed and loyal and trustworthy. That's the measure of success to me, that I can work with a team of people who I help and who help me, and go home happy at the end of the day."

—MARY MATALIN, POLITICAL CONSULTANT

"My definition of success is really very simple: that you've established a reasonable set of priorities, and a reasonable set of goals, and that you've accomplished those goals with a great degree of sensitivity, humility, and appreciation for the people who helped get you there."

—MICHAEL STRAMAGLIO, VICE PRESIDENT OF SALES AND MARKETING, MINOLTA CORPORATION

Years ago, in a popular store on Main Street, a shop owner placed a large grandfather clock in his front window. One morning shortly thereafter, he saw a man walk by, pull a pocket watch from his vest, adjust the watch to the clock, put it back in his pocket, and walk away. Every morning of every day of every week of every month of every year for the next four years, the shop owner observed this little ritual. Finally one day the shop owner was outside sweeping the sidewalk as the man passed by. He watched the man take his watch out of his pocket, adjust the time, and begin to walk away.

"Pardon me sir," the owner said, "but I just have to ask you one question. I've been watching you do this same thing every morning for four years. Can I ask you why?"

"Of course," said the man. "I'm the foreman down at the steel mill. I blow the quitting whistle at five o'clock every day, and I want to be sure my people get out on time."

"You're kidding," the owner replied in amazement. "I've been setting my grandfather clock to your five o'clock whistle all these years!"

The amazing thing is that the foreman and the shopkeeper could have been off by months. Five minutes here, two minutes there . . . It adds up. Who knows which of the men had the right time? Week after week, month after month, the two men simply followed their old habits, never bothering to check a reference or ask a question.

One of the biggest problems in our society today is that we play a lonely game called follow-the-follower. Like the steel mill foreman and the shop owner, we assume that the "other guy" has all the answers. Instead of conducting our own investigation, or finding someone who truly has the qualities we wish to emulate, we take on the group mentality. We do what others do, we talk the way they talk, we even think the same thoughts. We want to be liked; we want to be accepted. We want to be ourselves, yet we're afraid to be "different."

We start playing this game early on, when we insist on wearing the same sneakers and jeans that everybody else is wearing. We continue playing the game as adults when we start a new job and say, "Everybody else does it this way, and they've been doing it this way for years, so it must be the right way." Meanwhile, everybody is looking at the new guy to see how he does things, and when they see that he's doing just what they've always done, they breathe a sigh of relief and say, "We knew we were right all along."

There's nothing inherently wrong with following. One of the most effective methods of learning is by following a good example. Throughout the animal kingdom, the young learn how to survive by following and imitating the actions of their parents and elders. Humans, too, learn by example. High achievers are constantly studying other people and their methods of accomplishment.

The difference is that they are very particular about the people from whom they choose to learn. They look for people whose values match their own, and who have achieved excellence in their field. They surround themselves not only with markers of their own success, but also with models of the success of others.

"You are a product of your environment. So choose the environment that will best develop you toward your objective. Analyze your life in terms of its environment. Are the things around you helping you toward success—or are they holding you back?"

—W. CLEMENT STONE

SURROUND YOURSELF WITH MODELS OF SUCCESS

In chapter 1, we talked about surrounding yourself with markers of success—reminders of what you have previously achieved that let you know you have been successful in the past and can continue to be successful in the future. This is an effective tool to keep you motivated when disappointment or depression hits. Another tool you can use to provide inspiration and motivation is to surround yourself with models of success—positive ideas, philosophies, role models, and mentors.

And, as we also said in chapter 1 (and as we'll discuss in detail in the next chapter), one of the great laws of nature—what philosophers, prophets, great thinkers, and high achievers have said over and over again in many different ways—is that we become what we think about. We can't help but think about what surrounds us; therefore if we surround ourselves with positive images, we will necessarily reflect their positive influences. This is what I call the mirroring effect. What we see around us reflects back on ourselves. If everything we look at is dull, depressing, oppressing, and stifling, we cannot help but think dull, depressing thoughts. That is how we'll think of ourselves and how we'll live our lives. On the other miraculous hand, if we surround ourselves with the best and the brightest, with the energetic and the enthusiastic, our thoughts will automatically be brighter and more energizing, and our lives will reflect these positive qualities.

The world is full of raw materials that we can use as mirrors. It's up to us to mine for the gems. And there are gems to be found everywhere. Humankind has produced thousands and thousands of wise, intelligent, caring, energetic, motivated, successful women and men, living and dead, who have given us a fabulous legacy from which to learn and prosper. These people have been rich in word and deed. It is up to us to listen to what they had (or have) to say, and to study what they have achieved. Shining examples surround us. When we follow these examples, and cast aside the negative influencers, the doomsayers, the greedy and the selfish, we can ourselves become examples for others to follow.

We can't just wait for these shining examples to appear before us. We have to seek them out. Here are four examples of places you will find them:

◆ Explore the library. Role models don't necessarily need to be people we see around us every day. Read biographies. Go back into history. Look for those men and women who have achieved greatness and study their lives. Take notes.

If something they have said or done inspires you, write it down and put it somewhere you will see it frequently.

Literary agent Jeff Herman has used this method for a long time, and he has found it to be very helpful, especially when things aren't going smoothly. "Success is a long march," says Herman. "When you have the hunger to accomplish something, you measure time in a very different way. I often turn to books of history and books of conquest for inspiration. One is *The Long March* by Mao Tse Tung. Of course, I don't condone communism, but he created an army from nothing, with no resources, just his own hunger, to bring communism to China. He had a rag-tag army which was basically decimated by Western resources and was assumed to be all but dead. But he was measuring time in a very different way. He didn't give up, and he came back to conquer all of China.

"Another example is the Israeli war of independence in 1948. Another people who had no organized army or military resources, but they had the hunger to establish a homeland for themselves. Everyone who looked at it rationally assumed it was a lost cause. It was their relentless determination that enabled them to succeed against the odds. I often look at history and historical figures to see how they overcame situations which should have been fatal."

♦ Discover the world of audio tapes. When you're driving, when you're out walking, when you're exercising, whenever you have available listening time, plug in your earphones and get some good advice. Listen to many different people until you find someone who really sparks something in you. Then listen to that person over and over again so that the positive ideas, the inspirational messages, become a part of your inner psyche.

♦ Look to the people around you. Role models need not come from the ranks of the rich and famous. Success takes many forms; money and status are not the only criteria for measuring success. Are there people in your family, among your friends, or in your community whom you respect and admire? Many of the people interviewed for this book mentioned their parents' influence. Michael Stramaglio, for example, says that his greatest mentor was his father. "[He] gave me the basic appreciation of a job well done, a good day's work, doing things to the best of your ability or not doing them at all . . . all the things a father should instill in his children. On a personal level, it's a foundation I can't ignore."

♦ Teach yourself to be observant and to be discriminating. It's difficult to have heroes and roles models today. We put our "stars," whether they're sports figures, entrepreneurs, actors, or politicians, on high, high pedestals—and almost every day we watch another one slip, fall, and break our trust and hearts. We always want to put people in neat little categories, to see them as good or bad, right or wrong. When our heroes turn out to be fallible, complex human beings, we are hurt and confused. It's not always easy to understand how someone you admire can do something you can't respect. However, we can learn to "take the best and leave the rest": Emulate their positive qualities, appreciate the good they have done, and learn a lesson from the mistakes they have made.

If you don't want to play follow-the-follower, study the people you are looking to for knowledge and advice and ask yourself, "Is this person (or this group or this philosophy) I'm following going where I want to go?" If so, follow their lead. Study the way they conduct their lives. Watch how they dress, how they walk and talk. Think about the qualities they possess that you admire. Find ways to apply those qualities to your own life. Don't try to imitate or become these people, but learn from them.

KEEP YOURSELF OPEN TO THOSE WHO CAN HELP

We all need teachers, guides, and mentors in our lives. Often there are people around us who see in us what we cannot see ourselves. If we're willing to listen, if we open our minds to the possibilities these people are describing, we're likely to overcome the self-doubts that are keeping us from reaching our potential.

Now one of the most recognized voices in the country, Cousin Bruce Morrow stuttered and stammered in junior and senior high school. He was shy, he kept to himself, and he did not want to be called on to answer questions. But one of his teachers saw possibilities in the young Bruce Meyerowitz (his real name) and urged him to try out for the school's hygiene play. He did, and got the part of a cavity. "I went on that stage," says Morrow, "and suddenly the shyness was pushed aside. . . . Before that experience ended, I realized there was something on that stage that made me feel good, made me want to explore this more."

The teacher took Morrow under her wing and got him to audition for the all-city radio workshop, an organization that puts high school students in semiprofessional and professional radio environments. "As soon as that happened," says Morrow, "I knew that radio was going to be my life's work. . . . That was a very important part of my life."

School is often the place where we find our first mentors. Bruce Morrow is not alone in his story of a teacher's encouragement. William H. Danforth, in his classic book *I Dare You!* tells how he was a sallow-cheeked, hollow-chested, sickly boy until a teacher looked him straight in the eye and said, "I dare you to be the healthiest boy in class." That teacher not only encouraged a weak young man to become strong and healthy, his words became the foundation for Danforth's lifelong philosophy, daring himself and others to do and be more than they ever thought they could.

Having mentors early in life was so important to Dr. Rhoda Dorsey, president of Goucher College in Maryland, that she instituted an alumni mentoring program for her school. "We ask our alumni to volunteer some time so that students may come to visit them," says Dorsey. "First, the students come and talk about the alumni's job. Then they visit them a second and third time to follow them around and see what in fact they do on a daily basis. They visit a fourth time for a sort of summary recap.'' Dorsey feels that one of the benefits of a mentorship program is that the students can put themselves in their mentor's place, and get a much better idea of what the world outside the classroom is really like.

Dorsey had mentors of her own in college and graduate school. But it wasn't the actual information they gave her that made them essential to Dorsey's career and personal growth. ''What they did for me,'' she says, ''was to pay attention, to listen to me, and to give me the kind of confidence that says, 'Yes of course you can do it.' They believed in me. That's very important.''

In recent years, the importance of mentoring has also come to the attention of corporate America. Businesses all over the country are setting up formal mentoring programs so that newcomers will automatically have someone more experienced to explain the ins and outs of their particular business. But a mentor is often more than a teacher of business acumen; quite often he or she is a combination of a professor, a therapist, and Emily Post. As Michael Stramaglio explains, ''What often happens is that with the enthusiasm of youth there comes a certain amount of impatience. . . . Your enthusiasm sometimes outweighs your brain. You think you can do more than you're doing; you see too many frustrations in your path. . . . A mentor can teach you how to learn from frustrating situations, how to develop your people skills, and how to understand and appreciate areas of the business that may not be your strength. A mentor can work wonders in opening up your eyes and your imagination and controlling the impetuousness of being a young businessperson.''

We often look back at our lives and say, ''If only I knew then what I know now.'' That's what mentoring can provide us—the knowledge of people who have gone before us, who have already navigated the choppy seas and made the costly mistakes. In this country, the vast majority of businesses that fail do so because they didn't research their industry well enough. Mary Kay Ash believes this is so for many people who go into business for themselves. Before Mary Kay set up her megasuccessful cosmetics company, she had had twenty-five years' experience in other people's businesses. Her advice to anyone considering opening their own business is to "go to work for a company that's already doing what you want to do. Learn from their failures or from their successes before you invest your money and your time and your heart. I find so many people go out and borrow a hundred thousand dollars to open a business and they don't know what they're doing. The result is that within a few months it's down the drain, with a 'for lease' sign in the window. It's a shame and it's heartbreaking that people work so hard to set something up before they really know what they're doing. We don't need to make the same mistakes as our predecessors. Instead we can learn from their wisdom and experience."

> *"Personal relationships are the fertile soil from which*
> *all advancement, all success, all achievement in real*
> *life grows."*

> —BEN STEIN

BECAUSE YOU NEVER KNOW . . . EXPOSURE, CONTACTS, AND NETWORKING

Michael Stramaglio, Rhoda Dorsey, and Bruce Morrow all had mentors in their lives who served as shining examples. A mentor can be a guide and a teacher, but it's up to the "mentee" to take what he or she has learned and put it to use. Stramaglio, Dorsey, and Morrow took the spark that caring people saw in them and built it into outstanding careers.

You never know who is going to point you in a particular direction, give you a suggestion or an idea that may change your life. "It's up to you to take this idea or suggestion and let it grow. Follow it through, do your research," says Morrow. He recommends that everywhere you go, make contacts and ask questions. "Watch. Observe. Start absorbing energy.

Ask questions like crazy,'' he advises. ''Before you know it, things start to happen. I've seen it hundreds of times and it works. But you've got to go out there. No one is waiting for you. The world's not saying, 'A star is born.' You've got to do your own advertising.''

> *"He who has a thing to sell*
> *and goes and whispers in a well,*
> *is not so apt to get the dollars*
> *as he who climbs a tree and hollers."*
>
> —Anonymous

Doing your own advertising has always been the philosophy of Terrie Williams, president of one of the fastest-growing public relations firms in the country, with clients including Eddie Murphy, Bobby Brown, Janet Jackson, HBO, and the Coca-Cola Bottling Company of New York. Williams adamantly believes in reaching out to make contacts; it's how she built her business.

Williams didn't start out as a PR professional. She graduated *cum laude* in psychology from Brandeis University and holds a master of science degree in social work from Columbia. She was a social worker at New York Hospital when the great jazz legend Miles Davis was a patient there. Williams went up to his room and introduced herself. They struck up a friendship and Williams kept in touch. Davis eventually introduced her to Eddie Murphy, and the two became her first PR clients. At the time she met Davis, Williams wasn't even in public relations, much less considering her own agency. She did, however, consider making contacts the ideal method for giving herself options for the future.

''I think the key is to plant seeds,'' says Williams. ''I used to read everything I could get my hands on, skimming four or five newspapers a day. I subscribed to numerous publications. I kept in mind areas of interest to people I'd met. If I found an article I thought someone would like, I'd send it with a note that said, 'I thought you'd find the enclosed of interest.' I literally stayed in touch with people, not knowing exactly what it was I was going to do. So that when I did start my business, there was this awesome foundation that had been built, and I had amassed a really incredible network of contacts.

"I used to keep a log of every person I met with . . . and what the nature of our dialogue was about," says Williams. She would also keep these people posted about what she was doing, keep in touch from time to time, and let them know how much she appreciated them taking the time out to talk with her.

How do you meet the kinds of people you'd like to have contact with? You don't have to become a social climber, or live beyond your means trying to keep up with the lifestyles of the rich and famous. It's a matter of exposing yourself to a variety of situations. Be a participant, not an observer. Open yourself up to new experiences. You can kill two birds with one stone: Enjoy yourself by discovering new interests or by exploring old ones, while you're making valuable personal and professional contacts.

"It's important to set the stage for people to get to know you and what you can do. The only way you do that is if you're out and about," says Williams. "Go to functions. I used to go to things I was interested in—poetry readings and art exhibits—all the time. That's how I met people. I met some of the same people again and again, and relationships were established."

You never know how the various relationships you form will help you out. Norman King, author of seventeen books, creator of America's first media buying service, and chairman of American Capital Complex, Inc., sees networking as the way of the business world. "You meet someone and they introduce you to someone . . . and you start to move forward. . . . Years ago I met Frank Field [CBS-TV meteorologist and health and science expert]. We liked each other and stayed in touch. In certain markets, people recognize Frank in the street. So when I'm sitting at a table with Frank, all of a sudden my knowing him rubs off on three or four major world bankers. . . . They say, 'Look who Norman King knows.' Now these very same bankers have become part of my life . . . and other people see me with them and they say, 'Look who Norman King knows.' It's like the domino effect.''

You don't have to know someone famous to have this domino effect work for you. It's simply a matter of putting yourself out there, of seeking out people who are already doing what you would like to be doing, and asking them for help.

"We learn through association," says motivational trainer Bev Hyman. "We go from the known into the unknown. If you can only keep yourself open, then creative juices can flow. Who knows what value I can be to you and you to me. The whole story hasn't been told yet. There are many years ahead and we haven't got the faintest idea what we might do for each other someplace ten years from now—what we're going to learn from each other or what we'll mean to each other as human beings.''

These shining examples with which we surround ourselves are like comets lighting up the sky. If you ride on their trails for a while you'll be bathed in their light until you build up enough power and energy to be a star yourself.

FIND MENTORS OF YOUR OWN

In a *Reader's Digest* article called ''Someone to Watch Over You'' (Sept. 1992), Dave Thomas, founder of the Wendy's International fast-food chain, said, ''There are plenty of classy people out there who want to help. Instead of waiting for someone to take you under his wing, go out and find a good wing to climb under.''

This is excellent advice. It involves one of the underlying themes of this book: In order to reach your destination you've got to take the first step. Don't sit around and wait for others to help you—take action and you will get the help you need.

That's really what finding a mentor is all about—asking for help, advice, guidance. Most of us are afraid to ask for help. Somewhere along the line we've been taught that asking for help is a sign of weakness. We're supposed to be strong and independent, aren't we? We look at people who have made it to the top and we see them standing alone. We don't see the people around them who give them aid and support, just as we fail to see all the hard work that has gone before their public success.

The truth is that successful people know what their strengths are, and that they have to depend on others to bolster their weaknesses. They're not shy about finding others with more knowledge and/or experience and asking them for help.

So how do you go about cultivating mentors? Here are a few hints:

- ◆ **Be selective.** Study the people around you and find someone you like, admire, trust, and respect. Look for someone who has skills and experience you too would like to have.
- ◆ **Don't be afraid to call or write.** If you want help from someone you don't yet know, don't be afraid to try. Write to them. Don't just write a fan letter; let them know exactly why you chose to write to them and what information you're seeking. Make phone calls. Sometimes you can establish relationships with someone's right-hand person or secretary who can then help you establish a relationship with their boss.

  Most of us at some time have been in awe of someone else, intimidated by them, or afraid to approach them for fear of rejection. No matter how successful someone is, however, he or she is still a human being like everyone else. This realization hit J. Patrick Mulcahy, currently CEO of the Eveready Battery Company, early on in life. He was attending Camp Minnewonka, run by the American Youth Foundation. The focus of the camp was for youngsters to spend a week with high achievers. The week Mulcahy attended the camp, he came in contact with a U.S. senator, an Anglican bishop and a college president.

  ''The thing that struck me at the time,'' says Mulcahy, ''is that these people were no different than we were. They were just a little bit older and they had more experience.

And so what I learned was that if I want to achieve, all I
have to do is 'do it.' That's the difference between achievers and nonachievers. . . . When I go back now and talk to
the kids at this camp, that's the thought I try to put in their
minds. What's the difference between where I am now and
where they are? The only difference is that I found something I liked to do, and I went ahead and did it.''

♦ **Be persistent.** High achievers are available, but they're
also terribly busy. It took many, many phone calls and letters to arrange interviews with everyone profiled in this
book. With a few, like Boone Pickens and Senator Bradley,
it took at least four letters and twenty-five phone calls until
arrangements were finally made and settled. Although this
was a lot of effort, it made my meetings with those people
even more special than they would ordinarily have been.

Unless you are incredibly obnoxious, the person you are
trying to reach will probably appreciate your tenacity. Most
will be enthusiastic about giving back to someone who
doesn't give up. After all, that's how they made it.

♦ **Be specific about what you want to know.** Write down
your special areas of interest and any questions you have.
Don't be a pest or take up too much of your mentor's time,
but don't be afraid to ask. The people you're asking were
once in the same position you are, and can identify with
your thirst for knowledge.

♦ **Be willing and eager to work.** Ask your potential mentor
how you can be of help. Volunteer to work on a complicated project. Join trade associations, get on committees,
and do your share. Come up with specific plans of action
and ask your mentor for advice and suggestions.

♦ **Remember that one good turn deserves another.** The
best way you can say thank you to a mentor is to become
successful yourself. Always give credit to people who have
helped you along the way. And whenever you get the
chance, be a mentor to somebody else.

♦ **Realize that most people enjoy being asked.** This is true
in all areas of life. According to Mary Matalin, it is especially true in politics. ''You cannot succeed in this business

without mentors. It's not like science or art or law where you can read a book and learn 'how to do it.' In politics, you have to have mentors,'' she says. ''Kids are usually intimidated by their bosses or people who are advanced in their field. They shouldn't be, they should ask questions. . . .

''People who get to a certain level want to pass on what they've learned. They're always looking for people to be their alter egos. They're flattered to be asked. It's a nurturing thing; men and women both do it. Most people take kindly to helping other people—you'd be surprised at how much people really want to help.''

This is something that came up over and over again in the interviews—that people at the top were more than willing to share whenever and whatever they could. All of the people who spoke to me about their lives and their achievements took time out of their busy schedules because they thought that their experiences might be of benefit to others. Part of the satisfaction of realizing various levels of achievement is in being able to help those coming up behind you. As Michael Stramaglio of Minolta put it, ''One of the greatest things I enjoy is cultivating talent . . . watching people when they realize that they've actually done something beyond what they thought might be possible. That's really important. Helping other people achieve success is a motivator for me.''

I know this from my own experience as well. After a seminar or training session, people often come up to me and ask me questions or tell me how much the seminar has helped them. I see how excited they are and how ''pumped up'' they feel. That gets me higher than almost anything else in life. It's difficult to express in words how fulfilling it makes my professional life.

We all crave recognition. That's why many of us play the follow-the-follower game, because we want to be liked and accepted by our peers. But when you are recognized and singled out by someone who wants you to be their mentor, it makes all your hard work worth while. So if you have any fear or intimidation about approaching someone, remember that it is really their greatest reward.

MENTORS, MENTORS EVERYWHERE—WHETHER YOU KNOW THEM OR NOT

When we hear the word *mentor,* most of us picture one particular person with whom we develop a close relationship, and who guides us along the road to success. However, as this chapter has demonstrated, it's to your benefit to broaden your definition of what a mentor is. I consider Earl Nightingale a mentor, and I've never met or spoken with the man. But his tapes and writings continually inspire me and help me reach my business goals.

I became fascinated by his ideas and his motivational strategies. Every single word I heard had value to me. I played his tapes over and over again, at least one hundred times. Without even being aware of it, I started emulating his thoughts and ideas. I started speaking them and living them. I started picturing myself making my own audio program, to share some of my ideas and experiences. I pictured myself sitting in Earl Nightingale's chair to do the recording.

As I'm rereading this chapter, I'm thinking about how, not too long ago, my dream came true. I was sitting in Earl Nightingale's chair, facing the engineer who spent ten years working with him, recording my own audio program. After we recorded my program, he played some of Nightingale's original recordings I had never heard before.

I spent two years pursuing the Nightingale corporation to do an audio program. I approached four different people there who turned me down repeatedly before finally accepting me. Every time I got a reference letter, every time an article of mine appeared in a magazine, I sent them a copy. I sent them reviews of my book, and notices of my appearances on radio and television. Finally they agreed to record my material, not only because they liked what I had to say, but also because, they said, "We've practically got a file cabinet full of this guy's materials! If he's going to persist for almost two and a half years, he's gotta be good!" There is nothing like accomplishing a goal. And there is nothing like sitting in your mentor's chair.

If you find someone who inspires you that much, read his or her words over and over again, play the tapes, write down the main thoughts. Brainwash yourself in a positive way.

Remember, though, there are no absolutes in this world; there is not one right way of doing anything. Each of us has to find the way that's right for us. You watch other people to find out what it is that has made them successful, to feed that information into your brain, and then to determine what does and doesn't work for you.

This is true no matter what field you're in, be it entertainment, business, or sports. Bruce Jenner looked for role models when he became a sportscaster; he tried to learn from the masters, not to imitate them. "Why is it that you noticed Howard Cosell?" asks Jenner. "Why was he successful? Or Frank Gifford or Jim McKay? First of all, they all know their business. But they all do it differently. Each one knows his craft, but each one is an individual. You can't say that you're going to be a sportscaster just like Howard Cosell. It probably won't work for you because you're not being yourself. In any business, you've got to be yourself. But first, find people who do what you want to do. Listen to what they're saying and decide if that works for you. It may not, but you're going to learn something that day."

That is the whole point of surrounding yourself with shining examples—to learn something that can help you enhance what you already have, and to use the experience of others as the foundation on which you build your own achievements. This is certainly the attitude of David Lubetkin and Steve Weintraub, who took over a dying company and had to resuscitate it from the bottom up. Lubetkin remembered that when he was in the retail business, someone once told him that the best thing about retail was that you could just go into your competitor's store and see exactly how they became successful—how they displayed the goods, how the salespeople were dressed, how they were trained.

When the pair took over Industrial Edge USA, their goal was to take this company, which was "basically dead" and become one of the leaders in the industry within five years. One of the tools they used was to study other companies within their industry, and, as Steve Weintraub tells it, "take the best from each organization, try to implement it in our own company, and try to eliminate things we saw in their companies that we think can be improved upon. There's nothing wrong with taking good ideas from the best of your would-be competitors, and then improving upon them."

THE GREATEST MENTOR OF ALL

One mentor has not yet been mentioned—the greatest one of all, the one who will always be around when needed, the one you can count on when no one else is available, the only one who can decide what is best for you. That one, of course, is you.

We can, and should, look to others for aid, advice, and encouragement. But in the end, we must look inside, for it is only there that we will find the spirit of the true achiever. Inside ourselves we hold the energy, the desire, the will to keep going in whatever direction we choose. Inside ourselves, in our thoughts and in our hearts, we hold the belief that we can achieve our greatest dreams. We only have to look deep enough.

A Hindu legend says that once upon the earth, all people were gods. The people, however, ignored their divine spirits, sinned, and abused their powers. Brahma, who was the god of all gods, sadly decided that this divine spirit should be taken away from mankind, and stored in a place so obscure that no one would ever find it and abuse it again.

One of Brahma's gods advised that he hide it deep beneath

the earth. Brahma disagreed because, he said, man would eventually dig deep enough to uncover it. Another god suggested that they sink it down to the bottom of the deepest ocean. Brahma again disagreed, saying that eventually man would learn to dive deep enough to discover it. A third god suggested they carry it up to the highest mountaintop. "No," said Brahma, "for someday man will climb even the highest mountain on earth and find again the divine spirit." The other gods were at a loss, and had no more suggestions. "There is nowhere else to hide it where man cannot find it," they said.

"Yes there is," sighed Brahma. "We will hide it deep within man himself. He will never think to look for it there." And ever since then, man has been digging beneath the earth, diving into the ocean, and climbing the highest mountains looking for what is hidden deep within himself.

Out of all the people, books, tapes, tools, and techniques we turn to for help, the greatest resource of all lies within. And even though we may have help around us, it is ultimately this inner strength that will see us through, especially when the going is tough. Ask boxer Shannon Briggs.

"It's not that I don't look up to people, but I look up to myself too. There were a lot of times where I wanted to turn back and go the easy route, but I used my head. I forced myself to go to school. When my Dad died and my Mom was sick, I was pretty much on my own," he says. "There was a time when a friend of mine said, 'With all the things you've been through, I could understand it if you committed suicide. If it was me, I would have killed myself.' That made me see that I'm a stronger person than I thought I was."

Shannon Briggs looked inside himself and came out stronger for it. We all have it within ourselves to do the same.

If I had to figure out a way to continue my education without investing a lot of money, I'd start out selecting books that have to do with my interests, with what I want to accomplish. It doesn't have to take hours and hours of your time. You can benefit greatly by dedicating just fifteen minutes a day to reading. Keep a pad and pencil nearby and start writing down your ideas. Fifteen or twenty ideas a day is one hundred ideas a week—not including weekends. That's four hundred ideas a month, which is over four thousand a year. Guaranteed, you'll be surprised by what you come up with. Don't worry about whether or not you're making sense, or whether or not your ideas are practical. Just get them down on paper. Eventually you can start sorting them out, and pick out those ideas worth following up.

Select audio programs to listen to in the car, when you walk or jog, when you exercise, and when you're doing housework. We have so much available listening time. Subscribe to publications that have anything to do with your business or field of interest. You'll start picking up ideas and inspiration almost immediately.

You can use an idea or a philosophy as a mentor. When Mary Kay Ash was at a low point many years ago, she read Napoleon Hill's *Think and Grow Rich.* "That book turned me around," she says. "It had thirteen chapters. I read one every single week and tried to put into effect what that chapter said. By the end of the thirteenth week, I had turned my whole attitude around. I think it's very important to read inspirational books, like *Power Thoughts* by Robert Schuller—books that can get you thinking big and wanting to do great things."

I use quotes that I collect and put up on the wall or carry around with me. I have one taped to my desk that says "A person can succeed at almost anything for which he has unlimited enthusiasm." That quote reminds me that if I lack great skill in a certain area, I can use my enthusiasm to compensate. I keep quotes like that in front of me every day as part of my personal mentoring program.

Mentoring helps to create that unlimited enthusiasm. When you surround yourself with positive ideas, not just technical knowledge, you learn how to live a better life. And there's nothing better in this world than an education in the area of self-improvement.

Question yourself constantly: What am I surrounding myself with? How much am I investing in my mind? Who are the people with whom I'm surrounding myself? What kind of influence do they have? Do I believe in these people? Do they believe in me? Can I help these people in any way? Can they help me?

Mentoring is the automatic education you can keep in your pocket every day. It's the tool you can use to keep yourself updated on new and different ways to stay motivated or to help yourself become more effective at what you're doing.

The one thing you've got going for you—the one thing you own free and clear—is your mind. Don't take it for granted. It's your greatest asset in life.

> *"A good listener is not only popular everywhere, but after a while he knows something."*
>
> —WILSON MIZNER

Five Essential Facets of Chapter 4

1. Make careful choices about whom you wish to follow. Follow-the-follower is a lonely and potentially dangerous game. Look for people whose values match your own, and who have achieved excellence in their field.
2. Surround yourself with models of success. You become what you think about. If you surround yourself with positive images, you will find yourself moving in positive directions.
3. Keep your ears, heart, and mind open. There are many people around who are willing to teach us if we are willing to learn. It's sometimes easier for others to see things we are unable to see, so don't dismiss someone's advice or opinions without first giving them careful study.
4. Expose yourself to a variety of new and challenging situations. Network constantly. You never know who, out of all the people you meet, will be the one who can help you achieve your goals.

5. Remember where Brahma hid the divine spirit. Look to yourself to be your own greatest mentor. Do your research. Make things happen. Find your inner strength.

Think about actions you can take from these five ideas or others discussed in this chapter.

Six-Month Action Plan for Chapter 4

These are the benefits you will gain from completing this action plan:

♦ You'll learn from the credible people in the world—they've already done what you're trying to accomplish.
♦ You'll flatter them by asking for their help, and their advice is free.
♦ You'll make valuable inroads and connections.

Select ten people you admire and emulate, whom you would like to connect with in the next six months.

Design a letter, customized to each individual, asking for a time to speak. Use the letter you'll find in chapter 7 as an example, but be creative and add your own personal flair.

Here are some sample questions you might want to ask at a mentor interview. Add your own, of course. Ask open-ended questions (ones that require more than a yes or no answer). Before the interview, ask yourself what you'd most like to know.

♦ What motivates you every day?
♦ When did you discover this was what you wanted to do for a living?
♦ How did you get started?
♦ How can I learn what I need to know about this profession?
♦ Do you have any practical advice about getting started in this field?
♦ Do you set goals? If so, how?

♦ What are the three key attributes to being successful in this field?
♦ If you were going to start all over again and you were in my shoes, what specific steps would you take?
♦ What is your definition of success?
♦ Do you know anybody in this profession, or in any other, that you'd recommend I talk to?

Listen, serve, or move on. Listen to those people around you who are positive and successful. Serve people who are less successful than you by helping them move up. Move on when those around you are negative and pulling you down.

Remember that your greatest asset—your mind—is yours free and clear to do with as you will. Study, and take advantage of its incredible powers. The next chapter will give you an introductory tour of the fantastic world of the mind, and show you how you, like so many of our country's highest achievers, can use your brain power to unlock your hidden potential.

Chapter Five

DIAMOND MINDS:
THE INCREDIBLE POWERS OF THE
HUMAN BRAIN

"Sucrets? Sucrets are little green lozenges that are taken to soothe sore throats. They come in . . . What? Success? Not Sucrets? You want a definition for success? Oh. Well then: Success comes through living one's life with integrity, compassion, aliveness, and good humor. It's knowing you've done your best to reach your goals (even if they're not always fully realized), learned about life along the way, and built supportive relationships as part of the process. . . . For me, the final success I hope to judge my life by will include which friends I've made, whose lives I've touched, what difference I've made in the world, what challenges I've met and how I met them, and, of course, how much I've laughed and played and created."

—RITCH DAVIDSON, SENIOR VICE EMPEROR,
PLAYFAIR, INC.

"A person's ability to succeed depends on four basic skills:
1. Being a student forever—knowing that there is always more to learn.
2. Mapping alternative futures—successful people ask

*themselves where they will be several years from now,
and choose alternatives that will get them where they
want to go.*

*3. Updating your mission—being able to be flexible
enough to take advantage of new and changing
opportunities.*

*4. Expecting to succeed—some people make things
happen, some people watch things happen, and some
people wonder what happened. Most of those who
make things happen expect to be able to do it; they
develop powerful mental images of the behavior that
will lead them to the desired result.''*

—CHARLES GARFIELD, AUTHOR AND PEAK
PERFORMANCE EXPERT

There can be no discussion about human potential without
discussion of the human mind. The mind is, as everybody
knows, what separates us from all other species. No other living beings, though they contain hearts, lungs, stomachs, eyes,
ears, mouths, and even brains, have the power of the human
mind. No other living beings have the ability to change their
surroundings and their circumstances based on how they
change themselves. Only we have this extraordinary power of
transformation. We can start out poor and end up wealthy,
change ourselves from illiterate to highly educated, and turn
handicaps into advantages by using this wondrous tool handed
out free to each and every one of us.

Science is just beginning to understand how this wondrous
tool works. Human beings have existed for about two and a
half million years, yet we are still in the infant stages of discovery in the remarkable field of brain research. Ninety-five
percent of what we do know has been discovered within the
past fifty years. We are learning more every day, but there is
still a huge amount yet to be discovered.

In July 1989, President Bush signed into law House Joint

Resolution 174 designating the 1990s as the ''Decade of the Brain.'' The prediction is that by the year 2000, the Decade of the Brain will have yielded more knowledge about how the nervous system works and how to fix it than throughout all of history. Even scientists are in awe of how the mind functions. In his book *Bright Air, Brilliant Fire,* Gerald M. Edelman marvels at the patterns in which brain cells are arranged, and says that when one considers both the number and the arrangement of these cells ''in an object the size of your brain, and when one considers the chemical reactions going on inside, one is talking about the most complicated material object in the known universe.''

THOSE WHO USE THE GIFT LEAD THE WAY

This most complicated material object has been given to each and every one of us. It seems then almost sacrilegious not to take advantage of its wondrous powers. It doesn't take genius or paranormal senses to tap into these powers. We all do it every day. As you read this book, you are meeting many successful individuals who have learned to appreciate, and utilize, these powers.

You'll notice that each of the fifty people interviewed for this book has his or her own definition of success. Many of them mentioned, of course, the amenities of life—money, possessions, a comfortable lifestyle. But these are only byproducts of what success really means to them: satisfaction with one's life; doing what one loves to do; setting goals and achieving them; meeting challenges head on; achieving a balance between work and personal priorities; and giving back to others, for example.

Each definition is individual, unique, personal. That's because each definition is based on one person's life experience and perception of the world, as well as his or her genetic makeup. No two people can possibly see the world in exactly the same light, because no two people—not even identical twins—have exactly the same combination of genetic makeup and life experience. No two minds function in exactly the same way.

The average brain, which weighs about three pounds and is the size of two fists, contains over one hundred billion nerve cells, or neurons. These neurons are constantly sending messages back and forth to each other. The way this "message service" functions differs in every individual.

There's no use in comparing yourself with others around you and thinking they are better than you because they can do some things you cannot. Particular people may have skills and abilities you do not; we each have our individual gifts. It's up to you to find and appreciate the gifts that have been bestowed upon you. Your gifts are unlike any others' and you are the only one who can uncover them, develop them, and make them work for you.

A VISION OF SUCCESS

There is one very simple way to help make your gifts work for you, and it is one of the most common signposts of success. All the people interviewed for this book were able to see themselves as being successful even before they reached their goals. They had (and still have) a vision of success that they keep constantly in their mind's eye.

> *"Cherish your visions and your dreams as they are
> the children of your soul; the blueprints of your
> ultimate achievements."*
>
> —Napoleon Hill

Everything we do, everything we are, and everything we become comes from our incredible minds.

You become what you think about. There is no greater "secret" to success than this. It's what keeps me fired up. I constantly think about those things that I love to do and those people I love to be around. I study everything I can get my hands on about my business and about how I can improve myself and my life. I'm on a rampage of learning. I try to absorb as much as I can around me and then apply it to my life 110 percent.

You become what you think about. Set your mind to almost anything, and you can achieve it. As the saying goes, "If you argue for your limitations, you get to keep them." Tell yourself that you're too young, too old, too dumb, the wrong gender, the wrong race, the wrong height, or the wrong weight to achieve and you will be right.

"You will either live up to, or down to, your self-expectations."

—DR. ROBERT ANTHONY

There are, of course, limits beyond which human beings cannot go—we can't transform ourselves into other species or grow extra limbs when we need them. But each of us has within ourselves a great potential that can be reached if we so desire. Celebrated inventors, explorers, mathematicians, artists, entertainers, politicians, humanitarians, entrepreneurs, authors, athletes, teachers, scientists—they're all human beings, nothing more, nothing less, except that they achieved what they thought about most.

Athletes have used this concept for years. The greatest athletes are not always those with the strongest bodies. Sports superstars exercise their mental powers as well as their bodies. One such athlete is Franco Harris, who played an amazing thirteen seasons for the Pittsburgh Steelers. For him, there's no doubt that mental preparation is the most important part of the game. He credits his success on the field with the fact that he knew how to use his brain.

Franco Harris says that his vision was his greatest asset on the football field—and he's not talking about his eyesight.

"I was able to anticipate way down the line," he says. "I

could visualize a variety of situations and play them in my mind prior to the game.'' If a player made a defensive move during the game, Harris knew exactly what to do, because he'd already played out this scenario in his mind.

"As soon as I saw his move, my mind was already beyond him. I automatically knew what to do, and I was ready for the next move. I didn't have the speed of O.J., or the power of Larry Czonka—but I had the power of vision.''

This power of vision is given to all of us. The power of the subconscious mind is so strong that it really doesn't care what is true and what is false. In fact, the brain doesn't effectively discriminate between real and imagined events. We believe both in things that are real and in things that are not. However, we can use this phenomenon to our advantage. As I once heard a winning football coach say, "Treat a person as he is and he will remain as he is. Treat him as if he were what he could and should be, and he will become what he could and should be.''

Treat yourself as you could and should be, and you will surpass your own imagination. If you think about a positive outcome you have a much better chance of achieving it than if you picture a possible failure. This is how self-fulfilling prophecies are born. If you think you're successful, you are. If you think you're a failure, you are.

You can determine much of what goes into your subconscious mind by controlling your environment. Of course, you can't always control outside circumstances, but you can surround yourself with positive influences. A maxim in the computer world says, "Garbage in, garbage out." That goes for the mind as well. You can use your great power of vision to keep yourself stuck and limited, or you can use it to visualize a plan for success.

Just as much as we need to physically practice any skill we wish to master, we need to rehearse it mentally as well. In *Care and Feeding of the Human Brain: A Guide to Your Gray Matter,* Jack Maguire says that "mentally living through a specific physical challenge in advance allows our brain to prepare itself for optimum functioning at all levels when the time comes to perform that challenge for real.''

Niall Mackenzie, a young man who challenges himself in World Championship motorcycle racing, is the most successful British rider in Grand Prix racing since 1988. He has raced on tracks where the bikes reach speeds of more than two hundred miles per hour. Mackenzie trains year-round for his sport, running, mountain biking, and cycling. But when the season begins, his mind is totally focused on racing. ''At the racetrack, I make a lot of laps in my head,'' he says. ''I think about areas where I might be stronger than other riders, or weaker, or where I can improve. I think about the race and where a good place to pass might be or where someone might pass me. I think about the bike and I feel it going around the racetrack. And when I finish one race, I immediately start thinking about the next racetrack I'm going to, and start making laps in my head again.''

Scientists may not be able to fully explain this process, but they know that it works. Dr. Dominick Purpura, chairman of the National Foundation for Brain Research, says that ''the concept of the mental set and the rehearsal of a job, as athletes sometimes do, has a great deal of influence on the functional capacity of the brain. That mental rehearsal enables us to gain a deeper comprehension of a given situation, and to see the full implications of our planned behaviors.''

Successful people know how to tap into this incredible source of power and energy. This doesn't mean that they have genius IQs, or are necessarily any smarter than the rest of us. It does mean that they have learned how to think, and that they believe in their own ability to solve problems rationally and creatively.

Bruce Jenner overcame dyslexia and learning disabilities as a kid and became an American hero. Over the years, he learned to appreciate, and take advantage of, his own special abilities. ''I got a bad start. I had no confidence in myself at all,'' he says. ''But I found out as time went on that my greatest asset was my brain. I wasn't as physically talented as all the other guys, but I was always the guy who brought out the best with what I had. When other guys would fold, I would always rise to the top. It's not because I was stronger than they were, or because I was faster than them. It's because I was mentally confident.''

EXERCISE YOUR BRAIN POWER

The kind of mental confidence exhibited by Jenner, Harris, and Mackenzie applies not only to sports, but to every person in every area of life. In many respects, the brain is a muscle like any other in the body and requires that we "use it or lose it."

Our society has given up some of its brain power, however. We have neglected our responsibility to give our youngsters a head start in learning.

"The single most important thing one can do to improve the opportunities of a child and improve the health of a nation is to start all children with a formal education somewhere in the neighborhood of eighteen to twenty-four months," says Dr. Fred Plum, chairman of neurology and neuroscience, Cornell Medical Center, and member of the National Panel for Research in the Decade of the Brain.

"Look at what the brain learns in the first two and a half years: It learns to walk, talk, answer questions, be conscious of itself. Some children learn to read at three years of age. Parents should take maximum advantage of the fact that every day when they come home from work, their child's brain is going to be different than it was when they left in the morning. Connections are being made. The more connections that are made, the more one learns. And the more one learns as a child, the more channels are going to be open as an adult."

The brain must be stimulated and exercised for it to function at its highest capacity. "The brain doesn't just come ready for processing information," says Dr. Purpura. "It is built up by sets of neurons having fundamental circuitry, set up by our genetic apparatus, that determine the basic plan of the nervous system. But the basic plan is not enough. The nervous system has to be used appropriately for it to finally hone its capacity for information processing.''

Appropriate programming and stimulation are needed even from early infancy. The latest brain research has concluded that the earlier we start programming and stimulating brain circuitry the "greater the degree of cognitive potential." According to a thirty-million-dollar study by the Robert Wood Johnson Foundation, published in the *Journal of the American Medical Association* in 1990, newborn infants who were given extensive educational experiences in their first, second, and third years showed a definite increase in IQ of almost six to thirteen points over children not as extensively stimulated.

Both Dr. Purpura and Dr. Plum feel that there is a mistaken notion that television supplies much of that stimulation. Even the "good" television, like educational programs and PBS, is "like reading one paragraph of Socrates compared to a room full of comic books," says Dr. Plum. "Life is full of the stuff that abstractly fills the mind—like music, literature, films, complicated ideas and stories. Why should we be so interested in looking at a bunch of overweight adolescents playing football? Get the kids out there playing themselves. Teach them the games and sports so they can do them all their lives.''

Early stimulation and exercise of the brain can have a dramatic effect in our later years as well. "It's been established in some studies that even the onset of Alzheimer's . . . is delayed in populations where there has been a strong educational component in the early years," says Dr. Purpura. "It's as if those people have a reserve of good working synapses and connections. If Alzheimer's is going to attack you, it's going to come later and have less of an effect in the early years. . . . Therefore the more you're doing and continue to do, the more you exercise the brain, the less dramatic the effect of Alzheimer's in its early stages.''

Of course, the possibility of getting Alzheimer's disease is not the only reason we want to exercise our brains. It's been estimated that human beings use only somewhere between five and ten percent of our brain's capacity. Why settle for that? Why not try every possible way of raising that percentage?

Science has no idea how far human beings can go if they really try. What they do know is that there are definitely ways of improving both intelligence and creativity—two of the most important components in living a successful life.

Arthur Fry, scientist and inventor, is extremely interested in the area of creativity. He certainly loves what he does, and his excitement comes from ''finding out what people on the leading edge of research are doing with new materials and new products . . . and finding business applications for those new technologies and services. It's a fascinating area.'' It was this fascination with new products and business applications that led to his invention of the Post-it Note.

''Creativity is a means that both man and animals have to solve problems that would have stopped them—maybe even kept them from surviving—because they couldn't do something the same old comfortable way. They had to come up with something different. Creativity allows them to do that, and it's because of the way the mind stores information. It's not like a computer. In a computer, if one piece of information is missing, it stops the whole process. The mind stores and can visualize information in patterns. The creative mind doesn't have to have the whole pattern—it can have just a little piece and be able to envision the whole picture in completion.

''Another thing the creative mind can do is look at an existing pattern and say, 'Oh, I bet I can rip out this part of it and insert this other thing and it will fit.' Because we've stored a lot of patterns and a lot of information, all kinds of funny combinations are possible. And the more pieces we have, the more the unconscious mind can call on them when we're stuck.''

PUMP UP YOUR CREATIVITY

Everyone has the potential to have a creative mind, not just artists and scientists. We all use our creative brains as children, but the realities and responsibilities of adult life often stifle our creative impulses. High achievers are able to tap into their creative abilities to come up with imaginative solutions to difficult problems. Here are a few suggestions for exercising your own creative powers:

♦ **Allow your playful side to express itself.** Do something silly. Let your thinking escape the boundaries of practical reality. If you're in the middle of a difficult problem or project, take a break and simply goof around. You'll come back to the problem relaxed and refreshed, and be able to look at it from a new angle.

♦ **Give yourself time to find solutions.** We all want immediate answers, but they don't always come when we want them to. If a solution doesn't present itself right away, take a break. An answer will probably come to you when you're not consciously thinking about your problem at all.

Ritch Davidson is senior vice emperor (that's the title on his business cards) of Playfair, Inc., a company that teaches everyone from college students to corporate big-wigs how to use fun, play, and laughter to stimulate creative thinking. "It's important to take breaks for two reasons," says Davidson. "Number one is that studies have shown there is a clear link between laughter and greater creativity. It's also a diversion. We need to give our brains a break from what we're doing, and allow an opportunity for other processes in the brain to kick in. . . . Studies have also shown that when you take a break to play, when you laugh a little bit while you're learning, you're more likely to learn the information more fully and retain it longer."

♦ **Keep a pad, notebook, or tape recorder with you at all times.** How many times have you had an interesting thought or a creative solution while in the car, on a train or plane, or in the middle of the night while unable to sleep? How many times has that thought or solution gone right out of your head by the time you wake up in the morning or return home from your trip? If you keep a notebook or tape recorder handy at all times, you don't have to worry about losing what could be a valuable idea. You can keep a small notebook handy in your purse or pocket. And a tape recorder is particularly effective to keep in your car (so you can record your great ideas without pulling over or getting into an accident) or beside your bed (so you can record your thoughts in the middle of the night without even having to turn on the lights).

♦ **Challenge conventional wisdom.** Don't let the fact that something has never been done before stop you from creative thinking and experimentation. In 1943, Edwin Land was at the beach with his young daughter. He was taking photographs of her, when she, impatient as all young children are, asked, "Why can't I see the picture now, Daddy?" That question sparked Land's imagination, and the invention of the Polaroid camera. Question the things you see around you. Keep asking "Why not?" and "What if?" Don't confuse "this is the way things are now" with "this is the way things must always be."

Don't let others' opinions of what you can and cannot do determine your opinions of yourself. Beethoven's teacher told him he was hopeless as a composer. Walt Disney, who went bankrupt several times before he founded Disneyland, was once fired by a newspaper editor for lack of ideas. Louisa May Alcott, author of *Little Women,* was told by her family that perhaps she ought to look for work as a servant or a seamstress. And above his fireplace, Fred Astaire kept a memo written in 1933 by the director of his first screen test. The memo read, "Can't act! Slightly bald! Can dance a little!"

♦ **Listen to your own body rhythm.** Some people are very creative first thing in the morning, and slack off as the day goes on. Others are at their best in the middle of the night. Do you know when your most creative time of day is? Most of us have a pretty good idea. If you're a morning person, set aside a half hour first thing, before work if necessary, to write down your goals, create an action plan for the day, week, or month, or solve a sticky problem. If you're a night person, do it before you go to bed and write out an action plan for the following day.

♦ **Get yourself out of that old familiar rut.** Although following the same routine day in and day out may be comforting and in some ways efficient, it does not stimulate creative thinking. Sometimes even the smallest change in daily habits will get your mind thinking in new directions. We all need to take risks every once in a while. Things as simple as taking a new route to work, changing your breakfast cereal, or getting a new hair style can create new patterns of thinking and stimulate brain activity.

♦ **Suspend judgment.** Disregard the voice inside you that says, "This can never be done." Keep brainstorming. You may come up with some wild, impractical ideas; on the other hand, you may just find you've come up with something really incredible.

THE SNOWBALL EFFECT

It is our responsibility to monitor our thought patterns and develop positive ways of thinking. We spend a lot of time worrying about what has happened in the past and what might happen in the future, instead of concentrating on what actions we can take right now to improve our lives. Over the years, surveys have shown the approximate percentages of the things people worry about:

Things that never happen	40%
Things in the past that can never be changed	30%
Needless worries about our health	12%
Petty, miscellaneous worries	10%
Real, legitimate worries	8%

Ninety-two percent of worries are absolutely unnecessary. Of the eight percent left, there are some we can personally solve, and some that are simply out of our hands. When you find yourself spending large amounts of time worrying, ask yourself a few pertinent questions:

♦ Is this a legitimate concern?
♦ Is it something that *might* happen (whether I worry about it or not)?
♦ Am I thinking about times past in order to avoid confronting present problems or taking immediate action?
♦ Is this problem or concern worth the amount of time I'm spending thinking about it?
♦ Are there more important issues I could be concentrating on?
♦ Is there some way I can turn this around and find an opportunity hidden in this problem?

We are easily caught up in the familiar cycles of our lives. We wake up in the morning and do the same thing over and over again; it's not hard to see why we only use five percent of our brain capacity. The most valuable gift you can ever give yourself is to open your mind and to broaden your horizons. Try a new sport, take up a new hobby, learn a foreign language. Read poetry, write poetry, listen to reggae music, go to the opera. Explore your neighborhood, explore the world. Surprise yourself. The most rewarding thing you'll ever hear yourself say is, "I didn't know I could do this!"

Let in one idea and you let in a thousand. The more we learn, the more we're capable of learning. Ideas snowball on top of each other; each new idea is built on all the others that have come before. Earl Nightingale called this information age we're living in "an era of compounding advancement." Each time you open your mind to new ideas and new ways of thinking, the information that comes in to you is perceived much differently than before. You have a whole new foundation on which to create a successful life.

"All great masters are chiefly distinguished by the power of adding a second, third, and perhaps a fourth

step in a continuous line. Many a man has taken the
first step. With every additional step, you enhance
immensely the value of your first.''

—Ralph Waldo Emerson

A GREAT INVESTMENT OPPORTUNITY

You can make no greater investment than an investment into
your own mind. You can't expect to withdraw wisdom and
information if you don't make any deposits into your mind
bank. Start each day thinking, and your mind will continue to
think all day. Make the effort. As the scientists have told us,
we need to put effort into our mental as well as our physical
fitness. That might involve change. Most people are afraid of
change; they want to stay with what makes them feel comfortable and secure. But that security may be only an illusion.

For instance, many people today claim they have been ''victims'' of the bad economy. However, many of these people
are really ''victims'' of their own refusal to change tactics in
a changing economy. People are doing the same things they've
always done, despite the fact that the environment has
changed. The customer's needs have changed, but the company has not changed or adapted. Everyone assumes that what
was successful in the past is going to work now.

Companies think that way about their business, and individuals think that way about their lives. What they fail to see is
that change and risk help us grow. When we stop thinking
about what helps us grow, when we stop looking for new ideas
or new information, we don't just stay still—we move back-
wards.

Tap into your own brain power. Set ambitious goals for
yourself, and figure out step-by-step ways to achieve them.
When problems arise, write them down on paper and try to
come up with as many solutions as you possibly can. Include
everything you think of, no matter how silly or impractical.

Chances are you'll eventually come up with an idea, or a combination of ideas, that will work for you.

Keep a journal or diary—not for publication, just for yourself. Writing down a problem and its possible solutions in essay format encourages logic, clarity, and organization.

Expand your circle of friends and explore new activities, especially those that are not within your everyday routine. If you sit at a desk all day, involve yourself with an outdoor activity. If you're involved in manual labor, give yourself some quiet reading time or listen to calming music.

Ask yourself every day: What can I invest in my mind today? What can I do today to contribute to my having a healthier and happier life?

Earl Nightingale once told a story of a preacher who was traveling down a long country road. As he was traveling, he passed farm after farm, each one more desolate than the next. The few visible crops were withered and dying. The horses looked sickly, the pigs and chickens scrawny. The preacher drove on, greatly disturbed by what he saw.

Finally, after hours of travel along this same road, the preacher came upon an unbelievable sight—here was a farm that resembled a storybook picture. The grass was green, the corn was growing high and tall, the animals were in the pink of health. The farmer and his wife were sitting on the porch drinking lemonade. The preacher pulled up in amazement, got out of his buggy and said, "I've been driving on this road for two hours and all I've seen on either side of me was desolation. God has blessed you with such a beautiful piece of land."

"Yes," said the farmer, "God has blessed us with a beautiful piece of land. But you should have seen it when he had it all to himself."

The preacher then realized that every one of the farmers he'd passed had been blessed with a beautiful piece of land. It was what this particular farmer had done with his piece that made the difference.

Like those farmers, each of us has been given, free and clear, a beautiful piece of land—our minds. What we put into it determines what we'll get out of it. We become what we think about. Remember that the brightest diamond is often found beneath the roughest stone; if you give up digging too soon you will never reap the greatest rewards. Never give up on your own shining potential. It is given to each of us to use or abuse—the choice is yours to make.

"There exist limitless opportunities in every industry. When there is an open mind, there will always be a frontier."

—CHARLES F. KETTERING

Five Essential Facets of Chapter 5

1. Each of us is an individual with unique talents and untapped potential. There's no point in comparing ourselves with others; if we want to grow we need only compete with ourselves. Our obligation on earth is to discover and utilize our own uniqueness.
2. You become what you think about. Choose your influences and your surroundings as you wish your life to be, and know that as ye think, so shall ye become.
3. Use your mind to visualize future events. Focus on a successful outcome. Mentally rehearse any new job or task as you physically practice it, and you are preparing for success.
4. Apply creative thinking to any problems that might arise. Everyone has a creative mind—review the exercises on pages 108–110 for pumping up your creativity.
5. Focus on the positive. Ninety-two percent of all our worries are unnecessary. If you're constantly concentrating on failure and disappointment, that is what you will get. Your mind is the best tool you have available to create a positive, successful environment.

Think about actions you can take from these five ideas or others described in this chapter.

Thirty-Day Action Plan for Chapter 5

Read a book that focuses on your area of interest or on personal growth. Ask people you trust and respect for the greatest book they've read in those areas.

Find a motivational audio program to listen to on your headphones, in your car, while you exercise or clean the house.

Visualize yourself in successful situations. Close your eyes and create a scene or atmosphere that is vivid and full of details.

Introduce yourself to someone in your field of interest who can give you ideas or advice on how they achieved success and how you can achieve it in your own area.

Find a book of inspirational quotes. Every morning pick a quote and commit yourself to applying it to your life at least once during the day. If you find one that really resonates, copy it down and carry it with you, or paste it up somewhere you'll see it every day.

Finish this book and continue to do the action plans at the end of each chapter.

In this chapter, you've learned about the incredible powers of the human mind. In the next chapter, you'll learn more about how to utilize those powers by understanding how we learn, and discovering what an important part learning plays in reaching success. Peak performers are perpetual students. The next chapter will talk about learning in two different areas: how parents (and people who will someday be parents) can build a strong foundation of learning for their children; and how you can increase your own brain's muscle power, improve your memory, and enhance your creative thinking skills.

Chapter Six

THE CUTTING EDGE:
LEARNING HOW WE LEARN

*"I think success ultimately is learning. When I learn
and grow, I'm being successful. Even if I have a
business deal that doesn't work out and I don't make
a fortune on it—if I learn from it, then it was a
successful experience."*

—JACK CANFIELD, COAUTHOR OF *CHICKEN SOUP
FOR THE SOUL* AND *DARE TO WIN*

*"In my present job, success is helping others to
achieve their own goals. I think that's true of any
teacher's success: providing others with the tools to
go on learning to achieve their goals, and perhaps to
inspire them to more worthy goals."*

—DR. WILLIAM H. DANFORTH, CHANCELLOR,
WASHINGTON UNIVERSITY

Some people acquire valuable gems, put them away in a
safe-deposit box, and never enjoy their full value or beauty.
You can do the same with your diamond mind if you wish.
Or you can, like most successful people, constantly increase
the power and value of your most precious jewel.

A diamond, in its natural state, is cloudy and unshaped. Its value is determined by how it is cut, shaped, and set into a specific context. So it is with our precious diamond minds. How we "shape" the mind, the learning systems we set up, determines the level at which the brain will function. In order for it to function at its maximum capacity, we must set up optimal learning systems and discover how to apply our knowledge to the challenges of daily living.

In other words, we need to learn how we learn. In recent years, scientists, psychologists, and educators have begun to broaden their focus of study to include not only *what* we learn, but *how* we learn it. How do human beings take in information? How do we retrieve it? And how can we use this knowledge to increase our capacity for learning and for unlocking our hidden potential?

"Learning is not just an intellectual minuet. Learning opens possibilities, ideas, opportunities, and ways of thinking which can change one's whole life," says Cornell Medical Center's Dr. Fred Plum. Most of us are born with great capacities to learn. We are not all intellectually equal, but we are all able to take in new information, to form ideas, to change our lives. Learning is an equal opportunity employer.

In some respects, we can't stop ourselves from learning. We learn simply by living. All of our senses provide us with information. We observe. We interact. We experiment. We experience. Studies have recently shown that infants even as young as two and a half months can learn and remember visual sequences and simple mechanical tasks. Five-month-olds can grasp the basic concepts of addition and subtraction. Six-month-olds can recognize language, long before they know how to speak. Infants even seem to have an innate understanding of the laws of physics, of how the world is supposed to work (e.g., that objects can't hang in midair by themselves or pass through solid barriers). If this is how much we're capable of before we're even one year old, imagine what the adult mind can do!

I wanted to discuss the power of the adult mind when I went in to interview Dr. Plum. However, the first thing he said to me was that he would do the interview under one condition—that we address some of it toward the parents of this nation, because it is the only way we can assure ourselves of a healthy and prosperous future. He was passionate in his plea. I promised I would do as he asked.

You may not be a parent now, but it is likely you will become one. If not, you're probably an aunt or uncle. If you're none of these, I hope you're someone who cares about the future of humankind and that you will find a way to apply this information at some point in your life.

A LEGACY OF LEARNING

The babies in the studies mentioned above did not receive coaching to help them grasp sophisticated concepts. The scientists and psychologists were studying what babies already know. Their findings indicate that infants can probably start their formal education at a much earlier age than society has formerly advocated. However, as in everything else, moderation is the key. Knowing that infants can learn sophisticated concepts almost from birth doesn't mean we have to turn them into full-time students at three months old. But it does behoove us to be aware that they are learning all the time. Therefore, it is our responsibility to provide them with enough stimulation to keep their fertile minds growing, and to be careful that we provide a healthy, positive environment for this learning to take place.

The greatest gift a parent can give a child is the love of learning. This can be developed at any stage of life; however, children who love learning from the start have a great advantage over those who must develop it later on in life. Winifred Barnes Conley is a psychotherapist, educator, and president and CEO of the National Learning Laboratory in Bethesda, Maryland. She recommends that the best way for parents to foster a love of learning in their children is by loving it themselves.

"We suggest that there be family learning time," she says.

"While children are doing their homework, the TV should be off. Perhaps classical music could be playing. Parents can be reading, paying bills, or studying for a course they're taking. That way they're modeling learning as well as verbalizing it. It's what parents *do* that makes the biggest difference."

Children will imitate their parents' actions. Conley tells of one family that came to her because the children would not do their homework. It turned out that the father insisted on watching television from the moment he came home from work until the moment he went to bed. So the children were constantly sneaking away to watch television instead of doing their homework. It wasn't until the father gave up some of his tube time that the children began to improve their study habits.

Fostering the love of learning can, and should, begin long before children ever reach school age. According to Dr. Plum, the reason certain ethnic groups consistently test considerably higher on IQ exams is not because of any difference in brain capacity. It's because they come from a culture where learning begins early and remains a child's highest priority through his or her university years.

Learning can begin with the youngest of babies by providing them with new environments, new sounds and voices, new sensory experiences. This stimulation allows them to become familiar with the world around them and to feel freer to explore on their own later on.

Until the age of fourteen, the brain is like a sponge taking in information. It's important to establish learning patterns early, when the developing brain is most receptive. "The brain is maximally plastic up to the age of eight," says Dr. Plum. "Up until then, one can produce serious injury, for example to the language zones of the brain, yet the child will learn language with the other side of the brain. After the age of eight, it becomes increasingly difficult or even impossible to teach normal language to the nondominant hemisphere."

According to Dr. Plum, two elements of learning are important to all of us, and particularly to children:

♦ A lot of love and trust. If you can't trust your own environment growing up, how can you trust what you're learning? Why should you trust a book or a teacher if you can't trust your parent(s)?

♦ Communication. Children should be in a state of constant learning. Read to your children frequently. Take them places out of the ordinary, such as petting zoos, hands-on museums, and parks. Spend time with your child, and pay attention to his or her questions, no matter how silly they seem.

In fact, Dr. Plum feels there are no silly questions, even when we grow older. "One of the reasons I enjoy being around young trainees in my field," he says, "is that out of their naive views of things often come new ideas. There's nothing like seeing a problem from a fresh and different angle."

How can you encourage your children to want to learn and ask questions, and give them a head start on being the best they can be? Here are four suggestions for helping your children develop a good attitude, a strong character, and a love for learning:

♦ **Build on your child's particular strengths.** We often push our children into areas of our own interest, rather than finding out what they like and can do well. Children need to be accepted for who they are, not who we would like them to be.

♦ **Always have something good to say.** Praise the small successes as well as the large ones. If a child is learning to spell her name, for example, and gets three out of the five letters right, tell her how well she did at those three letters. Be honest in your praise, however. You might say, "You did that very well. You printed three of the letters beautifully. Keep going like that and soon you'll have your whole name printed."

♦ **Give gentle criticism followed by a suggestion for positive action.** It's easy for a child to confuse criticism of what he's done wrong with criticism of who he is as a person. We often make it even easier with remarks like, "That's not the right answer. How can you be so stupid!" It's all right to tell a child that something is incorrect, but then follow it up with a suggestion of how to do it correctly.

♦ **Use visualization techniques.** Adults use this method all the time, as we saw in the last chapter. Children's imaginations are even stronger than adults', so if your child is nervous or worried about performing a particular task, urge your child to practice often and then help her create a mental picture of her going through all the necessary motions, succeeding at each step, and then reaching her goal.

WHAT WE DON'T LEARN IN SCHOOL

Much of this chapter focuses on what parents can do to help their children improve their learning techniques. This does not imply in any way that adults can't use these concepts as well. For example, in the previous section, I suggested that one way you can help your child to learn is to build on his or her strengths. The same goes for you. We spend a lot of time in our lives trying to push ourselves into little boxes that other people have set up for us. Parents, teachers, advertising, and the media tell us we should like this, buy that, study this, be that. This book is devoted to encouraging you to be more of who you already are.

> *"To be what we are, and to become what we are capable of becoming, is the only end of life."*
>
> —ROBERT LOUIS STEVENSON

This is not something we learn in school. Schools are not set up to bring out our individual differences. They're set up to teach all children in the same way—even though we all have different ways of thinking and learning.

Mary Matalin was deputy campaign manager for President George Bush in the 1992 campaign. She was responsible for the overview and organization of all fifty state operations. She is extremely articulate and intelligent. Yet she feels her education let her down. She wants people to understand that our education system is not infallible.

"I know teaching has changed a lot since I've been there, but they did not teach me the right way," she says. "The way I was taught, you learned facts and you regurgitated them. Success was measured as a good grade on a test. That is not how the world works. That is not how I learn.

"I happen to be a visual learner, which I had to discover by myself. If a law professor is standing up in front of a class reading something to me, I don't get it. But if someone holds up a graph or shows me a picture, I readily understand it. . . . If you're reading and you don't understand something, that doesn't mean you're stupid. Read it, then take a pencil and 'draw' what you've read. . . . People don't understand that there are ways of learning beyond the traditional one we're taught."

Mary Matalin is absolutely right. Studies have shown that there are three ways we take in information: auditory, visual, and kinesthetic. Some people respond best to auditory cues, such as lectures and reading. Some need to see pictures or graphic representations. And some respond best when they are actually able to touch or have a hands-on experience. Each of us has one dominant mode of dealing with the world. If a person is visual, like Mary Matalin for example, telling her what to do will never be as effective as showing her what to do.

As parents, we need to make sure we cover all bases. Jack Canfield is an accomplished trainer and teacher and one of the nation's leading experts on peak performance and self-esteem. He's the author of several books, including *101 Ways to Develop Student Self-Esteem and Responsibility.* According to

Canfield, parents need to understand the three ways in which they need to communicate with their children:

♦ **Tell them:** Constantly remind them verbally what you like about what they do, that you love them, that they're competent, that they're unique and special to you.
♦ **Show them:** Take your children to interesting and unusual places. Spend time with them. Recent research shows that the average parent in America spends only twelve and a half to fourteen and a half minutes a day talking to each of their children—and eight and a half of those minutes are spent arguing! That leaves about four minutes to deal with values, morals, ethics, self-esteem, responsibility, etc. Spending time with children (not in front of the television), playing with them, listening to them, shows them you care.
♦ **Touch them:** Many parents are reluctant to touch their children, more so with boys than with girls. This reluctance often escalates as the children get older, and many of these children grow up hungry for affection.

In addition to the three modes of taking in information, there also exist seven different kinds of intelligence:

1. Spacial—as demonstrated by architects and interior designers
2. Kinesthetic—as demonstrated by dancers and athletes
3. Musical—as demonstrated by composers, classical musicians, rock stars
4. Empathic—as demonstrated by therapists, guidance counselors, social workers
5. Logical—as demonstrated by lawyers, researchers
6. Linguistic—as demonstrated by writers, speakers
7. Mathematical—as demonstrated by accountants, engineers

"Most people have one dominant type of intelligence, supported by a few others," says Canfield. "If you're a genius, you get three or four." Problems arise when a parent is a kinesthetic type, for example, and has trouble appreciating a child who's empathic. A father may think his son is a wimp because he spends his time wanting to talk about feelings instead of wanting to play football. That's why it's so important to understand that each of us, and each of our children, is totally unique, and to discover who that child is rather than try to make him into someone you think he ought to be.

HOW CAN WE LEARN IN SCHOOL—OR ANYWHERE ELSE, FOR THAT MATTER?

What does all of this mean? Now that it's been determined that there are seven categories of intelligence, am I stuck with the one I've got? If I have a "mathematical" mind, does that mean I'm pigeonholed forever because of some innate "talent" I possess? Not at all. Because in the end, it is not our intelligence category nor our particular talents that shape us; it's how we choose to shape them that counts.

Dr. Robert Bjork, chairman of Dartmouth College's Department of Psychology and chairman of the National Academy of Sciences Committee on Techniques for the Enhancement of Human Performance, researches human information processing and its practical application to instruction and the optimization of performance. In other words, he studies how we learn and how we can best apply our knowledge to real-life situations.

According to Dr. Bjork, "The typical layperson puts too much weight on innate or intrinsic talents as the sole force of individual differences. There are, of course, differences in people's capabilities. But what's often underplayed is how much performance has to do with experience, training, interest, and effort, and how much less it has to do with fundamental capabilities. . . . There's a mis-impression that you are lucky if you have 'the gift' and too bad if you don't. That's a defeating attitude; it's one of the things that limits where people go and what they can achieve."

Dr. Bjork and his committee's studies have led him to believe that there is something fundamentally wrong with the methods we have traditionally used to study new subjects and learn new tasks, especially when it comes to long-term retention of facts and skills. His studies indicate that training procedures in all types of situations are far less productive than they could be.

"The people responsible for training, and the people being trained, can easily be misled by the fact that what you see during training is *performance,* not *learning,*" says Dr. Bjork. "In fact, often the conditions that make you improve most rapidly are the conditions that lead to the worst long-term performance. Let's say I have some fairly complicated task that I'm trying to teach you. I break it down into various sub-tasks. A natural thing for a trainer to do is teach you one task at a time—and have you do that one thing over and over again until you seem to have it. That is known as massed practice (as opposed to spaced practice), meaning that the practice is bunched together in time rather than spread out over several sessions. Such massing of practice increases the rate at which people improve on a given task, but produces much less in the way of long-term ability."

In other words, you'll learn better by sitting down to study for one hour every day for a week than by trying to learn everything in one seven-hour sitting. That's why students who stay up all night and cram for a test can usually pass the exam the next day—but one week later they've forgotten all the material.

"Similarly," says Dr. Bjork, "I can get you to improve more rapidly if I fix some of the conditions under which I have you practice or test, and keep them constant. You'll improve much more quickly, but that will be disastrous in terms of long-term, real-world performance. Not only does it produce worse retention, it produces an inability to transfer your training and perform appropriately in new or altered conditions.

"What should happen during training is that I should keep changing the conditions under which you practice. That will slow down your acquisition, but it will actually accomplish the kind of learning, understanding, and ability to generalize that we're after.''

Dr. Bjork gives an example: Suppose you're a typical golfer who goes to the range to hit balls. You stand on a little platform that is completely level. You hit a dozen five-iron shots, ten seconds apart. You're not really aiming at anything. The shots look beautiful. So what do you do with the next one? You try to reproduce, based on short-term muscle memory, what you just did. And you probably hit another good one. Then, a few days later you're playing a round of golf with your friends, making terrible shots, and saying, ''I can't believe this! Just a few days ago I was hitting the ball so well!''

What happened? You're not taking into consideration the conditions on the course. Will anybody let you hit a dozen five-irons in a row ten seconds apart from a perfectly level line? Of course not. And the wind is blowing, there are trees on the course, everything's different. What's more, you're now aiming at something, and there's a little money on it. You were practicing under conditions that will never be available when you're actually playing the game. You won't be able to rely on short-term muscle memory to repeat exactly what you just did. Your practice, no matter how diligent, had nothing to do with how the game is really played.

This is the problem with much of the teaching we get in school and the training we get in vocational courses and corporate seminars. The training and the practice contexts are so different, and so far from overlapping real-life situations, they're almost completely irrelevant. Here then are two important hints to effective study or practice:

- ◆ **Practice under conditions that simulate reality.** ''You want the conditions under which you practice or train to be as messy and as complicated and as real as possible,'' says Dr. Bjork.
- ◆ **Spread your study or practice out over time.** Psychological studies have long shown that spaced repetitions produce twice the level of long-term retention as massed repetitions. Going over something more than once, in study

sessions that are spaced out in time and separated by other activities, produces far better long-term memory.

Learning how we learn is not only important for each individual, but for our society as a whole. We do, after all, shape the way our children grow and learn. A child is like a mined gem, ready to be polished. It's important for us as educators to discover the most effective ways of teaching the young and impressionable. It's important to us as parents so that we may raise our children to be happy, fulfilled, productive members of society. And it's important to American business so that we can train and maintain a skilled and satisfied workforce. In fact, some experts feel that until we improve our educational and training systems, America will remain far behind in a technologically advancing world.

It may be that in our society too much emphasis has been put on the kind of learning that has typically taken place in school, where subjects are clearly laid out and assigned for us and we're expected to do little more than memorize and recall facts and figures, names and dates. Creative thinking is often stifled, and sometimes actively discouraged.

The good news is that some schools are changing. There is much more emphasis on the techniques of solving problems instead of just producing the right answer. But we are still sorely lacking in educating ourselves and our children on how to learn, a concern of great importance to Dr. William H. Danforth, chancellor of Washington University in St. Louis, Missouri.

"The single most important thing you can do for yourself is learn how to learn," says Dr. Danforth, who is an expert both in education and in business. He is a trustee of the American Youth Foundation, and is on the board of directors of the Ralston Purina Company and the McDonnell Douglas Corporation. "The way the world is changing, one is going to have to go on learning and adapting all one's life. The facts that you learn in school won't carry you for very long. You have to learn how to get information, how to analyze and evaluate what you see and hear."

Dr. Danforth recognizes the importance of learning from others, but he also emphasizes the importance of learning to do your own research—to be able to go to the library and seek out the best opinions on a topic, and to put aside your own assumptions and figure out how people know what they know.

"One thing I tell every incoming class," says Dr. Danforth, "is that no one can learn for you, any more than someone else can eat for you. Learning is really a do-it-yourself affair. Teachers are just helpers, like coaches. You have to do it yourself, and you have to train yourself to do it."

Part of that training is to redefine what we mean by education, and to readjust our attitudes toward learning. The most successful people in our society are not necessarily those who have had the best formal education. Some did very poorly in school; some never graduated from high school or college. But somewhere along the road to success, their attitude about learning changed. They were quick to learn the lessons that life taught them about themselves, about other people, and about human nature. They practiced the skills they needed over and over again, and learned new ones whenever necessary. They didn't give up when the practice became boring or the learning difficult. They apprenticed themselves to masters in their field whenever possible. They read whatever they could get their hands on, seeking out any and all information they could find on their particular areas of interest and expertise. But above all, they learned to appreciate the value of learning itself.

Opportunities for education are all around us. Such is the view of radio personality Bruce Morrow. "A lot of people go to school today and think they're going to assimilate an education," he says. "But education is not in the books, not in the professor, not in the moments you spend in the classroom, not in that piece of sheepskin you get. Education doesn't happen *to* you, it happens *with* you. . . . School is going on from the moment you wake up in the morning to the moment you take your shoes off and turn out the lights. . . . Education is the development of curiosity and of our own power to take on the world."

"When every physical and mental resource is focused, one's power to solve a problem multiplies tremendously."

—NORMAN VINCENT PEALE

FLEXING YOUR INTELLECTUAL MUSCLE

Our curiosity, our power to take on the world, doesn't grow unattended. We must constantly feed it, walk it around, keep it exercised. Dr. Arthur Winter, neurosurgeon and director of the New Jersey Neurological Institute, says that you can actually "train your brain to preserve, restore, and improve your intellect" by keeping yourself intellectually stimulated.

In his book *Build Your Brain Power,* Dr. Winter dispels the long-held theory that we lose a great many brain cells as we age. He cites a study by Dr. Marian Cleeves Diamond that shows that the brain cells of mice "remain in number, even in old age, and are capable of being increased by an enrichment of their environment. . . . The same is undoubtedly true of humans."

Dr. Winter goes on to state: "In long term studies of humans, it has also been shown that people who continue to be active intellectually can actually improve on intelligence tests."

It is learning itself that enriches our environment. When a person who can't read learns to do so, for example, he doesn't just learn to put letters together to make words. He opens up whole new worlds. He increases tremendously not only his opportunities to succeed in the world, but also his ability to make a contribution to it. It's the snowball effect at work again. You never know where the one thing you learn today will lead you tomorrow.

The most successful people never stop learning. They don't sit back and say, "This is it, I've made it, there's nothing else to learn." They're constantly flexing, and thereby improving, their brain's muscle power.

This kind of attitude, this willingness to be a perpetual student, often leads to unexpected discoveries. Just ask Arthur Fry. He attends seminars "several times a month learning about new things five or ten years before they're in textbooks. A lot of what you learn you sort away and say, 'That's interesting, but I don't know what I'm going to do with it yet.' "

That is exactly what happened when Fry, singing in a church choir in St. Paul, was trying to mark his place in the choir's songbook. He suddenly remembered a seminar he had attended months earlier, where he had learned about a unique "low tack" adhesive. Fry wondered if he could use this adhesive to make a bookmark.

"It turned out to be perfect for paper," he says. "Had it been stickier, it would have pulled the fibers off. If it had been less sticky, it would not have held itself in place. Making the bookmark led me down the path of further discovery to the fact that they were great self-attaching notes." Thus, out of a desire to keep learning new things, the seemingly simple yet exceedingly useful Post-it Note was born.

"Every time we learn how to do something more efficiently, we displace several people from doing their job," says Fry. "But what happens then is that some of those people go on and find other ways to enrich our lives. . . . The only thing that's a constant these days is change; people have to learn to keep learning."

IF ONLY I COULD REMEMBER . . .

As several of the people interviewed for this chapter have stated, success in the '90s will depend on your ability to learn and adapt to changing times. When you learn something new, of course, it doesn't mean that you forget what you already know. It means that you add on to existing knowledge. That's why memory is so important to the learning process.

Dr. Bjork feels that one key reason that people don't "realize their capacities," is because we think of ourselves as some kind of recording device. When someone explains something to us, or we sit passively in a classroom, we expect that we're going to record the information through some kind of human video camera.

"As a matter of fact," says Dr. Bjork, "we don't work anything like a videotape recorder. The way we learn something new is to relate it or fit it in to those things we already know." This is in contrast to a videotape, where the more you have on the tape, the less room you have for something else; you often have to erase one program to record another.

Human memory, however, doesn't appear to have any limit on capacity. Prior knowledge doesn't use it up. "A good analogy for human memory is that it is like a scaffolding structure, where the more knowledge you have in a given domain, the more ways there are to interpret new things," says Dr. Bjork. "Knowledge creates the capacity for additional knowledge."

Human beings have a phenomenal capacity to take in new information, providing that we have the preexisting knowledge to interpret and store new ideas. Problems sometimes arise, though, when we try to access things that we have learned. One of the most interesting aspects of human memory is that the process of remembering is in itself a learning event. If you try to remember the name of your fifth-grade teacher, for example, you might end up in a real struggle trying to recall the name. But if you do come up with it, the very act of producing that name will facilitate greatly the likelihood that you'll be able to remember that name six months from now.

"The mistake everyone makes is that we spend way too much time on input and too little time on output," says Dr. Bjork. "A student will read a chapter three times, highlighting in three different colors until the only material that stands out is material that's not highlighted. That kind of process is nonproductive." Dr. Bjork suggests that you take a three-step approach to learning new material:

1. Read the material through once.
2. At the end of the section, try to summarize what the key points were. Rephrase, in your own words, what you've just read.
3. Try to generate another example related to the material, or make up your own "test" questions about what you've read.

"All of those processes are far more effective in terms of long-term memory," says Dr. Bjork. "Reading something once and then summarizing it yourself may produce twice the recall level of reading it twice. It also tends to reveal to us what we understand and what we don't understand. The act of retrieving the material from memory is in itself an important learning process. Much more potent than simply having something presented to you."

HOW GOOD IS YOUR MEMORY?

Do you ever hear anyone complain that they have difficulty learning new things because they have a terrible memory? Perhaps you've said it yourself; I used to. But now I'd like to share with you a simple exercise I learned that helped me develop my memory muscle.

I was an average student in high school. Although my parents always wanted me to study, I rarely did; frankly I didn't take it very seriously. I took a year off after high school, and I went back to school when I realized how important education would be to my future. This time I studied because I wanted to, not because it was my parents' idea. And this time I made the dean's list. One of the reasons I was able to do so well was because of a noncredit course called "Learning Techniques," which was without a doubt the most useful course I ever took throughout all my schooling. We're all taught the basics in math, science, and business, but you rarely see a program teaching people how to actually learn these subjects.

A wonderful teacher, Adolph J. Capriolo, taught the class how to read more effectively and the best ways to take a test. He taught us how to think, and how to understand situations more clearly. He also talked about memory techniques, in particular one called mnemonics. He taught us the following exercise, which, when practiced, can enhance your memory by as much as fifty percent.

First, memorize the ten words below in order.

1. Sun
2. Shoe
3. Tree
4. Door
5. Hive
6. Sticks
7. Heaven
8. Gate
9. Vine
10. Hen

It's not difficult to memorize this list because the words rhyme with the numbers, and you've learned them in order. Go through the list until you feel that you know it well. Now this list is going to help you remember another list of words or items, having no relation to each other, given to you in a completely random order. Ask a friend to give you any ten words right off the top of her head. Suppose the first word your friend gives you is *tractor*. Think of *number one: sun*. Then form a picture of the sun and a tractor. The more creative you are in your mental picture, and the more action that's involved in the picture, the better you're going to retain that word. For instance, you might picture the sun beating down on the tractor. It's so hot the paint on the tractor is melting, causing the field to start burning. So now you've got a fiery tractor sitting out in the hot sun in the middle of a burning field.

The second word your friend gives you is *birthday*. Go back to the original list and think of *number two: shoe*. Picture yourself having a birthday party. You take a bite of the cake, and inside is an old shoe. You can taste it, you're chewing on the leather and the laces are hanging from your mouth. Continue to create pictures for each of the remaining eight words your friend gives you. When you're finished, you can repeat the list of ten randomly chosen words back to her easily (She's probably forgotten one or two of them herself!). Not only that, if she asks what word number two was, you can quickly answer "Birthday." And if she asks what number *birthday* was, you'll know immediately that it was number two.

This exercise is a way of teaching one of the most important elements of improving memory: association.

> *"Memory is fired by association. When we perceive something . . . from that perception we are able to obtain a notion of some other thing like or unlike which is associated with it but has been forgotten."*
>
> —PLATO

PUTTING TWO AND TWO TOGETHER

In his book *Care and Feeding of the Brain,* Jack Maguire says that "our ability to remember something well rests on three principles: repetition, interest and association." The more you repeat something, the better you remember it. The more interested you are in a subject, the easier you will remember it, because you already have some of the scaffolding built on which to attach new facts. But perhaps the strongest memory links are associations—"connections we deliberately create between new information and information that is already familiar to us." If you want to remember a name, a date, or any information at all, it is much easier if you associate the new piece of information with something you already know.

Another strong example of association is what scientists call "state-bound knowledge." As Maguire explains it, every time we learn something new, it becomes "attached" to the state of consciousness in which we learned it. For example, if you learn someone's name at a party at which you had a particularly good time, that knowledge becomes attached to the state of consciousness you were in at the time of the party. If you want to recall that person's name, try to recreate the mood you were in at the party, and the name will come to you.

Suppose you study for exams every day in your room with the sun streaming through the window warming your back. When you actually take the exam, you will have a much easier time recalling the information you need if you can summon up the mood that you experienced in your room while studying, and the feeling of warmth on your back.

This goes right back to Dr. Bjork's suggestion of practicing under real-life conditions. If you learn a new task in one state of consciousness or environment, and you try to apply that task under totally different conditions, you will have a very difficult time. Therefore you must either change the conditions under which you practice, or strongly evoke your practice environment during real-life performance.

LEARNING TO BE SUCCESSFUL

Association is not only useful in learning facts, it is also an essential element of learning to be successful. Remember the phrase "you become what you think about"? Here it is again. Successful people are able to visualize themselves as being successful. But that doesn't mean they started out that way. Many had low self-esteem and basic insecurities when they were young. Eventually, however, they were able to learn to see themselves as successful, building each small success on the one before it.

Winifred Conley of the National Learning Laboratory uses a combination of association with past successes and visualization of future success to help her clients through difficult situations. "Suppose someone with a great amount of test anxiety is preparing to take his SATs on Saturday. I'll ask him what he thinks it will be like for him, what images he's having of taking the test. Then I'll say, 'You're already very success-ful—you've successfully created anxiety.' Then I'll have him stop, breathe, and take a break. I'll ask him to tell me about an experience he's had in which he was really successful in a way that was surprising and very pleasant. I ask him to de-scribe all the images, sounds, and sights that surrounded that success.

"Then I have him imagine walking into the SATs on Saturday. I ask him to create an image of him walking in the doorway, to see himself large and in color. I ask him to create a verbal script of what he will say to himself—not unrealistic things, but things like, 'I've prepared as much as I could, I'm going to do as well as I possibly can, and I'm going to give it my all.' "

Now this young man has two images of success he can use to keep his spirits and his enthusiasm going. He can use the feelings of success he's already experienced in other areas, and also use the kind of visualization we talked about in the first chapter to help him see himself as successful before he even takes the test.

There are many other examples of how this combination of visualization and association breeds success. Author Jack Can-field relates a story involving Gerald Jempolski, who became well known using imagery in working with terminally ill chil-dren in Marin County, California. Some people in the Marin County school system read about Jempolski in the newspaper and wondered if the same process would work with their re-medial reading classes. So Jempolski tested about twenty chil-dren with reading problems, and he tested a control group of another twenty children.

He took the children with reading problems through a vi-sualization process. He had them close their eyes and told them, "Imagine going into an elevator up to the tenth floor, stepping out into the lobby of a movie theater. Go over to the corner of the movie theater and you will see a bathtub. Kneel down and unzip the top of your head. Pull out your brain and wash all the negative thoughts out of it—thoughts like 'I can't read,' 'It's too hard,' or 'I'm too stupid.' Then put your brain back. Now walk into the theater, sit in a chair, and watch a movie of yourself reading well. Now get out of the chair and step into the movie. Look out at the book through your own eyes. You feel good, you hear the sound of your teacher's voice, you hear yourself sounding out the words phonetically, you see your parents smiling because you read so well. Now come back out of the theater and open your eyes.'' Jempolski then gave each student a cassette recorder and asked them to make a five-minute recording, in their own words, of what they had just experienced.

The children took their tapes home and listened to them for sixty days, every morning when they got up and every night before they went to sleep. At the end of two and a half months Jempolski tested the children in this group and the children in the control group. The children in the control group had improved one and a half months worth in their reading skills. The group that did the imaging and listened to their tapes improved their reading skills by one and a half to two and a half *years* worth!

Their visualizations and associations had allowed these children to rise way above their own, and their teachers' expectations. Of course, the one thing that this story leaves out is that all the while these children were imagining their success and listening to their tape recorders, they were also actively working on improving their skills. You can improve your chances for success through your mental processes, but unless they are accompanied by action, your dreams will remain unfulfilled.

"Not many years ago I began to play the cello. Most people would say that what I am doing is 'learning to play' the cello. But these words carry into our minds the strange idea that there exist two very different processes: one, learning to play the cello; and two, playing the cello. They imply that I will do the first until I have completed it, at which point I will stop the first process and begin the second. In short, I will go

on 'learning to play' until I have 'learned to play' and
then I will begin to play. Of course, this is nonsense.
There are not two processes, but one. We learn to do
something by doing it. There is no other way.''

—JOHN HOLT

EXPERIENCE, THE ULTIMATE TEACHER

We learn to do something by doing it. There is no other way.
Dr. Bjork provides an extreme example of the truth of this
statement: ''How many times have you sat in an airplane and
watched the stewardess demonstrate how to work an inflatable
life vest? Many times. Imagine, however, that the plane's
down in the water and it's dark and there's a smell of smoke
and people are screaming. What are the chances that you're
going to put that thing on right and remember what to pull
and what side goes front and what you blow in to inflate it?
All of those exposures where you were told what to do accomplish very little, in fact almost no, procedural learning. If
there was one trial where you actually got to do it, that would
be worth more than all of those passive exposures.''

We hear, we forget; we see, we remember; we do, we understand. In any learning procedure, the more we get involved
and jump into the job, the experiment, the sport, whatever it
is—that's when we really start learning the information. We
learn with our entire bodies. It's as if the information goes into
every cell, not only into our brains. The greatest learning experience is experience. Think about your days in school.
Which do you remember more clearly, sitting in the classroom
or going on field trips? Many museums across the country now
provide hands-on learning experiences for both adults and children. We learn best when we're aggressively interacting with
information.

To most effectively learn any new task or skill, we do best
when we go through these four stages:

1. Preparation
2. Practice
3. Application
4. Review

Many people want to go right to the application stage before doing any preparation or practice. Some people just prepare and practice their whole life and never "do" anything. And many of us never go back and review to see how we can improve our learning further.

You've read a lot in this book about educating yourself, about reading books, magazines, industry newspapers and newsletters, and about listening to audio tapes. I believe very strongly in learning everything you possibly can about anything in which you have an interest. But I also believe very strongly in action. I once heard someone say "I would rather be prepared and have no opportunity than have all the opportunities in the world and not be prepared." I disagree with that statement. I would rather have an opportunity for which I was not prepared, take a stab at it, and learn from my mistakes. Some people remain perpetual students because they are afraid to go out and face the real world. Some people prepare forever, but never take a chance.

This new information and research into learning how we learn is challenging all our educational and training systems. Children who are computer literate by the age of five are bored by the passivity of the old rote ways of learning. Scientists are studying advanced computer technologies, such as interactive learning programs and virtual reality, where 3-D simulators allow people to "step into" a new world of information. Whatever learning systems are developed, they cannot do the learning for us. As Dr. Danforth so aptly put it, learning is definitely a "do-it-yourself" affair.

"Learn as if you were going to live forever. Live as if you were going to die tomorrow."

—JOHN WOODEN

Five Essential Facets of Chapter 6

1. The most important elements of learning you can share with your children are love and trust and constant communication.
2. The only way you can truly foster a love of learning in your children is to be a role model yourself. Let your children see you reading, studying, working at home, etc. You can't expect them to learn good study habits while you're sitting in front of the television all night.
3. When you want to learn something new, remember that activity is more effective than passivity. Don't just read and highlight; read and rewrite in your own words. Verbalize your thoughts on the subject to someone else.
4. Make sure that practice sessions reflect reality. Practicing in unreal circumstances makes it difficult to repeat performance in real life.
5. We are learning all the time. When we put in one new piece of information and add it to another piece, we get more than just two pieces of information. We learn by association. The more experiences we have, the more associations we have on which to attach new information.

Think about actions you can take from these five ideas or others discussed in this chapter.

Thirty-Day Action Plan for Chapter 6

This is a memory action plan. The following is an extension of the mnemonics exercise we started earlier in the chapter. Once you're comfortable with the first ten words, you can go on to learn ten more. They are:

11. Elephant
12. Twigs
13. Throne

14. Fort
15. Fire
16. Silver
17. Seas
18. Apron
19. Knife
20. Baby

These words and numbers don't rhyme but they do have obvious associations. And you'll never forget number twenty. If you want to extend it, you can make up your own words. The more creative you are, the easier they will be to remember.

Here is another exercise for remembering people's names:

♦ Immediately upon meeting someone, repeat their name several times in conversation. Say, "Hello, Sue. It's nice to meet you, Sue. How do you know our host, Sue?"
♦ Use association. Find a trait or characteristic that reminds you of someone or something else. For instance, I recently met someone name Jay. He had a big nose. So I pictured a blue jay with a long beak. (It doesn't matter whether blue jays really have long beaks or not; and you don't have to ever tell the person what you were thinking.) These methods have helped me memorize the names of forty or fifty people at a seminar so that I'm able to call on each of them by name.

Now you've seen that education is everywhere, and that successful people are constantly learning. How do they keep themselves motivated when practice gets boring? For peak performers, the willingness to learn is born out of the love they have for what they want to achieve. In the next chapter we'll explore how you too can discover what it is you want to do in life, how to articulate your mission or purpose, how to research and prepare yourself to travel the road you've chosen, and how to take the actions necessary to turn your heart's dream into your life's work.

Chapter Seven

CUTTING TO THE CORE OF THE MATTER:
FINDING THE PASSION FOR WHAT YOU DO

"A successful person is someone who does what he or she desires to do, does it very well with quiet patience and determination. One size does not fit all. Each of us is an individual, and each of us can succeed as an individual with the love and support of those around us."

—ANN COMPTON

"I've heard so many definitions of success, but the one I like the best is that you can't tell the difference between work and play. If you enjoy what you're doing, it may seem to others like you work too hard. But if it's what you really want to do, and you enjoy doing it, it's not really work at all."

—BRUCE JENNER

Ask any truly successful person how he (or she) has done what he's done, and he'll tell you, "I worked hard. I made mistakes. I learned from them. I started again and I worked harder."

Ask any truly successful person *why* he's done what he's done, and he'll tell you, "For the love of it."

High achievers have a dream and follow it. Sometimes they have many dreams. But whatever they do, they do it with passion. This is true no matter what field or profession. There are people who are passionate about office products, about bicycles, about entertainment, about oil fields, about scientific discoveries, about teaching, about sports, about politics, about education, about plumbing supplies. People find their passions in the strangest places—but when they do, they are rewarded with great riches.

In the diamond industry, miners have to sort through twenty-three tons of raw material to come out with one carat of gem-quality diamond. And they don't always find the diamond right away. It takes much time, patience, and dedication to wash away the less valuable material and get to the gem beneath. The miners' mission is to keep washing, stripping, and sorting the raw material until they find the gem.

We are all like those miners—washing, stripping, and sorting our own raw materials so that we may discover the gem within. That gem is our calling in life, our mission, our purpose, our passion. It is what gives us that necessary spark to overcome obstacles, and keeps us going when the odds are against us.

Listen to how Dr. Mortimer Mishkin of the National Institute of Mental Health describes what keeps him going every day. "It is," he says, "a desire to discover something that has never been discovered before. To know something that no one else has ever known. To make clear some mystery and magic that has not been possible to clarify before. . . . Either you have wonder, either you believe that these questions are simply, awesomely interesting, or you don't. If you really are fascinated by how it is possible for the mind to comprehend the universe, how it is possible for the mind to create art and music and poetry, how it is possible to think thoughts and dream. . . . If you have these questions, then you ask 'What can I do to help figure these things out?' You've got to have this sense of wonder, otherwise there's no sense in going into this field.''

Obviously, Dr. Mishkin is someone who loves what he does, who finds his work ''simply, awesomely interesting.'' It's one of the reasons he is so good at what he does. Having a passion for what you do is not limited to any particular field or profession. An accountant can be just as passionate about crunching numbers as a scientist is about solving the mysteries of the universe. You can be a doctor or you can be a restaurateur. Vincent Sardi, owner of one of New York's most famous and treasured eateries, made the choice between those two professions when he was in college. His parents, who started the restaurant in 1921, wanted him to be a ''professional person,'' a doctor. He went to Columbia University as a premed student, working part-time in the restaurant. ''The more I worked here, the more I fell in love with Sardi's,'' he told me as we sat beneath the famous caricatures that grace the walls. ''I switched my curriculum to business administration and when I graduated, I came to work here full-time. . . . It was, and is, a hands-on operation. If you asked me what my hours were, I was just here. . . . If I didn't like it, I wouldn't be able to do it. But that goes for anything you do. If you feel that you're working, then you really don't enjoy what you're doing.''

It is not what you choose to do, but why you choose to do it that is important. We spend more than ninety-six thousand hours of our lives at work. Who wants to spend that many hours in drudgery and frustration? Certainly not Dr. Frank Field, CBS-TV's noted meteorologist and health and science expert. ''I think the key to succeeding in any business is looking forward to each day's work as though you're doing it for nothing, literally,'' says Field. ''There's nothing I enjoyed more than New York, when I was at NBC years ago, on a cold winter day, walking the six or seven blocks from where I lived, going up to my office on a Sunday morning. Looking down from my office at the ice skating rink with the snow falling, going through the mail, typing the responses. Then my wife would call and say lunch is ready. And I'd walk back through the snow. I'd finish my lunch, kiss her, and run back to the office. It was fun.''

When Dr. Field started to work in television, he fell in love with it because he could combine his own interests in science and teaching with ''a fun media. Here was an opportunity to make a good living and have a certain amount of creative freedom combined with the joy of doing something I loved. . . . To be able to do your 'hobby' and make a living at it is the most wonderful thing in the world.''

If your purpose in life is to make money and have lots of expensive toys and perks, that's fine. There's nothing wrong with being rich or with being able to afford the things that give us pleasure. Perhaps that's why you picked up this book—to learn the secret money-making methods of the rich and famous. Sorry to disappoint you. If you ask successful people to describe themselves in terms of their success, they rarely talk about money. Or if they do, it's mentioned as a by-product of their achievements.

That's why all the get-rich-quick scams and the ''no money down'' infomercials don't make many people rich. Ignoring the issue of whether or not these money-making schemes actually work, most people who buy into these plans do not follow through by putting in the time and effort it would take to make them profitable. And why not? Because it has nothing to do with their real purpose in life. The people who buy into the program suddenly discover that, even though the possibility of making a lot of money exists, there is nothing about this program that excites them or ignites their passion.

In the 1980s, many people thought they could live their lives solely in pursuit of financial success. It was a sociological experiment that failed miserably. Apparently, human beings cannot live by greed alone. It is part of our makeup to look for happiness and fulfillment as well as material comforts.

''Get very good at what you love to do, because you can never get good enough at something you are not suited for.''

—DR. ROBERT ANTHONY

FINDING A SENSE OF PURPOSE

John James is a psychotherapist, an ordained clergyman, a business consultant, and coauthor of *Passion for Life*. It took him many years of searching before he found his niche, before he discovered what he had to offer that made him feel good about himself. It is his opinion that "within us all is a hunger to transcend our barriers, our inadequacies and our problems and to want to reach for something that's right and healthy. That hunger within us is like a spark that we need to ignite. . . . We are all hungry to be on a path with heart, which means we're emotionally committed to what we're doing; to bringing about something that's important to us in the future, something that has meaning beyond comfort, something that gives us a sense of purpose in life."

According to James, there are five steps we can take to find our purpose:

1. **Listen within.** Discover your dreams, your passions, and what is really exciting to you; move toward those things that are positive and motivating and to which you find yourself continually drawn.
2. **Begin the adventure.** Set clear goals and plans, take some time to really think these plans through, and take the steps to get yourself started. "Where people usually get stuck, though, is their resistance," says James. "All the feelings or reasons why it won't work or how they can't get going or how it's impossible to find the time, the money, the energy. . . . An important part of beginning the adventure is to figure out how to make a friend of this resistance, . . . how to use it and defuse it." You can ask yourself several questions to get started:

   ♦ What do you want to do that will enhance your life?
   ♦ How will you know when you've "made it"?

♦ What are you willing to do to bring it about (not what you should do or could do, but what are you willing to do)?

♦ How might you sabotage yourself, and what can you do to prevent yourself from getting in your own way?

For instance, you might set a positive goal, then sabotage yourself by getting so busy you have no time to move toward it. You might counteract that sabotage by setting aside a specific time of the day or week during which you will take at least one step toward your goal, no matter how small.

3. **Persevere.** It's easy to get discouraged when plans don't produce immediate results, and it's easy to get distracted. As we reach for new goals, we have to keep asking ourselves, "Is this a path with heart? Is it one I want to take, or am I doing this to please someone else?" If it is truly a path with heart, it is possible to persevere through almost any adversity.

4. **Learn the positive lessons.** Going through adversity often teaches us necessary survival techniques. But if we're not careful, we may learn only cynical lessons such as, "You can't trust anybody," or "If you want something done, do it yourself." We need to search out the lessons that help us reach a positive goal. "Keep thinking 'What have I learned that's *right* from this process?'," says James. " 'What am I learning that's good about me, about other people, or about life, that I can use?' "

5. **Incorporate these lessons into your life.** There's no greater teacher than experience. Everything that happens to us contains a lesson that can help us find a path with heart. We must learn to recognize these lessons, and use them to help us move forward in the direction we choose to go.

ONE CHOICE OUT OF MILLIONS

We all know someone like this: Sarah is bright, intelligent, funny, hard-working. She got good grades in school, and people like her. Yet she drifts from one job to another, enthusiastic for a short while about each new opportunity, then unhappy and restless. When you ask her why she keeps moving around, she answers, "I just don't know what it is I want to do!"

Sometimes the choice comes easily. Bruce Jenner discovered sports in elementary school. Lt. Col. Dennis Krembel was six years old when he took his first airplane ride and from then on he knew that he would spend his life flying. Some people have obvious musical or artistic talents that point them in a definite direction early on. For most of us, however, the choices concerning what we want to do in life are more difficult to make.

Joe Montgomery didn't follow a straight line to becoming a successful business owner. Founder and CEO of Cannondale Corporation, manufacturer of high-quality, lightweight, aluminum frame bikes, Montgomery was very much a wanderer during his early years. He dropped out of college. He went to New York to study music. He got married and divorced. He dropped out of two more colleges. He went down to the Caribbean to sail other people's boats and try to figure out what he wanted to do. While there, he met a man who worked on Wall Street, who told Montgomery to give him a call if he ever wanted a "real" job. He did, and a year later he was working for what is now Prudential Bache.

Montgomery soon realized that Wall Street wasn't for him. What he really wanted was to "make something," he says. "But it gave me the opportunity to work for some very intelligent people and to see how businesses, especially small- and medium-sized businesses, were financed and managed."

Working on Wall Street in the '70s, Montgomery became aware of a newly forming niche known as leisure-time industries, such as camping and bicycling. Since he had always been an avid cycler, Montgomery combined his business knowledge and his love for improving existing equipment by starting Cannondale.

Like most successful people, Montgomery used the knowledge he gained from all his previous experience as a foundation for his ultimate endeavor. Even though he knew a career on Wall Street wasn't for him, he used his time there to absorb information for future use.

Having taken a circuitous route himself, Montgomery has advice for others who may be searching and wandering. "When we're young we think of ourselves as immortal," he says. "We don't think about the fact that we're running out of time at eighteen and at twenty-two just like we are at fifty-two, which is what I am now. Young people fail to imagine their lives as they want them to be. . . . They need to say, 'What do I want my life to look like when I'm forty? When I'm sixty?' It's purposeful daydreaming.

"And you've got to put it on paper, write it down. . . . You need a plan. It's like a painting; you need to be drawing what it's going to look like for you down the road. You may change it a thousand times. But the more detailed you can make that picture in your mind, the more likely you are to achieve.

"If you know what the future is going to be like, the chances are you're going to be better prepared for it. . . . If you design your future, the likelihood of your achieving your goal, as it evolves and changes over time, is five, ten, maybe fifty times more likely to happen."

> *"Plant the seed of desire in your mind and it forms a nucleus with power to attract to itself everything needed for its fulfillment."*
>
> —ROBERT COLLIER

IT'S NEVER TOO LATE

It's not only the young who can benefit from "purposeful day-dreaming." This is a valuable tool for anyone who is unsure of which road to take, which calling to follow.

Charles Garfield has made his life's work studying high achievers and how they work. Author of several books on the subject, including *Peak Performers* and *Second to None,* Garfield recommends two ways to find your "mission"—not only what area you want to work in, but what you want to accomplish once you get there.

He suggests that you look back into your past at the times you did your best work, the times you were most fulfilled, the times you felt best about yourself and what you were doing. Write them down.

"Most folks who are not high achievers by nature or by predilection will look back and see those times as due to God, to good luck, or to somebody else's assistance," says Garfield. "They won't own their own participation in it. People need to go back to the times in which they've done their best work . . . and ask themselves what it was they contributed to each of these times that was common to the different situations. . . . They usually find that they had a similar role in each of those occasions where their best work occurred. Those consistent roles end up being the common thread that suggests what your best arena of peak performance is likely to be."

For instance, suppose you are a computer repair person who normally works alone, making more contact with machines than with people. You're looking to make a change in your life, but you don't know "what else you can do." You make a list of the experiences that have been most successful and given you the most satisfaction in all areas of your life.

Going over your list, you realize that the times you were most fulfilled were when you were (1) coaching the Little League team and (2) sharing your skills and abilities with others, either explaining what you had done or showing them how to do it themselves. So when you look back at the times you were most proud of the work you'd done, you were motivating and teaching others. This may be a good direction for you to follow: You might want to explore such possibilities as becoming an instructor of computer maintenance and repair, a computer consultant, or even a technical trainer for computer salespeople. There are myriad directions in which you could go. The idea you had in your mind that computer repair was the only thing you could possibly do was obviously false.

Once you have discovered the areas in your life and work that give you consistent satisfaction, you can make choices and decisions that will lead you in that direction. According to Garfield, the first step you take is internal. You begin by creating "a visual image of a positive future. . . . You've got to be able to see it in your mind's eye. And you've got to be able to get a strong sense of what life you'll be living and what work you'll be doing."

The next step is to clarify your "mission," to create a statement of purpose that says, "This is what I want to do, and this is why I want to do it." This statement should also be written down, so that you can refer to it when things are tough and times are slow. It should answer the question we all have at various times in our lives, "Why am I doing this?"

"If you ask why," says Garfield, "you have to talk about a deep level of commitment. When people don't stay motivated, it's because they don't have a clue as to what the deeper purpose of their commitment is—and it just isn't powerful enough to sustain the amount of work it takes to become a peak performer."

Jack Canfield, another leading expert on peak performance, says that it's easy to get excited about any goal, dream, or passion. It's a lot harder, though, to actually sit down and do the work necessary to succeed. "The question really is how to stay pumped when you meet adversity, or when the going gets dull. You've got to go back to your vision. Ask yourself, 'Why am I doing this?' You may be doing it to make a difference, or to make a million dollars, but there's some purpose behind your behavior. Behavior is always purposeful. Even a kid with a knife in an alley who's trying to get your money has a purpose. It's when you lose sight of your purpose that you get bored and stuck."

Canfield tells a story about a marathoner who has no legs. In order to compete, he swings forward on both hands, pulls

his body up and lands on his trunk, then leans forward again—
and does that for 26 miles. By the time he's done his hands
look like hamburgers, they're torn and bleeding. People constantly ask him how he is able to keep going, how he keeps
himself motivated. "Look at your hands," someone said to
him after a race. "You must be in great pain." The runner
answered by saying, "Every time I would take my eyes off
the next three hundred feet in front of me, my hands would
hurt. But as long as I had my eyes three hundred feet down
the road, knowing that's where I was going, I wouldn't think
about my hands. My goal was to finish the race." It was his
sense of purpose that kept him going, despite his handicap and
despite his pain.

RESEARCH AND DISCOVERY

Once you've looked inside yourself, created a vision, and established a mission, it's time to look to the "outside" world
to help you make those difficult life choices. Charles Garfield
recommends taking a look at "the people in your life, and the
people you read about, who are living lives that are interesting
to you; people who are making the best out of their own
lives."

When you put your own accomplishments together with
what you admire about others, you begin to see a pattern and
a possible life-focus emerge.

"Don't trust your perception from a distance," says Garfield. "Actually meet with as many of the people as possible
and test out whether or not they are as happy as they appear
to be."

Sounds like excellent advice. But how do you go about
meeting these people you admire so much? If they're so successful, won't they be too busy to see someone they don't even
know? Won't they be annoyed that a perfect stranger is asking
to take up their valuable time?

Everyone's time is valuable—including yours. If you think

seeking advice and information is a waste of anyone's time, don't even make the effort. If you believe in the value of tapping into the wisdom of experienced professionals, chances are someone else will believe in the value of sharing that wisdom. It's not necessary to ask for an hour-long face-to-face meeting. A five-minute phone conversation may be all you need.

Your first order of business is to make a list of all those people you'd like to contact. Start with people you know, or know that you can contact through friends or acquaintances. Then add on people you've read about in books or magazines or seen on television.

Finally, if you know what field you're interested in, but don't know whom to contact, go to the library and do some research in the following areas:

♦ If there is a particular company that is an industry leader, check to see if the library has a copy of the company's annual report (or call the company directly and request one), which will include profiles of the company's top executives.

♦ Check trade journals and professional publications for articles about interesting and influential people in that field.

♦ Look for the associations that are attached to the industry in which you're interested; high-ranking association officials could be of great help to you. If you don't know which groups would be most beneficial to you, look through the *Encyclopedia of Associations* for ones that apply to your area of interest.

♦ Refer to other directories and reference books in which you'll find valuable information, including:

   ♦ *The Fortune Directory of U.S. Corporations*
   ♦ *Poor's Register of Corporations, Directors and Executives*
   ♦ *Thomas' Register*
   ♦ *Who's Who in America*
   ♦ *Who's Who of American Women*

THE ALL-IMPORTANT LETTER

Once you've made your list of potential advisors (including names, titles, addresses, and phone numbers), you're ready to make contact. The best way to go about contacting someone you don't know is to write to them directly. Here are six important points to keep in mind when writing such a letter:

♦ **You are not asking for a job.** You're only seeking advice and information. Be sure this is clearly stated in the letter.

♦ **You're writing to this particular person for a specific reason.** Perhaps you were referred to this person by a mutual acquaintance. In that case you might say, "John Smith suggested that because of your long and successful history in this industry, you would be the perfect person from whom to seek advice." If you're contacting this person without a reference, include something about them you discovered during your research. You might say, "I recently read an article about you in *Business Week* and I was especially impressed with your quote about . . ." Anyone receiving this letter is sure to be impressed with the fact that you've done your homework.

♦ **You're a serious, committed individual.** Include a little about your background, and why you're interested in getting information about this particular profession.

♦ **You have specific questions in mind.** There's no need to include the questions in the letter, but you do want to give the contact a hint of what you expect to gain from this meeting or interview.

♦ **You will not take up much of your contact's time.** If you live near enough for an in-person meeting, indicate that you're only asking for fifteen or twenty minutes. If you want a phone interview, let him or her know it will be short and to the point. Most people, especially when they realize the research you've done before meeting with them, will give generously of their time.

♦ **You will follow up with a phone call.** Mention a specific date on which you will call to set up an interview appointment.

Here is a sample of an effective letter:

June 22, 1993

Mr. James Expert
President
SuperSales Inc.
500 Main Street
Anytown, USA

Dear Mr. Expert:

I recently read an article about you in *Achievement Magazine* where you were quoted as saying, ''Intense customer service is the secret behind every successful salesperson.'' You then gave the ten most effective steps to improving customer service. It's this kind of insight, plus your years of experience both in the field and as a trainer, that convinced me you are the most qualified person around to give advice to newcomers.

Although I have been a teacher for the past eight years, I've come to realize that I have great interest in sales and sales training. Any advice you might have about what I might need to do to enter and succeed in this field would, I'm sure, prove invaluable.

I'm not asking for a job in your organization. I'm seeking only 10 or 15 minutes of your time for advice and information. I will call you on July 10th to set up a convenient time.

Sincerely,

Tim McDonald

Be sure you follow up on the tenth. You may not get through on the first try. You may not get through on the third or fourth try. After several more attempts, you may get turned down. But you'll probably be surprised at the number of people who are impressed by the kind of initiative and persistence you've shown, who feel flattered and honored by such a request, and who are happy to "give something back."

This is basically the way I contacted all the people interviewed for this book. Sometimes I was referred to them by other people I had interviewed, and sometimes I simply wrote them a letter introducing myself and my book and asking for a bit of their time. Very often the fifteen minutes they thought they could spare turned into forty-five minutes to an hour of delightful and insightful conversation.

THE GRASS IS NOT ALWAYS GREENER

So far, we have been talking about finding the passion with the assumption that it lies in something other than what you are doing right now. This isn't necessarily so. Many people who feel temporarily bored, overwhelmed, or stuck in a rut do not need to make large-scale changes. Sometimes all it takes is a commitment to making the most of the situation in which you currently find yourself.

I have been in sales all my working life. I love selling, and at one point when I was younger, I was a "sales juggler," selling several different products at once. I sold home improvement products over the phone at night; on the weekends I sold real estate; and during the day I sold advertising for a start-up fashion magazine. I was used to a fast pace and a quick sale.

Then I took a full-time job selling office copiers. The first year and a half was a difficult time for me. The quick sale was gone. This was a service-oriented business; the sales cycle could take anywhere from thirty days to several months before you got an order. I was an average performer. I had my good months and my not-so-good months. But I felt something was missing. For the first time I questioned whether or not this was the right field for me.

Then one day I read an article that suggested interviewing satisfied customers on a tape recorder and using these testimonials to show other prospects how you might help them. I decided to try it—and it turned my selling life around. Now when prospects said, "I'm not familiar with your brand name," or "I can get it for less," I could say, "I can understand your concern. Other people have felt that way too. But I'd like you to hear what some of my customers have to say about using our products."

My prospects were impressed and I got totally "pumped up" hearing first-hand the benefits my customers were receiving. Once again, I became enthusiastic about selling, and my enthusiasm was catching. I had been selling two copiers a month; I was now selling ten. For a year and a half I couldn't get into the business—and then the business got into me.

Sometimes we're so busy looking around for what else we could be doing, we fail to see the opportunities right in front of us. I resuscitated my passion for sales by finding a unique and creative way to differentiate myself from the competition. The testimonials from satisfied customers I was playing for prospective buyers did more than assure them they'd get the service they deserved, it put my energy and enthusiasm back on track. So before you give up on something about which you were once so passionate, seek out the opportunities you may have overlooked.

Dr. William H. Danforth of Washington University has this advice: "A lot of people are hesitant to do things because the times don't seem just right or the situation doesn't seem just perfect. . . . The world has never been perfect. The situation will never seem just right. In the final analysis, you have to act out of determination and courage. You're never assured of success. You have to be willing to say that if things aren't just the way you want them to be, you'll do your best to change them, to *make* things be the way you want them to be. . . . You make the most of what you have."

Many times when we're bored, restless, disappointed, or depressed, we assume we have to become another person entirely, to make a 180-degree shift, to do something completely different. This is often a false assumption. Frequently it's not *what* we're doing that's the problem—it's *how* we're doing it.

If you're dissatisfied with what you're doing, take a look at it from a fresh point of view, as if you were a stranger viewing your situation for the first time. Ask yourself:

♦ What can I do differently here?
♦ What simple step can I make today toward change?
♦ Is there some aspect of this job I have not yet explored?
♦ What's unique about my skills and/or personality that can make me stand out from the competition?

Sometimes, in order to get out of the rut we're in, we need "a shock or a shovel." The shock often comes when we're laid off or fired, threatened with firing, or even when we're moved around within the company. I had a shock of my own, and it was the best thing that ever happened to me.

After four years of working as a corporate trainer, I was told that my position was going to be eliminated. Many people told me I should interview for a regional sales position or another job with the company. But I decided to go out on my own. I saw this as a perfect opportunity to make a change in my life. But if it hadn't been for the "shock" at that point, I don't know if I would ever have done it.

Sometimes it's not even a shock that you need, it's a shovel. The excitement you crave may be right in front of you. You just need to dig deep enough. Ask yourself:

♦ How much do I really know about what I'm doing now?
♦ How can I use what I'm doing to help other people?
♦ Who can I interview in my company or my industry who can give me a broader view of what I'm doing now?

Instead of jumping ship and going somewhere else when the going gets rough, look for ways to improve the situation at hand. Sometimes things come to life when we cultivate them. It's like a garden—if you just sit and look at it, nothing's going to grow. But if you water it, weed it, and cultivate the seeds, you may be surprised at what you find in bloom.

*"Two roads diverged in the yellow wood
and I took the road less traveled by
and that has made all the difference."*

—ROBERT FROST

THE ENTREPRENEURIAL ATTITUDE: DEALING WITH A CHANGING WORLD

Wherever you find your passion, whether you continue along your present career path or make a complete turnaround, you need to consider the realities of the current economic situation.

An old saying has it that the secret to success is in learning to do one thing and doing that one thing better than anyone else. That old saying no longer exactly applies. It's still possible to do one thing better than anyone else, but it is no longer advisable to make that one thing the *only* thing you do. That kind of narrow focus creates blinders, and can actually be a handicap in today's changing world.

One of the main reasons people get stuck in circumstances they feel they cannot change is that they don't know what else they could possibly do. They see life as one dreary highway with the same dull scenery always ahead.

Successful people see many roads ahead—and if they don't see one they like, they build their own. They know there is more than one way to get where they're going.

Scott DeGarmo, publisher of *Success* magazine, has profiled many of the most successful people in America. A common thread he sees is the entrepreneurial attitude.

"People no longer have all their choices made for them within an organization," he says. "The rapid advance of technology is changing the shape of organizations; people are becoming more self-reliant. We are entering into an entrepreneurial society.

"In an era in which there is the opportunity for everyone to create their own scenarios of success, they should be armed with as much knowledge as possible. Successful individuals are seeking a whole range of disciplines and skills and knowledge. . . . People are developing entrepreneurial attitudes about their own lives, and are getting a sense of almost unlimited potential in terms of what they can do with their lives.''

LEAVING NO STONE UNTURNED

Each of the people interviewed for this book possesses this sense of unlimited potential, this entrepreneurial attitude. They have created their own scenarios of success by opening themselves to the opportunities around them. One of the things radio personality Bruce Morrow enjoys most about his life is its multifaceted nature.

"A lot of people make a big error,'' he says. "They put blindfolds on thinking they're a race horse. They don't want to use their peripheral vision. But without vision on either side, they're going to get into a lot of trouble. They get specialized in life very quickly. Those are the people who are bored with their work. . . .

"I've never been bored a day in my life. . . . I look to the left, I turn my head completely around, I want to see what's doing behind me. If there's a tablecloth, I want to look underneath because I want to see what the table is standing on. When the refrigerator closes, I don't trust it. I want to find out if the light is really out. You can never stop looking. The person who stops looking and is satisfied is not really exposing himself to his fullest. . . .

"You're not born with passion. You're born with desire and intelligence and curiosity. Curiosity then develops into ambition and that develops into skill. Skill and curiosity and ambition develop into passion. With passion you develop a desire to continue going and you walk into work saying, 'Boy I'm glad I'm here.'

"We're all put here for a reason. If you're not interested in finding the reason, you'll never have passion, and without passion you're going to be very bored and disappointed in life. Life offers a tremendous amount of trees, and your branches can spread any way you want. No one can stop you.''

Management consultant Beverly Hyman has felt that way all her life. ''I often didn't know exactly what my objective was. And I often didn't know exactly what the specific route to success was,'' she says. ''I didn't know precisely where I was going. I have a view of my own career as a scattering of many seeds, like sowing a field of wildflowers. You're not quite sure exactly what's in the seed packet. All you know is you've got fertile ground and you've got strong motivation, and you're willing to put the labor in to till up the soil, enrich it, fertilize it, lay down the seed, water it, and devote yourself to it. But it could be many things simultaneously. You don't always have to follow a linear path.''

When Hyman was taking her master's at Hofstra University, she was teaching a course in the English department, teaching a course in the school of business, supervising student teachers in the school of education, and running a writing clinic at night. One evening around nine o'clock, her officemate came in and saw her with her evening students in the writing clinic and said, ''What the heck are you doing? You're doing so many different things! Plus you have a two-year-old at home and you're taking a master's and you're trying to get a television program. What are you doing?''

Hyman replied, ''I don't know what I'm doing. All I know is that I'm planting all these seeds and I'm going to harvest some of them. I can't say right now which ones I'm going to harvest. But somehow all these experiences that I am throwing myself into and all these people I'm meeting and all that I'm learning will all come together.''

Bev Hyman had faith and confidence that eventually she would find the path that was right for her. She didn't let someone else's view of her life choices stop her from finding her own way.

Neither did Jeff Herman. Jeff is a very successful literary agent in New York who held down several different jobs before he decided to go out on his own as an agent. When I asked Jeff (who just happens to be my agent) what advice he had for people who were searching to find their passion in life, he told me the most important thing was "not to let other people draw walls for you. Don't let other people tell you what can or can't be done, or what you can or can't do. Once you start buying into other people's walls, you're no longer your own person, you don't really belong to yourself anymore. Listen to them to learn, but don't let them set the agenda for you, or tell you who you are. . . .

"You have to get in touch with what it is you like doing. You may not know what that is right away. You have to be willing to try a few things. You may go through three or four jobs by the time you're twenty-five, but then you have to be willing to let go, move on and try something else. Sometimes it's easier to take these risks when you're younger. When I started my business, I was naive in a positive way because I didn't know what I was up against, I didn't know that there were things I needed to be afraid of. I didn't know that there were things that were going to be difficult. That's an advantage you have when you're young.

"I don't think you always have to overeducate yourself. There's nothing wrong with inventing the wheel all over again. My experience was that because I didn't have an education in some areas, I ended up inventing the wheel for myself, and I evolved a way of doing certain things I may not have done otherwise. So you don't necessarily have to look for other people's footsteps. Your footsteps may create something better."

> "All you need in this life is ignorance and confidence and then success is sure."
>
> —MARK TWAIN

Finding your passion is like mining for gemstones. It takes a lot of exploration to come up with a rough stone, which must be cut, shaped, and faceted to reveal its brilliance and beauty. When a beautifully cut, multifaceted diamond is held up to the light, it works as a prism. The light is dispersed and broken up into the spectral colors of red, orange, yellow, green, blue, and violet. Without the facets, the stone would have no "fire." This fire, caused by the facets, is what makes the diamond so special and so valued.

We, too, enhance our value and release our inner fire, or passion, when we become multifaceted. This doesn't mean we must be a Jack or Jill of all trades. It means that we must expose ourselves to as much as possible, in as many areas as possible. It means keeping ourselves open to new experiences, and it means having a respect and a passion for learning itself.

Senator Bill Bradley of New Jersey is a prime example of how a passion for learning can lead to success. Raised in a small town in Missouri where his father was a banker, Bradley was always interested in learning. In junior high, he would often study into the early morning hours. His mother was determined that he be a well-rounded "gentleman." She arranged for him to learn to play the trumpet, the French horn, and the piano; sent him for swimming and golf lessons; saw that he learned how to ride a horse, how to type, and how to box.

Bradley feels that being exposed to so many different things in his childhood helped him to find his niche. He was able to try many different things, and eliminate those areas where he had little talent.

An All-American at Princeton, Bradley went on to become an Olympic gold medalist as captain of the 1964 U.S. basketball team. He attended Oxford University as a Rhodes scholar, played pro basketball (including two NBA championships), and ran for the U.S. Senate in 1977. According to a 1990 *Rolling Stone* article, Bradley's first action as Senator-elect was to poll "every knowledgeable source he could find and ask: 'What does it take to do the job—very well?' "

In this as in everything he undertakes, Bradley had two goals: to learn everything there is to learn about a particular endeavor—whether it's the sport of basketball or the game of politics—and then to do it extremely well.

Before I met Senator Bradley, I was amazed and impressed

by all his accomplishments. During our meeting, I discovered he was down-to-earth, genuine, and giving. I'm now not only amazed at his accomplishments, I'm amazed at the person he has become through them.

"You must have a certain pride in your work, in your ability to do something well," says Bradley. But for him, the greatest stimulation is the learning itself. "There is a great enjoyment in learning more about the world around you," he says. "Learn more about how a city functions, or what goes into the defense budget, or how you actually organize a computer system or business. Learning how to do something has a real satisfaction built into it."

TEACHING YOUR CHILDREN WELL

As much as we owe it to ourselves to become multifaceted, we have a greater responsibility to our children to expose them to as much as life has to offer. A child may be a poor student, but a gifted artist. If this child is never exposed to good art, or given the opportunity to draw, she may never know she has this talent. We have a duty to show our kids that there are many options for them out in the world.

This is definitely Bruce Jenner's philosophy. He has always had a firm commitment to youth, including the physically and mentally handicapped. He battled dyslexia as a child, and feels that his exposure to sports was a major turning point in his life. He encourages all children with problems to explore many different areas until they find the one in which they have a special talent.

"I've got eight kids," he says, "and I think it's my responsibility to expose them to as many different areas as I can. When you get older, you take that responsibility onto yourself. I think of it as having a little computer in my brain. I feed it information, and then decipher what works for me."

It's being open to all possibilities that has allowed Jenner to become an Olympic athlete, a highly respected sports commentator, entrepreneur, commercial spokesperson, television personality, actor, producer, and author.

"The hardest part of life is finding what you want to do," he says. "So many people don't expose themselves, don't get out there and find things. What do you do if you don't know what it is you want? First, take the few things you know you have going for you."

When a handsome friend of Jenner's came to him for advice about what to do with his life, Jenner said, "You're a great-looking guy, and you have confidence in the way you look. Use that. Get into commercials or modeling. Just start doing something. Use your assets just to get going, and branch out from there."

"There's a saying," says Jenner, "that some very ordinary people do some extraordinary things. You talk to anyone who's been successful in their area and they're really ordinary people. But they've worked very hard and they have a great belief in what they want to do."

"You've got to go out on a limb sometimes because that's where all the fruit is."

—WILL ROGERS

PASSION IS NOTHING WITHOUT THE COURAGE TO TAKE ACTION

We live in an amazing country. The American Dream is famous all over the world: that anyone can be whatever they choose to be. This is not true in all other areas of the world. Here, we often take this freedom for granted. We let our chances slip by. We're afraid to take risks and we let others' opinions, or our own fears and inhibitions, hold us back.

"People are blessed in life if they find a career for which they feel passion and excitement," says Dr. Fred Epstein, chief of pediatric neurosurgery at New York University Medical Center. "Then you have to have the courage to go for it, because so often what we have a passion for puts us out on a limb which could break. I've always been intrigued when I see many people who are much smarter than I am, and they have limited professional success. Very often it's because they have been unwilling to go out on a limb, to take chances.

"When I look back at my own career, which is still unfolding, I would say that nineteen out of twenty of my ideas haven't worked. But the twentieth has been good, and has been able to save lives. One has to be willing to face failure and ridicule and keep spewing out ideas. . . . When I interview people for our neurosurgical training program . . . I tell them that everybody can take a little piece of turf and make it better. That's what I think the commitment of human beings should be. . . . If you find an area for which you have real passion, that is the main ingredient for success."

Earl Nightingale once said, "The secret to successful living is freedom, and the secret to freedom is courage." Don't be afraid to take chances. Stand up for those things in which you believe. Go after your dreams and keep searching until you find what you want.

Bev Hyman tells a story about a professor she had as an undergraduate who was "the nastiest SOB. But he taught me a lot of things because he had very high standards. We were once assigned a paper and one of the students said, 'But Professor, I'm not interested in writing a paper on this.' And the professor said, 'Of course you're not interested in it. No one is ever interested in anything. If you're lucky, when you're in the library and you're in the middle of your research for this paper, for a brief period of time you will become powerfully engaged by it. It will interest you. And then when you're finished writing the paper, five minutes later it won't interest you.' Interest is something that is galvanized by the act of doing. If we're going to sit around and wait to feel what our passion is, we're never going to find it. You have to go out and pursue it. The harder you pursue it, the more you're likely to find it. And the more you put into it, the more you're likely to experience it.''

The next time you get tired or discouraged, or find difficulty getting interested in what you're doing, think about this piece of advice from Bruce Jenner:

''You've got to get up in the morning, look life square in the face, and get on with it. The number one thing is, never underestimate yourself. Too many people say, 'I'm not good enough for this job.' Once you've said that, you're not good enough. Don't be afraid to take chances. The things you want are right there in front of you. The sad thing is, most people don't know they're out there. But all you have to do is reach out, grab them, and haul them in.''

"We are shaped and fashioned by what we love."

—GOETHE

Five Essential Facets of Chapter 7

1. Look into your past and think of times when you did your best work and were most fulfilled. Write down those experiences, exactly what you were doing, and how you felt about it.
2. Write down your mission or purpose in life. Write a paragraph about what you want to accomplish, based on your passion. Put this sheet of paper somewhere you can see it every day.
3. Once you have an idea of what you want to do, the process of research and discovery begins. Read everything you can get your hands on. Make contact with people in the industry. Write, follow up, and be persistent.
4. Leave no stone unturned. Expose yourself, and your children, to many different things until you find the ones that spark your interest. Plant seeds in many areas that interest you without worrying about exactly how they will come together. Don't forget to explore the possibility that the

diamond you seek may be buried in your own backyard. Frequently it's not what we're doing that's the problem, it's how we're doing it.

5. Use Bill Bradley's two-step method: (1) Learn as much as you can about your areas of interest; (2) Do it to the best of your ability.

Think about actions you can take from these five ideas or others discussed in this chapter.

Thirty-Day Action Plan for Chapter 7

To help you find your areas of interest, fill in the blanks:

I feel happy when I'm_____

_____

I feel passionate when I'm_____

_____

I feel energized when I'm_____

_____

Time goes by very quickly when I'm_____

_____

If I had one year to live, what would I do?_____

_____

_____

If I won ten million dollars, what would I do for the rest of my life?_____

_____

What careers or business opportunities exist where I can combine the times in my life when I was the happiest, most passionate, etc. into a way to make a living?

_____

_____

_____

Fill in the ten blanks below with positive statements about yourself (i.e., I am: athletic; I am: outgoing). You'll find out what your basic strengths are. Combine them with the answers to the questions above, and you should come up with several areas about which you are enthusiastic and passionate.

I am:_____

I am:_____

I am:_____

I am:_____

I am:_____

I am:_____

I am:_____

I am:_____

I am:_____

I am:_____

Cut out magazine and newspaper articles and photographs that interest you. Put them into a file folder and/or make a collage out of the photos. After thirty days, go through the file and analyze what all the clippings have in common. This will also give you a good idea of your true areas of interest.

Once you have found your passion, how do you turn it into reality? In the next chapter, you'll learn that if you want your "path with heart" to lead to real-life satisfaction, you must walk along it one step at a time. And the only way you can know where each step must lead is to set goals that match your passion, break large goals down into small achievable steps, create visual references of where you want to go and what you need to do to get there, and make a strong commitment to achieving your purpose.

Chapter Eight

"PLANNING" THE STONE:
Setting Goals for
High Achievement

"Success is attaining realistic goals, and not responding too negatively when goals are not attainable. I believe to be successful is to be able to recognize one's limitations as well as one's capacities."

—Dr. Dominick Purpura

"Success is making the most of your abilities and discovering new abilities along the way. It's also working toward a goal. The working toward it is more important than the attaining of it. As soon as you set a goal for yourself and begin working toward it, you are a success."

—Scott DeGarmo

How do you make a dream become reality? How do you turn your passion into a tangible commodity? Step by step and day by day. Nothing is ever accomplished in one fell swoop. The finest achievements are made step by tiny step, one following another until the task has been accomplished.

Dreams become reality when we set goals for ourselves. They give us direction and focus. They break down impossible undertakings into achievable tasks. They help us keep our vision clear and our footing steady. A goal accomplished is not just another step toward a destination; it's a building block in the foundation of our self-esteem.

Turning a dream into reality is like turning a rough stone into a beautiful gem. It can be a long, difficult process. In the diamond industry, the first person to deal with a stone, and perhaps the most important, is called the planner.

Planning how a stone should be cut is often much more exciting than the actual cutting. It can take months, or even years, of study to decide just how the stone should be cut. If cut incorrectly, a potentially priceless stone can shatter into thousands of worthless pieces. No one in the diamond industry would even *think* of cutting a stone before it had been planned.

Human beings are not always that careful with their own lives. If people planned their lives in as much detail as they planned their vacations, they would be much further along the road to success. Imagine saying to yourself, "I want to go to Disneyland." Even though you've never been there before, you just get in your car and start driving. You haven't looked at a map. You haven't thought about how much money you'll need to get there. You don't know how far away it is. You've forgotten your spare tire. How long do you think it will take before you get lost, run out of money, get a flat tire, give up and go home?

Successful people know that in order to get anything done, you have to plan. You must set goals for yourself in order to move ahead. In fact, some people, like super-salesman Joe Girard, believe that everything they've accomplished is due to the goals they set for themselves.

"You have to say over and over: 'If it's to be, it's up to me,'" says Girard. "The world won't do it for you. What I got, I got from guts. I got it because I wanted it. The whole secret of life is to know what you want, to write it down, and then commit yourself to accomplishing it. Make dreams come true. Take a picture of what you want. If you want to go to college, what college? Go to that college and take a picture of it, have about four of them made. Put it on your car visor, put it on your mirror, in your wallet. Look at it every day.

"This body does not move without a plan. I plan each second, each day, each moment. I bet if I stop ten people coming out of the house and ask them, 'What are you going to do today?' they'll say, 'Jeez, I don't know.' I know what I'm going to do. Before I go to sleep, and I do this every night, I outline what I'm going to do tomorrow. Then I do what I set out to do the night before, plus ten. I give 110 percent."

THE "PASSION PLUS" EQUATION

What is a goal, anyway? It's a target, a focal point, the end toward which you direct your efforts. It's a vision, a quest, a *possible* dream. And for our purpose—achieving success—it's a dream, vision, or quest that coincides with our innermost desires and passions.

You don't just pick a goal out of a hat, follow it, and become successful. The plain truth is that if a goal is not important to you, you will not put in the necessary effort to see it through to the end. If you don't care very much about getting to Disneyland, you may give up your trip after only an hour or so of driving. But if you really, passionately want to get there, the fact that you don't have a map, you run out of money, and/or you get four flat tires won't stop you from trying.

What will happen, though, is that you'll discover you need to devise a strategy in order to reach your destination. You'll need to research alternative means of transportation, and find out how much money you will need. You'll have to devise ways to make that money. You may have to go home and start all over again. But chances are eventually you'll arrive at Tomorrowland—because it meant a lot to you.

Passion plus planning equals success.

When we are passionate about a goal, we think about it all the time. And as we learned in chapter 1, we become what we think about. If our thoughts are scattered all over creation, we will wander through our lives with no ballast, nothing to give us stability or control. If our thoughts are focused toward a particular objective, they will act as a magnet pulling us in that direction.

Goals give us focus and energy. They are our internal batteries, keeping us going against the odds.

We're not strangers to setting goals. Every one of us has set—and achieved—a goal at one time or another. As a child, you may have put your pennies in a bank, saving up for that special toy. Or as an adolescent, you may have worked an after-school job to get money for dates, clothes, or even a car. We set goals without even being aware of it: We want to get to work on time, to improve our tennis game, to buy a new CD player. Anyone who passes a test, graduates from school, learns how to drive a car, gets a job, a raise, or a promotion knows how to work toward a goal and achieve it. What we don't know is how to apply these same concepts toward what we really want out of life.

The late Earl Nightingale, whom I've mentioned frequently, was one of the pioneers in the motivational tape industry and founder of Nightingale-Conant, the largest producer and distributor of audio tape programs in the country. He's been a great inspiration to me in many areas, and particularly in setting goals. In his program "Lead the Field," Nightingale says that when we want something badly enough, such as a car or a refrigerator, we know how to get it. We devise a system and we follow it. What we don't understand, he says, is that "it is a system, and that if it will work for a refrigerator or a new car, it will work for anything else we want very much just as well."

Passion plus planning equals success. This is truly a case of mind over matter. When we put our mind to what matters, we can achieve our goals.

SEVEN STEPS TO SETTING GOALS

Taking action on something about which we are passionate can seem daunting, perhaps even terrifying. But, as with everything else in this chapter, if you break down the process into its logical components, you'll see that it is not so very daunting at all. Seven steps are involved:

1. Find out what you like to do. What's important to you? What's your passion? What is it you'd like most to accomplish?
2. Get the facts. Once you've found your passion, the research begins. Find out everything you can from books, tapes, people in the industry, magazines, trade papers, newsletters, etc.
3. Set up a plan of action. What are the steps you need to take? Develop a step-by-step procedure and write it down. Everything that gets done in life gets done in stages. It's the little things you do along the way that count. If you're not sure which steps you might need to take to achieve your goal, you can use a process Jack Canfield calls future pacing. "You go into the future and look back. One of the ways to decide what the 'to-do's' are in your life is to pretend you've already achieved them and then look back from the future and say, 'What did I have to do to get here?'"

   All the steps you take are like signposts, each one a signal that you're getting closer to your goal. You're successful as long as you keep moving toward your goal.
4. Set a timetable. Write out a realistic time frame for accomplishing each step in the process and/or the final goal. A timetable lets us know how much time to put into each step. It also keeps us motivated and moving—it's like lighting the fuse before the dynamite goes off.
5. Begin. Just do it. Dive into it. Get the experience. Even if

you're not totally prepared, get the experience so that the next time you will be prepared. Experience is our best teacher. Many of the greatest ideas in the world are still lying dormant because the people who had them were afraid to take a chance.

6. Make constant reevaluations. Look at the plan on a weekly or monthly basis to see how you're doing. It may be necessary to adjust the plan because of unforeseen obstacles. Be sure your plan is flexible enough to allow for changes. Here is what Dr. Edmund J. Sybertz of the Schering-Plough Research Institute has to say about how he and his staff set their goals: "Professionally, we set goals that are based on what achievements we want to make in a year's time. Each year we write these out and form our action plan. . . . It's very straightforward: What is our goal? What is the expected outcome? What is the timing—when do we expect to have that outcome? What are the action steps that go into achieving this goal? These goals help us focus our attention on what's important. We tend to go back to them and maybe change them—on second and third reflection, things that were important at one point are now less important. We do this at least twice a year."

7. Never give up. Too many people have lost their dreams because of lack of will, focus, or passion. The top five percent of any profession are the ones who are so passionate about what they want that no matter what feedback they get, no matter how many times they fail, they rethink, replan, and redo, because they believe in themselves and in their goals.

"Obstacles are those frightful things you see when you take your eyes off your goal."

—HENRY FORD

CHANGING THE OVERWHELMING TO THE ACHIEVABLE

Sometimes we resist setting goals because we've never done it before. We're comfortable going along our current path, and outwardly content with our lives. We've gotten along in our haphazard way so far, why rock the boat? We're afraid to set goals because we're afraid we might not achieve them.

Sometimes we're reluctant to set goals because the road ahead seems unbearably long, filled with hurdles and obstacles impossible to overcome. We can't imagine how we could ever find the time, the money, the space, the resources. . . . We are defeated before we even begin. We think that reaching a goal requires one great, giant leap; a leap we're not sure we're ready to take.

All goals are reached one step at a time. Once you have a goal in mind, once you have painted a clear, detailed picture of what you want to accomplish, you can then take the small steps necessary to follow through. Barbara Sher and Annie Gottlieb write in their book *Wishcraft: How to Get What You Really Want,* "Most of us have a distorted notion of how things actually get done in the world. We think that accomplishment only comes from great deeds. Great deeds are made of small, steady actions, and it is these you must learn to value and sustain."

Scientists and inventors are experts at breaking down tasks into small steady actions. They start out with a clear destination and they know the only way to get there is to keep their eyes directly on the goal.

"The Chinese have a saying that 'if you leave from a port and steer on course, you shouldn't be surprised if you arrive at your destination,'" says inventor Arthur Fry. "In the United States we have a simpler saying: 'The train only goes where you lay the track.' People get where they are because they very carefully laid the track and walked along it—for good or for bad. . . .

"If I want to go about reaching a goal, I do a lot of library research and talk to knowledgeable people. The more you ask questions, either of yourself or of other people . . . the better you set the path to discovering new things. When I first set up Post-it Notes, I made samples. Then the question was how to go from there to providing Post-it Notes to the world. We set up a critical path diagram (see illustration). You think of all the steps that might be required to get from here to there and then think What will it be like once I get there?

"The diagram served as a planning and control mechanism for the process. The box shows the task to be accomplished. The numbers on the top represent the time frame in days to accomplish that task. The numbers on the bottom are the days in the schedule during which the task is to be accomplished. The letters on the bottom of the box also say who is to do that task, such as TS (Technical Service), ENG (Engineering), or MKTG (Marketing). The most critical path in a diagram is the series of steps that take the longest. Constant care must be taken that the things that feed into it are done promptly so that the project is not held up.

"This sort of diagram is a system that was developed by the Government Services to plan and keep track of large projects. It is just a formalized version of what we do in life. . . . I think, 'If I want to play tennis on Saturday morning I need to phone my friend and make reservations, but I also must get balls first and restring the racquet, which means I have to fix the flat tire on my car right away.' "

We don't give ourselves enough credit for the "small stuff," for the individual steps we take. It's only by breaking down large, seemingly unattainable goals that we can make them attainable. For instance, writing this book at times seemed an overwhelming task, especially at the beginning. Three hundred manuscript pages to fill and not a word written! Pretty daunting. The only way to get through it was to break the overall goal of writing a book down into smaller and smaller achievable goals until the job was finished.

Here is an acronym for the word *goals* that may explain just how goals work:

Critical Path Diagram

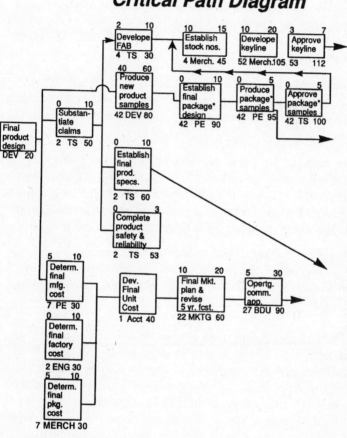

Gather as much information as you can on your goals. Read books, articles, listen to tapes, and interview people who have achieved the goals you're setting.

Organize a step-by-step plan. Make sure your steps are in a logical sequence. Write it down! Post the plan on the wall. Look at it morning and night. Your subconscious mind works wonders.

Action speaks louder than words. You'll never hit the target if you don't pull the trigger. Experience is our best teacher. This is the most important step, and the one that is the most underutilized.

Look back at the plan. Are you on track? Do you need to change your direction or add new steps? You can learn from any setbacks along the way and try again with new information. Failure isn't failure as long as you're learning from it and using the input for a better approach next time.

Set new goals. You should constantly have new goals to shoot for. We are at our best when we are climbing, stretching, and challenging ourselves. Happiness and rewards lie in the journey, not in the destination.

The first step in any plan is to *write down* your overall, or long-term goal. My goal was "to write a book utilizing all my experience and the experience of dozens of highly successful people to help others find their passion and realize their potential so that they may attain their own success."

The next step in any plan is to determine the intermediate goals that will have to be taken in order to accomplish that goal. The intermediate steps for writing this book were:

Write book proposal
Interview successful people
Do research
Write chapters
Edit/Rewrite
Turn in manuscript

Each of these intermediate goals can be broken down into even smaller steps, or short-term goals. For instance, the first two intermediate goals were broken into:

—Write book proposal:
    Organize possible chapters
    Collect adjunct materials (my resume, public relations clips, articles, etc.)
    Write sample chapter
    Send to agent

—Interview successful people:
    Break down into categories (politics, sports, etc.)
    Make a list of possibilities
    Network for possible contacts
    Make sure tape recorder is working
    Buy extra tapes
    Put together sheet of contacts
    Send out letters asking for interviews
    Make contact calls
    Set up interview appointments
    Conduct interviews

I made a similar list for every intermediate goal I had written down. This accomplishes three things:

♦ It takes the idea of ''writing a book'' out of the realm of fantasy and into the realm of possibility.
♦ It gives me a fairly realistic picture of what it will take to achieve this goal. Given that information, I can then decide whether or not I want to continue in this direction. I may decide to go on, or I may decide that it's not worth the effort, or that I don't have the time right now, but that I will look at the plan again in six months.
♦ It breaks down an ''impossible'' goal into small, achievable steps. If I decide to go ahead with the project, I can then set daily, weekly, or monthly goals to accomplish each step.

These are the basic steps of goal-setting. You can find this information in many different sources. It may seem dry and

academic. It may remind you of making an outline for a school
paper. It's very organized and "left-brained." I know that many
of you will read this passage, in fact this chapter, and say, "Oh,
that sounds like a good idea," and forget all about it. However, I
urge you to try it just once. Think about something you'd really
like to do or have. Write it down. Write down the intermediate
and short-term steps it would take. Then feel what happens.

What is difficult to convey in this book or any other is the *energy* that setting goals and writing them down generates. They
literally propel you into action. They give you focus and direction and provide you with something to hold on to when you're
crossing over rocky patches. A goal can be the spark that ignites
the fire within, and the fuel we need to keep that fire burning.

> " 'Would you tell me, please, which way I go from
> here?'
>   'That depends a good deal on where you want to
> get to,' said the Cat.
>   'I don't much care where—' said Alice.
>   'Then it doesn't matter which way you go,' said the
> Cat.''

> —FROM *ALICE'S ADVENTURES IN WONDERLAND* BY
>   LEWIS CARROLL

TO REACH YOUR GOALS, FOLLOW THE MAP

There is no stronger incentive to reaching your goals than to
have a visual representation of your progress in front of you
every day. Such a visual aid can help you focus on the activities necessary to achieve your goal, and can provide immediate feedback on your progress. The visual aid I use is called
the MAP system.

Here is how it works. You start out with a two-by-three-
foot cork board, a set of map tacks or push pins, and twenty

to thirty business-card-size pieces of paper or cardboard. Across the top of the cork board are headings that represent the various stages necessary to reach your goal.

A MAP board can be devised for any type of goal, and may include any number of stages. For an example, let's use the goal of getting a job. Your first step would be to research and choose particular companies at which you would like to work. Once you have targeted those companies, you would call them up to find out the name of the specific person who has the power to hire you, his or her correct title, address, and telephone number. When you have that information for five to ten companies, you are ready to begin using the MAP board. In this example, our board might include the following headings:

STAGE 1: INTRODUCTORY LETTER. Send each targeted company a letter (similar to the one in chapter 7), but this time let the executive know you are available for employment. Include one or two past accomplishments, and one or two benefits the company would receive by hiring you. Mention a date on which you will call to set up an interview appointment.

STAGE 2: FOLLOW-UP CALL. Call on the proposed date to set up an interview appointment.

STAGE 3: FIRST INTERVIEW. Meet with the potential boss face-to-face.

STAGE 4: CALLBACK INTERVIEW. A second interview with the potential boss, or with others in the company.

STAGE 5: JOB OFFER. This stage is completed when you have either accepted or rejected the job offer.

Suppose you've researched ten companies at which you would like to work. After sending a letter to each one, you would fill out a "company card" which would include the name of company and date of completion for each stage. This is what a company card would look like:

Company name:_____

Stage Completed: Date:

_____Stage 1   _____

_____Stage 2   _____

_____Stage 3   _____

_____Stage 4   _____

_____Stage 5   _____

Once the card is filled out, it is then posted on the MAP under the Introductory Letter column. One of the most important steps in the MAP system is recording the date at which each stage has been completed. That way you'll know if a card has been sitting under one heading for a long period of time, and that some action should be taken to either remove the card or move it along to the next stage.

Here is an idea of what your MAP board might look like after several weeks (each lettered square represents a company card):

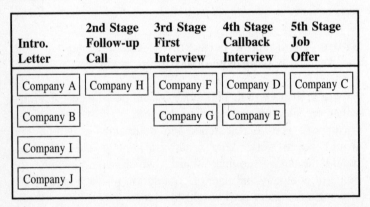

Intro. Letter	2nd Stage Follow-up Call	3rd Stage First Interview	4th Stage Callback Interview	5th Stage Job Offer
Company A	Company H	Company F	Company D	Company C
Company B		Company G	Company E	
Company I				
Company J				

This system can be customized to work with any goal. Instead of having company cards you can make up cards that represent your own intermediate and short-term goals. MAP boards help you focus in three different areas:

♦ To determine the various steps and stages you'll have to go through to reach your goal.
♦ To provide a visual representation of the steps you have already accomplished.
♦ To move ahead in areas where less progress has been made.

Seeing the board every day reminds you of the actions you need to take in order to keep moving toward your ultimate goal.

HOW TO MAKE GOALS WORK FOR YOU

I find the MAP system an invaluable tool for planning and growing my business. But if this system doesn't appeal to you, don't be too concerned. Most of the people interviewed for this book had their own ideas and systems for setting goals. Some were as simple as listing items on a page, and some were much more complicated. Mary Kay Ash helps everyone in her company achieve their goals by furnishing them sheets of paper entitled "The Six Most Important Things to Do Tomorrow."

"It's very easy every night to think about the things you didn't get done," says Mary Kay. "But if what you have to do is right there in front of you when you wake up in the morning, you can just start with number one. You list your tasks in order of importance. Usually I put the one I don't want to do most at the top. Once I have that done, the rest of the day is easy. You scratch off each task as it's accomplished. By the end of the day, if you haven't finished all six tasks, you put the leftover ones on the list for tomorrow. There's something very rewarding about scratching each of the items off your list. It makes you feel as if you've accomplished something. If you don't have a goal, how are you going to know when you get there? Or if you can get there?''

Rhoda Dorsey, president of Goucher College, uses goal-setting as a form of time management. ''I set a lot of goals,'' she says. ''If you lead a busy life, you have to set goals during the day. . . . I live my life with a calendar. My challenge every day is to get through everything with flying colors and to get everything done. Because I like to plan and think ahead, I use the calendar as a means of making sure that what I need to be thinking about and doing now, even if I won't need it until next week, gets done. It gives me time to do all the planning and the prework I have to do for any event.''

Paul Pavis, entertainment director at Harrah's, uses goal-setting not only as a means of prioritizing his incredibly busy schedule, but as a management tool for his employees. ''In business, we all have tasks we have to accomplish on a daily basis,'' says Pavis. '' 'A' priorities are things I must do today in order to keep my job, 'B' priorities are things I should do today, and 'C' priorities are things that are nice to do. I know what my priorities are for tomorrow when I leave today. . . .

''Getting ready for work is an hour-long ritual of a shower and a shave and selecting what I'm going to wear and all the time . . . I'm running the list in my head of what has to be done that day. And I carry a little notepad [some people use tape recorders] in case I have to remind myself of what has to be done today. By the time I hit the door at work . . . I'm ready to do what it is I have to accomplish that day. I have four colors of folders in my in-box: red, yellow, green, and blue. Red is ''got to be done today.'' Yellow is medium-priority, interoffice correspondence. Blue is correspondence that needs to be answered, and green is ''get to it when you can.''

Pavis believes so strongly in the power of setting goals and objectives, he demands that his staff constantly set and review their own short- and long-term goals. He demands of his subordinates, and insists that they demand of their subordinates, that every year they answer the question, ''What are you going to accomplish next year and how are you going to do it? By what date are we going to be able to look at it and say, 'Yes, you did it,' or 'No, you didn't'?"

"I ask my managers, 'What do you think you're going to be doing five years from now? Even if you don't know the name of the job,' says Pavis, 'at least get a vision in your head of the style of life you're going to be living.'

"I believe this is very important. The last person who worked for me as a box office manager a year ago had never done that before. She was thirty years old and nobody had ever made her look down the road. She had been at Harrah's since she was twenty-two, she had done all kinds of different jobs in marketing and bus operations and clerking and employee activities, and basically she was just getting blown around by the breeze. Managers would say, 'Nobody else will do that, let's get Fran to do it.' Setting goals was difficult for her because nobody'd asked her to do it. I had a conversation with her. 'I want to know what kind of car you're going to be driving, what kind of house you're going to be living in, what it's going to feel like. Get something in your mind and hold it out there as a target to strive for.' It took her a while, but she did it. Now she's in charge of marketing operations in a new facility we own in Illinois and she's never looked back."

In contrast to this is literary agent Jeff Herman, who says he's never really sat down and written out his goals. "I didn't come into this business knowing what a literary agent was. And I didn't really study what other literary agents do; I ran on my own instincts. I came from a public relations background. I never really stopped to think, 'Can I do this, is it realistic for me to do this?' I just came in with a lot of stamina and a lot of drive and a lot of ambition about what I wanted to accomplish. But it wasn't really an intellectual process. I never really sat down and wrote goals.

"Some people benefit from rituals, like writing down goals. Just like there are certain people who follow certain religious rituals—it keeps order in their lives. We all have different personalities. Some people need a great deal of daily discipline to get from A to Z. I'm gifted in that I can keep a lot of details in my brain; I have an automatic filing system in my head. I keep notes, I write down who I want to call or who I want to network with, but it's a loose system. You have to find what works for you. Not everyone needs to sit down and make a business plan or make a list of goals. Some people function on a very intuitive level, we just sort of know where we're going.''

Goal-setting is a tool. Use as much of it as you need. You may be more like Jeff, who doesn't formally set goals, but is guided by the deep passion he has for what he wants to accomplish. Or you may be more like me, functioning best with MAP boards and visual reminders of the steps I need to take. The best method is the one that's the best for you.

IT'S NOT WHERE WE FINISH, IT'S HOW WE GET THERE

What happens if you never achieve a particular goal you're striving for? Does that mean you should consider yourself unsuccessful? Earl Nightingale's definition of success is that it is the ''progressive realization of a worthy goal.'' In other words, it's not where we finish, it's how we get there that counts. Every time we take even the smallest step toward achieving a goal, we are successful. A student working toward his college graduation is not only successful on commencement day. He's successful every time he goes to class, studies, takes a test, and learns something new. A woman whose goal is to become salesperson of the year is not only successful when she is handed the award, she is successful every time she works an hour later than usual, sends out letters of thanks and appreciation, or does an extra service for an old and valued customer. Although society may view success as the diploma or the award, the real accomplishments were made with every small step taken.

"What you get *by reaching your destination is not as important as what you* become *by reaching your destination."*

—Dr. Robert Anthony

It is in taking these steps that we find happiness and fulfillment. That is certainly the way Bruce Jenner feels about life. "If we don't have goals, we stand still in life," he says. "You can get up today, do what you have to do, have your three meals, and that's the end of it. To me, that's no fun. The fun part is to have a goal."

Jenner leads an incredibly busy life. He is very successful in all his endeavors, yet he is never complacent. "I never want to be stagnant in life," he says. "I always want to have something that gives me a reason to be on a journey. . . .

"There have to be things that you're striving for. If your life is just nine-to-five every day, with your two days off a week and your two weeks off a year, there's no excitement. No energy. I don't want to live like that. I want energy. I want things to do. I want hills to climb, journeys to be on."

VALUES, COMMITMENT, AND WHAT'S IN IT FOR ME

Each of our lives is a journey. Some people prefer to stay on well-traveled, clearly marked highways. Others would rather take side trips and clear new trails for themselves. There are many ways to travel, none of them better than the other, as long as you are happy with the route you've taken and continue to move forward along it. Problems arise when:

♦ You get stuck in a rut and can't seem to get out of it;
♦ You find yourself traveling the same roads over and over again, purely by habit, and no longer find the scenery enjoyable;

♦ You've gotten off at the wrong exit and can't seem to find your way back;

♦ You're so completely lost that you no longer have any sense of direction.

When any of these situations arise, ask yourself the following questions in order to continue the journey. Write your answers down, and keep them somewhere accessible so that you can review, revise, and rewrite as necessary.

1. **Where am I now?** The answer to this question doesn't involve long years of self-analysis. It does involve, as with any journey, pinpointing you present location so that you can determine the best way to get from where you are now to where you want to be. Depending on what your goal is, you may need to look at your current assets—finances, education, family, career, etc.—and figure out which area(s) you need to improve and enrich before you can get what you want. For instance, if your goal is to go back to school, you will have to look at all the areas mentioned above to determine if you have enough money to go back to school, and if not how you will earn it, how the time spent at school will affect your family, and what they can do to support you in your efforts, and so on.

2. **Where do I want to end up?** The research you did for "finding your passion" in the previous chapter will have given you some possible destinations. Human beings like to know where they are going. A few people choose to live their lives wandering from here to there, always at loose ends. If that is your choice, and that choice makes you happy, that's fine. But most of us prefer to have a more defined existence. Knowing where we want to end up helps us define and focus our lives, and gives us a sense of purpose and accomplishment.

3. **Why do I want to go there?** Answering this question often helps clarify what your goals really are and how you can best achieve them. Be as honest with yourself as possible.

Suppose your goal is to become a teacher. When you ask yourself why, your answers may include: "It's what I love to do," "I want to share my knowledge with others," and/or, "It's what my parents want me to do." Put these answers in order of their importance to you. If answer number three is first on your list, this may not be an appropriate goal for you. If your top answer is to share your knowledge with others, teaching may be a good outlet, but you might also consider writing a book or becoming a speaker. If "It's what I love to do" is your highest priority, your chances of accomplishment are very high.

4. **What's the best way to get there?** This answer may require research. If your goal is career-oriented, for instance, you may need to go to the library, interview people in the industry, rewrite your resume, or compile a portfolio. If your goal is financial, you may need to save a particular dollar figure each month, or get sound investment advice. Whatever your goal, this step should provide you with several options so that you can choose the one that will work best for you.

5. **What do I expect to be, get, or have happen when I arrive?** Answering this question can help keep you motivated toward reaching your goal, and also help you visualize yourself already there. The more specific you are, the better. If your goal is to learn to speak French, for example, picture yourself in an animated conversation with two sexy Parisians. Hear them speaking, hear yourself answering back effortlessly, and enjoy the rapport. Keep this vision in front of you daily and it will provide you with motivation and momentum toward your goal.

Answering these questions involves three important criteria for setting goals: values, commitment, and benefits.

♦ **Values:** We all have values, or standards by which we measure our personal success, happiness, and satisfaction in life. Everyone's list of values is different; what's of great importance to me may not carry the same weight for you. One person's values might include adventure, ambition, and political power. Another's might be creativity, family life, and physical fitness. Obviously, these two people would have very different goals in life.

Mary Matalin has always had her own way of setting goals. "Some people set job goals. I always set value goals," she says. "My value goal was to have a job where I didn't look up at the clock until 4:00 in the afternoon. This is a product of growing up in the steel mills, where you punch in at 8:00 a.m. and at 10:00 a.m. you're looking for your first coffee break, and by 10:30 you're counting down to lunch and after lunch you're counting down to the 3:00 break. My goal was to have a job where I didn't do that. That meant something that was fast-paced and interesting—which is how campaigns work."

When setting goals, it is necessary to keep your personal values in mind and ask yourself, "What is most important to me?" Unless a goal is relevant to that which you deem important, it is unlikely that you will attain it. Goals that you set for any other reason, such as peer pressure or other people's expectations, are doomed to fail.

♦ **Commitment:** The achievability of any goal is in direct proportion to your commitment to its attainment. If you think about a goal every day, if you make at least one tangible step toward that goal, if you continually ask yourself the five questions posed above, you will achieve results. Some commitments are easier to keep than others; temptations always arise to lead us away from our intended destinations, and/or obstacles block our paths. Writing down your goals and keeping them someplace you'll see them every day helps keep commitment strong. I also share my goals with the people around me. That way, I'm not only accountable to myself, I'm also accountable to the people I've told. By verbalizing my goal to someone else, I'm reinforcing it for myself.

♦ **Benefits:** A good salesperson makes a sale by finding out what's most important to a customer, and then letting the customer know how her product or service will fill those needs. When we set goals for ourselves, we often have to sell ourselves on the idea before we can make a deep commitment to it. If there's nothing at stake, nothing to be gained, there is no incentive to keep working toward the goal. Every time you set a goal, ask yourself "What's in it for me?" The stronger and more clearly articulated the answers, the more likely your commitment will withstand the bumps and blows it may receive along the way.

For instance, if your goal is to go back to college and get your degree, write down a list of benefits you will receive. Your list might look something like this:

♦ Get a better job
♦ Support my family
♦ Increase my confidence and self-esteem
♦ Learn new subjects
♦ Meet new people

Then if you should run into difficulties in class, get a low grade, or even have to drop out for a semester, you can go back to your written list to remind you what you'll get when you've accomplished your goal.

THE ULTIMATE GOAL OF SETTING GOALS

Unlocking your hidden potential pertains to your entire development as a human being. All goals do not have to pertain to work. They can apply to sports and exercise, general health, social, financial, and creative areas. Michael Stramaglio of Minolta sets goals in two areas: his work and his personal life.

"My goal-setting tasks revolve around two separate issues, and I can't separate them from each other," he says. "In practical business task-setting or goal-setting, what I do specifically is every single week, I identify exactly where I am in relation to my annual goal. Being in sales and marketing, I have a very strategic set of goals that I have to hit. . . . Every Sunday afternoon . . . I reassess each one of the sales goals, the marketing goals, the advertising goals, and the financial goals [as well as] project status in . . . advertising, sales, marketing, and finance. . . .

"If you don't have your goals written down, and if you don't continually reevaluate them and rewrite them, you don't have a plan. You don't have goals. What you have then is just a wish list.

"I have my own personal goals which include my family and how I want to provide for my family. For example, there are goals about giving back to whatever communities or groups that have been responsible for helping you along the way. My wife had leukemia. Six years ago she was told she had six months to live. So we spend a lot of time supporting the leukemia foundation because without them she wouldn't have been inspired or been given the products she needed to survive. I would feel a complete failure if we didn't recognize those responsibilities to the community."

The ultimate goal of all our lives is to be happy and fulfilled. Goal-setting is simply a tool we can use to help us on our way. There's no need to overwhelm yourself by setting too many goals at once. We all have many areas in which we'd like to improve or enrich ourselves, but it's not necessary to try each of them at once. Too many projects will not allow you to give each of them your best efforts; some will necessarily suffer.

If you have a number of goals you want to reach, work on one or two at a time—then as soon as you are nearing one destination you can begin planning for the next journey. This is how Michael Stramaglio manages his division. "As I realize that I am actually going to be attaining a goal, or that my group or my division is going to be attaining a goal, I've already pushed it up again. Having achieved the recognition or the benefits of that goal, I'm already past it. . . .

"That is probably the most critical aspect of success. Making sure that you challenge yourself and the people that work for you and that you encourage them by giving them the recognition that they deserve for a job well done. But as a manager, at the moment they are in fact getting that recognition, I'm already past it, having just set a new set of goals.''

Finally, it's important to remember that whether or not you reach your goal is less important than knowing you did your best to work toward it. In his book *Living Beyond Limits,* Jerry Lynch includes a reminder that ''to measure yourself by the outcome of your goals is a sure set-up for self-imposed misery. What you are *inside* is the true measure of your character and worth.''

And what we are inside determines the nature of the goals we set for ourselves. The best goals are those that benefit not only ourselves, but others as well. As Dr. William H. Danforth put it: ''I like people who set the worthy goals, the noble goals that go beyond themselves. Not selfish goals, like having the biggest house or the biggest car. You have to have short-term goals, but you can orient those toward your longer-range goals—to do what one can to make the world better during our brief lifetime.''

Goals are simply markers or guideposts. They are not meant to be indelibly written and immutable. As in all things in life, flexibility is the key. Arthur Fry gives a very good reason for that: ''I'm always setting goals and writing to-do lists, but they're always very flexible and open-ended. . . . If I'm going to discover the future, I can't be rigid. The future will always be about an eighty-percent extension of what we know right now. Automobiles are different than they were when my grandfather first got his, but they're still automobiles. Twenty percent of the future will be brand new to the world, have never existed before, and will tremendously impact our lives. . . . If you don't leave time open to explore and look at things, you're going to walk right by them. It's okay to be confused and uncertain sometimes. These are things that lead us to our greatest discoveries about ourselves and our lives in general.''

Goals should be chosen with great care and concern. Be prepared to get what you go after. Whatever it is that you really want can be achieved if you write it on the page and engrave it in your mind.

> *"By the mile, it's a trial*
> *By the yard, it's hard*
> *But by the inch*
> *It's a cinch."*
>
> —ANONYMOUS

Five Essential Facets of Chapter 8

1. Remember the "passion plus" equation. Make sure there's a passion tied into your goal. The more passionate you are about the goal you're trying to achieve, the greater your chance of achieving it.
2. Review the seven steps of setting goals:

   ♦ Find out what you like to do
   ♦ Get the facts
   ♦ Set up a plan of action
   ♦ Set a timetable
   ♦ Begin
   ♦ Make constant reevaluations and adjustments
   ♦ Never, ever give up

3. If you set up a goal that is difficult to reach or too much to handle all at once, break it down into small steps that are achievable one by one.
4. Create a MAP—management activity plan—or some other type of goal board. A board is a visual reminder of what our goals are, and the steps we have to take every day, week, and month. It also provides a subconscious reminder, so that your goal is in your mind even when you're not looking at the board.
5. Understand the three criteria for setting goals. A goal has to have:

♦ Personal value to you
♦ Commitment
♦ Benefits

Think about actions you can take from these five ideas or others discussed in this chapter.

Thirty-Day Action Plan For Chapter 8
You get what you set.

Goal:_____Date of completion:_____

What books, tapes, newspaper or magazine articles can I collect so that I can become an expert at what I'm trying to

accomplish?_____

_____

Who are people I can contact who have accomplished this goal already so that I can benefit from their advice and

input?_____

_____

What are some obstacles I foresee that might stop me from

achieving this goal?_____

_____

What are some resources I can use to overcome these
obstacles?_____

_____

Break the goal down into at least five smaller stages:

    1._____

    2._____

    3._____

    4._____

    5._____

Post the stages on the wall or somewhere you will see them
every day.

Write your main goal down on a small card and carry it in
your wallet or stick it on your refrigerator. Ask yourself
every day, "What can I do today to get closer to my goal?"

What five major benefits can I receive from achieving this
goal?

    1._____

    2._____

    3._____

    4._____

    5._____

Make copies of this action plan and use it for every goal you
have.

Now you know the essentials of what it takes to be successful. One factor is still missing, however, although you've
caught glimpses of it in all the previous chapters. It is that you
must share some of what you've been fortunate enough to
develop for yourself. Success that is selfishly hoarded cannot
truly be called success.

Chapter Nine

HE WHO DIES WITH THE MOST TOYS . . . :
THE VALUE IS IN THE JOURNEY, NOT THE GEMS

"I feel successful when I'm very much in the middle of things. For example, I feel successful as a mother when I'm in the middle of the comings and goings of my daughters and their lives. Being a successful professional is feeling that there's an ebb and a flow, that there are new people to meet, new clients, new challenges, new problems to solve. . . . It's about my own ingenuity, about using resources I didn't know I had, about my own endurance, my own pain, my own joy. And in the process of finding out all these things, of saying, 'I didn't know I could do that!'"

—BEVERLY HYMAN

"Success means that at the end of the day or the end of the week, you can look back and know that you've accomplished something. There's a certain thrill that comes from creativity, from knowing that you're moving in a positive direction, and from feeling that

you're contributing to other people in a very
constructive way."

—Jeff Herman

Imagine, for a moment, that it is the end of your life. You're in a large room in your custom-built mansion with priceless art on the walls. You're lying on satin sheets in a brass bed, covered by a goose-down comforter. All around you are precious jewels, expensive trinkets, closets full of designer clothes, drawers full of money. What's wrong with this picture? You are all alone.

Is that success? Most of us would answer, "No, of course not." Yet we sometimes get so caught up in the pursuit of "things," we forget what is really important in life. As I'm sure you've realized by now, this is not a book about being poor but happy. Neither is it a book about making millions of dollars. It is about using everything you have been given, and everything you can get, and doing something worthwhile with it.

Charles Garfield has made his life's work studying peak performers—how and why they do what they do. What he found is that contrary to what many people think, money is not a sufficient motivator for high achievement.

"Money is necessary," says Garfield. "Anyone who says it isn't doesn't live in the same world the rest of us do. But there are clearly more powerful motivators—recognition, challenge, personal development, life fulfillment. There are all sorts of things that are more powerful than money. Money is a resource that allows you to get the other stuff. Many people just work for money and they don't have a clue as to how that money translates into a higher quality of life."

Garfield cites as an example that scores of very wealthy, very miserable people do nothing but work all day long to get more money.

"There is a tremendous difference between money and wealth," says Garfield. "Anybody can quest after money; it's just collecting dollar bills. Some people get a lot, some people get a little. . . . Wealth is understanding what that money translates into in terms of improving the quality of your life. People always start talking about success, saying "I want the Rolex and I want three luxury cars and that boat." And you find them not using them, not enjoying them, and they say to themselves, "I think I climbed the ladder but it was up against the wrong wall."

Not too long ago a very popular slogan was plastered on bumper stickers, mugs, and T-shirts around the country. It read, "He who dies with the most toys wins." There are times when we all feel that way. But if you've been reading the definitions of success that begin every chapter, you know that no one interviewed for this book repeated this sentiment. Money was always the by-product of their achievements, the bonus they got for a job well done.

None of these successful people started out wealthy. It's not as if they don't care about, or can afford to be without, the financial rewards. But in the end, it's not what they care about most; nor is it how they define success.

My own definition of success has changed over the years. Early on, I thought it meant possession. But now that I have my own business, now that I have a family, now that I have met and talked to so many truly successful people, success means something very different to me. Now, I know I'm being successful when I can give something back to other people, whether it be an actual helping hand, an idea, a tool, a technique—anything that makes their lives easier and more fulfilled.

My thinking really started to turn around when I read, "Catch a passion for helping others and a richer life will come back to you," in William H. Danforth's *I Dare You!* Whenever I find myself getting off track, I realize that my center of focus is turned inward, toward selfishness. As soon as I turn myself around, everything comes back to me tenfold when I focus on helping others. The more I can enrich other people's lives, the greater my success becomes.

> *"Our most valuable possessions are those which can be shared without lessening, those which, when*

shared, multiply; our least valuable possessions are those which, when divided, are diminished.''

—FROM *I DARE YOU!* BY WILLIAM H. DANFORTH

There are many, many ways of giving back. I am a teacher and a trainer; I give back in that way. You can give to charity, do volunteer work. You can mentor someone starting out in your profession. You can compliment people, say please and thank you, treat people kindly and honestly. But you can't even begin to give back unless you are giving yourself the very same treatment.

When your goal is to be the best that you can be, you can help others do the same. As you've read all the preceding chapters, you have gathered advice from peak performers in all areas of life as to how you can live your life most successfully. Their advice has been worthwhile and helpful, I'm sure, but I am now going to divulge to you the ultimate, absolute, last word, final secret to success in life: gamble, cheat, lie, and steal.

♦ Gamble. Gamble your best shot in life. Take a risk. Go after what you want and give it your all.
♦ Cheat. Cheat those who would have you be less than you are. Success is the best revenge.
♦ Lie. Lie in the arms of those you love, those who surround and support you—family, friends, teammates, colleagues, associates. Treasure the people who treasure you.
♦ Steal. Steal every second of happiness you can. There is nothing more precious.

Gotcha there for a minute, didn't I? I bet you thought I'd lost my marbles. Well, it only goes to show that there is something good hidden inside everything, no matter how bad it seems at first glance. So, using my definitions, gamble, cheat, lie, and steal all you want!

"When all is said and done, success without happiness is the worst kind of failure."

—LOUIS BINSTOCK

GAMBLE

As far as we know, we only have one shot at this life. Nobody wants to let it slip by, to be left at the end with nothing but sorrow and regrets. Life is not meant to be lived looking backward, thinking about what might have been done differently. All we have is this present moment and we owe it to ourselves to be living it now one hundred percent. Here are two ways to make that happen:

1. Serve the people as best you can. No matter who you are, no matter what business you're in, everyone has a customer. What can you do to increase your service?
2. Put in the best effort possible. As simple and corny as it sounds, you get a wonderful feeling from hard work. Knowing you have done your best at something, regardless of the outcome, makes you feel alive and energized. It also allows you to enjoy the times when you aren't working. You can stop at the end of the day satisfied that your work is done, and your time is now your own.

Giving everything you do your best shot comes back to you twice over. First, it gives you the satisfaction and fulfillment of accomplishment. And second, you will always get something back from taking a considered risk. Even if it doesn't come out as you planned, you will learn something from the effort. It may feel like a risk to jump into something one hundred percent, particularly if it's something new and different, but you never know how it will pay off. Especially if you think more about serving others and less about how you will fare in the situation.

"Always give people more than they expect and it comes back to you like a tidal wave," says Jack Canfield. "Someone once told me, 'Always give people twenty-five percent more than they expect.' For instance, he wanted to have a pool built. He asked for an estimate. When the pool man said, '$10,000,' he said, 'Great. I'll pay you $12,000. But what I want is for you to build this pool as if it were going into your own backyard.' What he got was the best-quality, best-built pool in town.

"Most people do the opposite. If someone says he'll paint your house for $800 you say, "How about $650?" He might do the job for $650, but what are you going to get?"

This "give them more than they expect" philosophy is something that Jack Canfield and I have in common. In my seminars and training sessions, I always try my hardest to go beyond what my clients expect. Why? One, because I believe I owe it to them, and two, because I know if I do, I'll get asked back and/or referred to other clients. It's good for me and it's good for them, a classic win-win situation.

"It's the old saying that what goes around comes around," says Dr. Philip T. Santiago, New Jersey's Chiropractor of the Year for 1990 and a member of the medical staff for the U.S. Olympic teams in 1992's Barcelona games. "The name of my business is service. All it takes is giving less than one hundred percent one time. Bad news about you spreads a lot faster than good news. It's just not worth the risk. People have to get to know you, to like you, and most of all, to trust you."

Giving one hundred percent effort to what you're doing can be the most positive force in your life—as long as you maintain a balance with other areas. When super-athlete Bruce Jenner was in the Olympics in 1976, he was so obsessed with his training, practice, and performance, he "gave up" the rest of his life. He now sees things in a different light, and never wants to get himself into a similar situation.

"I see people in the business world who are so obsessed with the game of business, it takes away from the rest of their lives," Jenner told me. "There's a time for business, for getting ahead, for doing what you have to do. And those eight hours, or however many they are, have to be totally focused on what you're trying to accomplish. But you can't give up the rest of your life, your friends, and your family. Because when you're laid out in your casket, there aren't going to be too many business partners standing over you. Don't get so obsessed with business that you can't enjoy life.''

> *"My crown is in my heart, not on my head,*
> *Nor decked with diamonds and Indian stones,*
> *Nor to be seen: My crown is called content;*
> *A crown it is that seldom kings enjoy.''*
>
> —WILLIAM SHAKESPEARE

CHEAT

Cheat those who would have you be less than you are. You can always find people willing to tell you, ''It can't be done.'' It doesn't even matter what ''it'' is. Someone is bound to have plenty of reasons it won't work, and plenty of time to share them with you.

Some people will be jealous. They won't want you to succeed. They think that if someone else succeeds, it will lessen their chances. They don't know about the law of abundance in the universe: There is plenty of room for everyone, and the more abundance you create, the more there is to spread around.

There are those who make themselves less than they are. They convince themselves that they are losers, that they can do nothing right, that they may as well not even try to make things better because they will certainly fail. If you want to live your life as a loser, there are any number of ways you can do it. But remember, failure is something that happens to you, not something you are. Even if nothing you've ever done before has come out right, there is always hope for the next time—provided you have learned from what has gone before.

There are also those who make themselves less than they

are by behaving as if they are more than everyone else. I'm sure you've met people like that—people who think they know it all, who think they are somehow above the rest of humanity. The most successful people I met during interviews for this book—the ones you'd think would have the most reason to have inflated egos—were always the most unassuming, the most down-to-earth, the most ready to lend a helping hand. It's easy for success to go to your head, and you have to work consciously to prevent that from happening.

Jeff Herman became quite successful as a literary agent within a relatively short period of time. It might have been easy for his ego to take over. But Jeff is very aware of that trap, and likes to keep himself "on level ground."

"A lot of people in this business do affect a certain attitude of superiority," he says. "But to me that's just a measure of their own inferiority. It's better to be natural, and assume that almost everyone is your superior. . . . There's always something I can learn from someone. There's always some way that I can be amused, entertained, or interested. As long as I remind myself to be humble, and that everybody's my superior in some way, I can get a lot from them, and give back as well. I can grow professionally and personally by watching what other people do and how they deal with their lives."

You can learn from both the positive and the negative you see in people. If you don't like how someone else deals with his or her life, learn from what you see. Conduct your life differently. Forget about those who would have you believe that you must be selfish to get anywhere. Don't be influenced by those who don't understand the concept of sharing, of giving back. Make your own decisions about how you will live your life. That's what author Robert Shook did. When he was an aspiring writer, yet to be published, he was introduced to a gentleman who had recently had a book out on the market. Shook took the man and his wife out to dinner. He told the man that he had been sending out a manuscript and had received several rejections.

"Perhaps you could give me the name of your editor," Shook said. "At least that way I could tell him you recommended me, and maybe he'd take a look at my book.''

The man replied, ''You know, it took me six months of shopping my book around, and I went through all kinds of hell before I could find somebody who would publish my book. Why should I make it easier for anybody else?''

''That night I said to my wife,'' Shook now says, ''if I ever get a book published, if anybody ever calls me up and asks me for help, I vow that I will give it to them. Why should anyone else have to go through the hell that I've gone through?'' Shook has made good on his promise. He's helped at least forty writers get their first book published.

Shook also gives back in other ways. He works with inner-city kids, helping them to write a book. He's told them that when they get the book published, the royalties will go into a trust for their college educations. ''These kids, some of whom were ready to drop out of school, are now excited and enthusiastic about this project. It makes me feel great—there's not enough money in the world that can make you feel that good.''

Robert Shook is cheating those who would have him be stingy with his caring attitude and with his expertise. We often think that in order to get ahead, one has to be cutthroat and concerned only with self-preservation, especially in the corporate world. One would think, then, that as CEO of the Eveready Battery Company, J. Patrick Mulcahy would be steeped in the dog-eat-dog philosophy. Not so. From his point of view in senior management, people get ahead by helping others get ahead.

''In the corporate world, you're always networked,'' he says. ''You're linked to the success or failure of other people or of the organization. Therefore, unless you're exceptionally brilliant or the founder of the company, you have to recognize that you're simply one part of the total body. And that you're much better off trying to help others succeed rather than stepping on them in the hopes they'll fail.''

This is teamwork at its best. It's how the most effective teams work in any situation. In sports, for example, even star players like Wayne Gretzky, Michael Jordan, and Bo Jackson have to learn to make their contributions to the game as part of a team. People who tell you that the best way to success is to concern yourself only with "number one"—yourself—are forgetting that no one ever makes it alone. This is true in politics as well as in sports. Although the public only sees the candidate win or lose, there is a whole team of people backing her up—and no one on that team can afford to be bringing the others down.

Mary Matalin explains it this way: "The personal qualities I grew up with—loyalty, dogged perseverance, and familial fealty, are all present on a campaign. You're constantly motivated by helping—it's a very synergistic effort when campaigns work—and the only way they do work is when the whole is greater than the sum of its parts. If you get a team you're used to working with, you can read each other's minds. You trust each other and you're loyal to each other. There's nothing more gratifying than coming out at the end of something, even if you lose, if you individually and your team together have done the best they can, with everybody giving 110 percent."

"I believe you can get everything in life you want if you will just help enough other people get what they want."

—ZIG ZIGLAR

LIE

Lie in the arms of those you love. This world is all about other people. It's human nature. We are not meant to be solitary creatures. We are meant to have people around us to love, care for us, and support us. We are meant to have people around whom we love, care for, and support. We all know that there are negative people around. Avoid them whenever possible. Actively seek out those people who enjoy living, who support creative thinking and bold ideas, who are actively pursuing dreams of their own. Those are the people from whom we get our greatest inspiration.

One such person is Dr. Fred Epstein, chief of pediatric neurosurgery at New York University Medical Center. Dr. Epstein operates on children with brain tumors, many of whom have been diagnosed as terminal by other doctors. He believes it is the love and support of one human being for another that often gets a child and his or her family through the most difficult of times.

"What keeps me motivated is that we're all human beings. We share the same planet and want the same things for our kids," he says. "I have never felt that as a physician or surgeon, I am in a different element—professional, social, or scientific—than the families I'm taking care of. I feel that if they had the opportunity, they would do what I do equally as well. I've always recognized my own fallibility, and I have always felt that the single most important thing for a family, when you're trying to help them through this cataclysm in their lives, is to show them you care. A television interviewer once asked me if I was someone who gives false hope, someone who could be accused of being too upbeat. I think it's a legitimate criticism. But it's the only way I can do what I do."

Caring about people is the only way Dr. Epstein can do what he does. That is inspirational. If everybody felt that way about their jobs and their lives, what a world this would be! It's hard to imagine that there is really any other reason for being here on earth. For his book *Life After Life,* author Raymond Moody interviewed many people who have had near-death experiences. They all related similar experiences: After supposedly being declared dead, they would leave their body, go through a tunnel, and be greeted by a beam of light. And they would be asked two questions—"What did you learn in this lifetime?" and "How did you expand your capacity to love?" It would seem that these are the two ultimate measures of a successful life.

No one was asked what their profession was, or how much money they made. No one was questioned about where they went to school (or whether they went to school), what kind of clothes they wore, or how much their sneakers cost. They were asked how much they learned and how much they loved.

It's important for all of us to have people in our lives with whom we can communicate, people who will be there for us when we need them. Boxer Shannon Briggs has had his ups and downs in life, but to him, what counts more than any knockout is his friends. "A true friend is worth more than anything you can imagine," Shannon told me. "One thing about me, I'm always trying to help somebody. Not that I want you to remember this, but I know that if I help you, I might need you someday. I might meet a person today, they might tell me some sad story and I might fall for it. But I'm doing it for a reason. Because if I ever need them, hopefully they'll be there for me. . . . I know what it is to need help. I know how important it is to have somebody."

Sometimes we don't even realize that there are many people around us who are willing to give support. Take a good, hard look at the people in your life. There are probably many folks who have been reaching out over the years, saying, "Try it, come on, go for it. Here, let me give you a hand." Even in tough times, even in poverty and in pain, there are always people around who are willing to walk at least partway down the road with you.

We have thousands of opportunities to be kind to others, to reach out to strangers. We've always got that ability within us, regardless of our environment or our position. And when we utilize that ability, the energy that is released is truly unbelievable.

"Treasure the love you receive above all. It will survive long after your gold and good health have vanished."

—Og Mandino

STEAL

Steal every second of happiness you can get. As Earl Nightingale once said, the guy who first uttered ''life is too short''
should get an award. Life is full of heartache and tragedy.
That's the way it is. We can change our circumstances to a
great degree, but we can't change everything that happens.

We have no choice but to make the best of it. There is no
alternative. Life is precious. We often forget that, and it takes
a jolt to the system to remind us. I had such a jolt a few weeks
ago. A company I had consulted with for several years recently
hired a new training director. The CEO of the company told
me it would be a good idea for me to introduce myself to this
man and let him know of the work I had previously done. I
did that. We had a meeting; we got along very well. I kept in
touch, wrote him a follow-up letter, told him I would be glad
to help him in any way I could. He was to get back to me
within thirty days. Two weeks later, I received a phone call
from someone in the company telling me that this man had
passed away over the weekend. I hardly knew the man, but
the shock of his passing made me stop and think, made me
take a fresh look at my life, made me realize there is no time
to waste in anger, in hatred, or in useless worry.

It often takes such a dramatic event to make us realize that
life itself is the most precious possession of all. That is exactly
what happened to Jack Lehav, founder and president of Remarkable Products.

In 1969, Israel was involved in a war of attrition with Egypt,
following the Six-Day War. The fighting went on for months
and months and the casualties piled up. As an officer in the
Israeli army, Lehav had to serve in the Suez Canal.

''I will never forget one very nasty day,'' Lehav relates.
''We were shooting at each other in an absolutely crazy battle.
All that separated us and the Egyptians was the Suez Canal,
200, 250 yards of water. All of a sudden through the periscope—you could look through a periscope from the bunkers

into the canal—I look and I see something that I've never seen before. Two huge whales flipping in the water, calmly swimming in the Suez Canal. I said to my guys, 'Stop shooting.' And all of a sudden the Egyptians did the same thing on the other side.

"All of us raised our heads and looked into the water, and for a ten-minute period there was an absolute awe. Everybody stopped what they were doing, which was fighting and killing and shooting and bombing, and looked at this miracle of nature going by, tranquil, like it had nothing to do with the war between us. And I'm standing there, a very young person, and I said, 'Look what two whales can do to two nations!' It's vividly, vividly strong in my mind. As the whales headed south and disappeared from us, slowly all of us went back to the bunkers. A very good friend of mine, another young officer, stood out there and kept on looking. I was standing next to him, but a little bit lower. I screamed to him, 'Get down!' but I was too late. Within a tenth of a second, which is all it takes in a war, a bullet went through his head and he was dead.

"Something very strong happens to you in life at that moment. In wartime you really make close friendships with people, then in one second a friend is in your arms and he's dead. I realized we come to this planet for a short visit. It could be ten, twenty years, it could be eighty or one hundred for the very few and the very lucky. And you get a chance to contribute, to do, to set yourself goals, and you never know when it could end. It could end for you tomorrow, at a traffic light because somebody didn't stop because he was drunk, on an airplane where you have no control over what will happen, or anywhere.

"I realized then and there, 'Hey, mister, you have a chance. You don't know what this chance is like. Go and get the most out of it.' "

"Just as a wave cannot exist for itself, but is ever a part of the heaving surface of the ocean, so must I never live my life for myself, but always in the experience which is going on around me. It is an

*uncomfortable doctrine which the true ethics whisper
into my ear. You are happy, they say; therefore you
are called upon to give.''*

—ALBERT SCHWEITZER

Five Essential Facets of Chapter 9

1. At the end of his or her life, no one ever said, ''I wish I'd
   spent more time at the office.''
2. Here is the secret to success:

   ♦ Gamble. Gamble your best shot in life. Dare to take
     risks, to live the adventure you were meant to live.
   ♦ Cheat. Cheat those who would have you be less than
     you are. Surround yourself with those who would buoy
     you up and encourage your growth and success.
   ♦ Lie. Lie in the arms of those you love. In the end, all
     we have is one another. Don't take the love you give,
     or the love you get, for granted.
   ♦ Steal. Steal every second of happiness. Live every day
     as if it is your last, for you never know when that day
     will come.

3. Live in the present moment. The two ways to make that
   happen are:

   ♦ Serve the people as best you can.
   ♦ Put your best effort into everything you do.

4. Always give people more than they expect.
5. Remember the test you will be given at the end of your
   life:

   ♦ ''What did you learn in this lifetime?''
   ♦ ''How did you expand your capacity to love?''

Think about actions you can take from these five ideas or others discussed in this chapter.

Thirty-Day Action Plan for Chapter 9

Every day, for thirty days, do something to help someone else—without their knowing it.

Make a list of the people who are most important in your life. Refer to this list frequently so that you don't neglect or take any of these people for granted.

Make a list of the people who have given you a helping hand along the way. Have you thanked them? Is there something you can do for them now?

Every day, in large and small ways, give people more than they expect.

We're almost at the end of the adventure. It's now time to reflect and review. The appendix following this chapter is a list of the forty-five essential facets of success culled from each of the preceding chapters, plus some more of the insightful definitions of success from the wonderful, giving people I interviewed for these pages. Read their words over and over again. They know what they're talking about.

I wish you all the best—and to be the best—in everything you do. Let me know how it all turns out. Please write to me with any successes, or any ways this book has affected your life. You can write to me at:

FTS INC.
250 RIDGEDALE AVE
SUITE Q5
FLORHAM PARK, NJ 07932
ATTN: BARRY J. FARBER

Albert Einstein, one of the greatest thinkers of all time, was thought by some to be an alien from another planet because he was so much more advanced than anyone else on earth. He studied not only physics, but metaphysics as well. Who better, then, to answer the ultimate question: Why are we here? When he was asked that question, Einstein answered: "To serve mankind."

How can we best serve mankind? By finding out what it is we do best. By discovering and exploiting our potential. By being passionate about our work and our lives. By utilizing our talents to aid others. By reaching the goals we set for ourselves without trampling on others, by claiming the rewards of being the best that we can be, by using success to improve not only ourselves, but the world around us, and by realizing— and cherishing—the value of being a diamond in the rough.

Appendix

THE DIAMOND COLLECTION

THE FORTY-FIVE ESSENTIAL FACETS OF SUCCESS

1. Enthusiasm is the great equalizer. It can help us over obstacles, and can often make up for deficiencies or lack of skill in a given area.
2. Two steps are necessary to keep enthusiasm going:

   ♦ learning as much as possible before we take action; and
   ♦ reviewing our accomplishments and successes.

3. Remember the three *D*'s of a positive attitude: discipline, desire, and dedication.
4. Focus on the positive. In any negative situation, failure, or setback, look for the good that has come out of it and the lessons that can be learned. Whether you are born to be a "fifty-gallon barrel" or a "ten-gallon barrel," be sure you fill it up to capacity.
5. Surround yourself with markers of success, key achievements or goals, or anything that can focus you on the positive when things are tough.
6. The major antidote for depression is action.
7. The key to "coming back" when you're slowing down is all in the hustle. Give that extra effort that leads to the three *C*'s—confidence, consistency, and competence—which together equal success.

8. Give one hundred percent all the time. Ask yourself after every endeavor, Did I give it my best? Remember William H. Danforth's motto: To be our own selves at our very best all the time. Knowing you put in your best at work allows you the guilt-free pleasure of enjoying your leisure time.

9. Remember that luck is when you're learning, when you're doing the research, when you're working late, when you're working harder than the next person, when you're putting in that extra effort. Other people see luck in the wrong place; they see it in the positive outcome. We know where it really is—in the hard work and the effort.

10. Practice resistance training for the brain. Whenever you're doing something that's tough and painful, but must be done, remember that what we resist most is what builds us the most. That's what builds character. That's what helps us when we're suddenly hit by an obstacle. We build our substance and stamina through the resistance training. It's getting through the tough little steps and stages that build character, not going over the finish line.

11. Failure is the ultimate learning tool. Every disappointment teaches a positive lesson—you just have to look for it. It's only when we make the same mistakes over and over again that we have failed. It is in times of adversity that we grow the most.

12. Success is our greatest revenge. When people are discouraging or critical, use your "I'll prove them wrong" energy as a motivator to push you into action.

13. Once you perceive a problem or an obstacle, learn from it as quickly as you can and then move on. Don't bathe in defeat. If you've made a mistake, understand that you'll do it differently next time. Dwelling on previous failures causes you to fail in the future.

14. *Fear* is the acronym for false evidence appearing real. Therefore, the first step in taming any fear is to analyze what is real and what is not. It is the unknown that frightens us, and our imaginations fuel our fear.

15. Preparation and action are the greatest combators of fear. The only way to conquer any fear is to study all you can,

and to prepare in every possible way. You can reduce your fear by increasing your knowledge and focusing your nervous energy on the preparation instead of on your imagination.

16. Make careful choices about whom you wish to follow. Follow-the-follower is a lonely and potentially dangerous game. Look for people whose values match your own, and who have achieved excellence in their field.

17. Surround yourself with models of success. You become what you think about. If you surround yourself with positive images, you will find yourself moving in positive directions.

18. Keep your ears, heart, and mind open. There are many people around who are willing to teach us if we are willing to learn. It's sometimes easier for others to see things we are unable to see, so don't dismiss someone's advice or opinions without first giving them careful study.

19. Expose yourself to a variety of new and challenging situations. Network constantly. You never know who, out of all the people you meet, will be the one who can help you achieve your goals.

20. Remember where Brahma hid the divine spirit. Look to yourself to be your greatest mentor. Do your own research. Make things happen. Find your inner strength.

21. Each of us is an individual with unique talents and untapped potential. There's no point in comparing ourselves with others; if we want to grow we need only compete with ourselves. Our obligation on earth is to discover and utilize our own uniqueness.

22. You become what you think about. Choose your influences and your surroundings as you wish your life to be, and know that as ye think, so shall ye become.

23. Use your mind to visualize future events. Focus on a successful outcome. Mentally rehearse any new job or task as you physically practice it, and you are preparing for success.

24. Apply creative thinking to any problems that might arise. Everyone has a creative mind—keep yourself mentally fit by exercising your creativity.

25. Focus on the positive. Ninety-two percent of all our worries are unnecessary. If you're constantly concentrating on failure and disappointment, that is what you will get. Your mind is the best tool you have available to create a positive, successful environment.

26. The most important elements of learning you can share with your children are love and trust and constant communication.

27. The only way you can truly foster a love of learning in your children is to be a role model yourself. Let your children see you reading, studying, working at home, etc. You can't expect them to learn good study habits while you're sitting in front of the television all night.

28. When you want to learn something new, remember that activity is more effective than passivity. Don't just read and highlight; read and rewrite in your own words. Verbalize your thoughts on the subject to someone else.

29. Make sure that practice sessions reflect reality. Practicing in unreal circumstances makes it difficult to repeat performance in real life.

30. We are learning all the time. When we put in one new piece of information and add it to another piece, we get more than just two pieces of information. We learn by association. The more experiences we have, the more associations we have on which to attach new information.

31. Look into your past and think of times when you did your best work and were most fulfilled. Write down those experiences, exactly what you were doing, and how you felt about it.

32. Write down your mission or purpose in life. Write a paragraph about what you want to accomplish, based on your passion. Put this sheet of paper somewhere you can see it every day.

33. Once you have an idea of what you want to do, the process of research and discovery begins. Read everything you can get your hands on. Make contact with people in the industry. Write, follow up, and be persistent.

34. Leave no stone unturned. Expose yourself, and your children, to many different things until you find the ones that spark your interest. Plant seeds in many areas that interest you without worrying about exactly how they will come together. Don't forget to explore the possibility that the diamond you seek may be buried in your own backyard. Frequently it's not what we're doing that's the problem, it's how we're doing it.

35. Use Bill Bradley's two-step method: (1) Learn as much as you can about your areas of interest; (2) Do it to the best of your ability.

36. Remember the "passion plus" equation. Make sure there's a passion tied into your goal. The more passionate you are about the goal you're trying to achieve, the greater your chance of achieving it.

37. Review the seven steps of setting goals:

   ◆ Find out what you like to do
   ◆ Get the facts
   ◆ Set up a plan of action
   ◆ Set a timetable
   ◆ Begin
   ◆ Make constant reevaluations and adjustments
   ◆ Never, ever give up

38. If you set up a goal that is difficult to reach or too much to handle all at once, break it down into small steps that are achievable one by one.

39. Create a MAP—management activity plan—or some other type of goal board. A board is a visual reminder of what our goals are, and the steps we have to take every day, week, and month. It also provides a subconscious reminder, so that your goal is in your mind even when you're not looking at the board.

40. Understand the three criteria for setting goals. A goal has to have:

   ◆ Personal value to you
   ◆ Commitment
   ◆ Benefits

41. At the end of his or her life, no one ever said, "I wish I'd spent more time at the office."
42. Here is the secret to success:

   ◆ Gamble. Gamble your best shot in life. Dare to take risks, to live the adventure you were meant to live.
   ◆ Cheat. Cheat those who would have you be less than you are. Surround yourself with those who would buoy you up and encourage your growth and success.
   ◆ Lie. Lie in the arms of those you love. In the end, all we have is one another. Don't take the love you give, or the love you get, for granted.
   ◆ Steal. Steal every second of happiness. Live every day as if it is your last, for you never know when that day will come.

43. Live in the present moment. The two ways to make that happen are:

   ◆ Serve the people as best you can.
   ◆ Put your best effort into everything you do.

44. Always give people more than they expect.
45. Remember the test you will be given at the end of your life:

   ◆ "What did you learn in this lifetime?"
   ◆ "How did you expand your capacity to love?"

ADDITIONAL DEFINITIONS OF SUCCESS

MARY KAY ASH, Founder of Mary Kay Cosmetics:

First of all, find something to do that you just love—something you do well, or something that you would like to do. Then find someone to love, and third, find something to look forward to. And when you get all those things put together, you will be a success, no question.

TEDDY ATLAS, boxing trainer:

The trick to being successful is just like the trick of winning the lottery: You have to be in it to win it. You have to have a realistic goal, then set in motion the steps to success. Success means you chose what you wanted to do—whether it was to become president or a solid employee. To know that you didn't conveniently underachieve to avoid the stress. To be honest with yourself and know that you have achieved what you wanted to do.

DR. ROBERT BJORK, chairman, Department of Psychology, Dartmouth College; chairman, National Academy of Sciences Committee on Techniques for the Enhancement of Human Performance:

Success is making the most of your potential. We all have various capacities we could develop. If you have an impairment somewhere, it might lead you to redirect your energies and work on other areas where you can realize your potential.

WILLIAM CLEMENTS, two-term governor of Texas:

The first thing a person needs to be successful, in my judgment, is that they have to be able to live with themselves, and be honest in that evaluation. And if they're not really happy within themselves, then they're not successful.

DR. WINIFRED CONLEY, president and CEO of the National Learning Laboratory:

Success is knowing what you want. My motto is "no judgment." It's not What's the right thing to do, What's the best thing to do, it's What do I want? Then you can create the images and internal dialogues that will help you get it.

RHODA DORSEY, president, Goucher College:

Making a mark. First of all, making a mark on my students in the classroom, and then it has been making a mark on this college. I certainly haven't done it alone, but I have helped. Something constructive, I don't mean a negative mark.

DR. FRED EPSTEIN, chief of pediatric neurosurgery, New York University Medical Center:

My definition of success is twofold. First, if you're doing something that gives you professional satisfaction. If you can look back on your career and say "I'm very pleased with what I did, I really wouldn't have wanted to do anything different," I think that's success. The next standard of success is that you make things a little better in the field that you have chosen. You don't have to make a major difference. If you have expanded your understanding of what you're pursuing, that's success.

DR. FRANK FIELD, CBS-TV meteorologist and health and sciences expert:

You're successful when you go to bed happy with what you've done during the day, and wake up the next morning anxious to get back to what you know is going to be another exciting day. And after thirty-five years, my job is just as invigorating today as it was then. It's fascinating to me to walk in and get into a hot argument with the news director, who is one-third my age. And we really get into it. When I go out and sit with my peers, who are retired, I can't stand it. They're living in a totally different environment. I still work and compete in a world of teenagers and young people. I'm out there doing this every day and it's exhilarating.

ARTHUR FRY, scientist, inventor:

I know some people who are very highly paid who aren't happy with their lives and don't have a lot of satisfaction with their work. I can't say that is a complete success. There are a lot of elements that go into success; having a balance between your personal life and your business life is important. I know a fellow who was a technician in our group. He's now retired. He makes a fraction of what other people that I know make, but he's out getting exercise, he's seeing his kids, he's enjoying himself. He's got more things to do with his life than some people who are in much better shape than he is, physically or financially. His life is full and satisfying so I think this man is a pretty successful person.

JOE GIRARD, "World's Greatest Salesman" (*Guinness Book of World Records*):

What success means to me is being the best in the world. When I first got a job selling cars, I used to watch the number-one guy there like a hawk, the way he walked, the way he moved, the way he dressed, the way he greeted people. And I'd stand near his office and listen to the way he talked to people on the phone. . . . I put his picture on my desk. He was my motivator. I finally beat this guy because I wanted to. . . . The whole secret of life is to know what you want, to write it down, and then commit yourself to accomplish it. Make your dreams come true.

FRANCO HARRIS, business owner, Football Hall-of-Famer:

What really makes me feel that I've achieved something is that I'm able to provide jobs for people. Also that I'm able to take my product to a market that hasn't been developed and develop it to its fullest. I can't say that I have been successful at that yet, because I'm in that process right now. When I look at my football career, it was beyond my wildest dreams to have accomplished what I did accomplish. I did it without knowing that I had such talent and would reach such heights. But now I do believe in myself for doing those things.

DR. IRENE KASSORLA, psychologist amd author:

You are successful when you keep focusing and trying, when you make a friend of failure, and when you fall down, get up and start trying again.

DANIELLE KENNEDY, national speaker and trainer:

Success is a constant process, a journey. It's a balance among six areas: spiritual, mental, physical, financial, familial, and social. Sometimes it's like walking a tightrope, and it definitely has to be enveloped in internal peace. If you've got peace inside and you've got the outside elements coming together, that's about as close as you're going to get to a Garden of Eden in this world.

NORMAN KING, chairman of American Capital Complex, Inc. and author:

My literary agent says happiness and success are a good night's sleep and regularity. I say it's money and laughs. The more money you have, the easier it is to have laughs. If there are no laughs, it's terrible. Luckily, there are laughs without money.

KRESKIN, mentalist:

My definition of success has very little to do with money. It doesn't matter if you have three cars or five cars, or three houses, or one house with twenty-two rooms. How many rooms can you be in at one time? You can only be in one. You begin to realize that success doesn't have to do with the fact that you own this kind of bookcase or this kind of house. If you're really honest with yourself, you've only borrowed all the things you own. They're only temporary. The time's going to come when you don't have them anymore.

Success really means that you have some people in your life with whom you can communicate and with whom you feel a richness—without money—that gives you a sense of fulfillment. There are sports figures you hear of who have an entourage that follows them around. It's tragic. If a person says he has fifty friends, I will show you a very lonely person. Friendship is something that takes years to cultivate. If you can count on one hand a few people that you consider lifelong friends, you have the signs of the fulfillment of life. And then to know that what you're doing has added in some way to someone else's life.

JACK LEHAV, founder and CEO, Remarkable Products:

Success is being happy with what you do. Like what you do. Like the people that you associate with, your friends, your family. Discover the beauty of close relationships. Do the work—and it's work—to find the best part of human beings. Every one of us, even the most rotten person who was nasty to you because he had a rough morning before you came, or some distant relative that you think is a nasty rotten character, try to find the nice side to him. It's a lot easier to deal with that side.

DR. MORTIMER MISHKIN, chief of the neuropsychology laboratory at the National Institute of Mental Health:

I guess there are two measures that I would use. One is if you feel yourself that you have made progress in understanding something that had never been understood before. Two, if your peers think so. You can't depend only upon yourself because you could be fooled. But if your peers think so too, that's success.

JOSEPH MONTGOMERY, president and founder, Cannondale Bicycles:

I think there are two requirements for success. The first is that you find joy in your work. Beyond the typical day-to-day frustrations, there should be a fundamental enjoyment in what you do and the environment in which you do it.

Secondly, whether the influence is large or small, your efforts should have a positive effect on society. I know a stonemason—a real craftsman—who builds beautiful stone walls. He creates something that is pleasing to the eye, that in some small way makes the community a better place. And he finds great pleasure in his work. While he might not fit traditional notions of ''success,'' I'd say he's one of the more successful people I've met.

BRUCE MORROW, international broadcaster and musicologist:

You're successful when you want to wake up in the morning and walk outside and smell the roses and stay out and look around, look to the left and look to the right and come home at night feeling very good about yourself. That's success.

There's also another part—the physical comforts of life. To some people that's not important. To me, it's important. Part of my success and feeling good about myself has also afforded me the opportunity to have the toys that I love in life. I don't measure success by that, but it's very comforting to know that I can do anything I want in the world. That's a part of success.

J. Patrick Mulcahy, CEO, Eveready Battery Company:

From a personal standpoint, success is looking back and having delivered on those things that you said you were going to deliver on. For example, success in the family might be getting your kids to be independent and college educated. . . . So I think it's simply how you view what you've done against the race of life, in a sense.

Paul Pavis, director of entertainment, Harrah's Atlantic City:

I would define success as supporting and developing your family through doing something that fulfills your own needs.

Boone Pickens, chairman and CEO, MESA Inc.:

My daughter is a child of the '60s, making money is embarrassing to her. I said, let me explain this to you. If I were a football coach, I would be judged by my win-loss record. If I don't win, I'll lose my job. Very simple. She agreed that was right. Then I said, if I was a preacher, I have to have a unified church and the congregation would have to feel that I'm making progress in their religion. If I don't, they'll get another preacher. She said that was right. I said, if you're going to run a company, you've got to make money. . . . If I'm not successful, they'll get somebody else to run the company. She seemed to understand that.

DR. FRED PLUM, chairman of neurology amd neuroscience, Cornell Medical Center:

Success means maintaining your good health, both physical and mental. It's also the pleasure of having a good job and being allowed to work hard at it.

DR. PHILIP SANTIAGO, chiropractor, member of the medical staff for the U.S. Olympic teams in 1992's Barcelona games:

What motivates me is the fun of doing things, getting things accomplished. Meeting people—people who are pumped up about what they do. That pumps me up. My definition of success is just liking what you do. It's not necessarily money. Money is nice, I'm not stupid. I want my toys. But that's not my motivation.

ROBERT SHOOK, author:

Success to me is being able to see my three grown children do well and be happy, and giving back to people. . . . When I was a young man, when I was just able to make a living and pay my bills, I said, "Gee, I'm really doing well." But once you have the basics, money becomes less and less important.

DR. EDMUND J. SYBERTZ, JR., Distinguished Research Fellow, Cardiovascular Pharmacology, Schering-Plough:

There are multiple elements to success, and these are not in any particular order: One is excellence in whatever task you're involved in. . . . Another is achievement, actually going out and achieving, completing something. Then there's personal satisfaction in what you're doing, and achievement that is in the context and consistent with an overall framework of moral values. You can't be successful unless you have inner peace in terms of how you've succeeded. For myself, it's important for me to attain achievement with trust, and with appropriate commitment to other people.

STEVE WEINTRAUB, CEO, Industrial Edge USA:

To me, success is being satisfied with what you've been able to achieve and accomplish in your life.

TERRIE WILLIAMS, president of the Terrie Williams Agency:

I think it's important to realize that there must be a balance in one's life. You need to focus a good deal of energy on who you are as a person. This thing called success doesn't mean anything unless you have a good sense of who you are.

DR. ARTHUR WINTER, neurosurgeon and director of the New Jersey Neurological Institute:

Success to me is the comfortable feeling I get about myself when I'm working with other people. . . . When I go out somewhere and run into former patients, there's a certain amount of pleasure in knowing that I do something for others. I've gotten more out of life than I ever thought I would. For instance, I recently designed a catheter that goes into tumors in the brain and stops the tumors from growing. These people who have brain tumors have terrible headaches. So success to me is coming up with ideas and making things a little bit nicer for other people.

Bibliography

Anthony, Robert. *Think and Win.* New York: Berkley Books, 1992.

Covey, Stephen R. *The Seven Habits of Highly Effective People.* New York: Simon & Schuster, 1989.

Danforth, William H. *I Dare You!* St. Louis, Mo.: American Youth Foundation, 1991.

Davis, Wynn, ed. *The Best of Success: A Treasury of Success Ideas.* Lombard, Ill.: Great Quotations Publishing Co., 1988.

Donaldson, Margaret. *Human Minds: An Exploration.* New York: Penguin Press, 1993.

Druckman, Daniel and Robert A. Bjork, eds. *In the Mind's Eye: Enhancing Human Performance.* Washington, D.C.: National Academy Press, 1991.

Edeleman, Gerald M. *Bright Air, Brilliant Fire: On the Matter of the Mind.* New York: HarperCollins, 1992.

Farber, Barry J. *State of the Art Selling: 100 Top Sales Performers Share Their Secrets for Success.* Hawthorne, N.J.: Career Press, 1994.

Ferris, Timothy. *The Mind's Sky: Human Intelligence in a Cosmic Context.* New York: Bantam Books, 1992.

Garfield, Charles. *Peak Performers: The New Heroes of American Business.* New York: Avon Books, 1986.

————. *Second to None.* Homewood, Ill.: Business One Irwin, 1992.

Gschwandter, Gerhard. *Superachievers: Portraits of Success from Personal Selling Power.* Englewood Cliffs, N.J.: Prentice-Hall, 1984.

Hill, Napoleon. *Think and Grow Rich.* New York: Fawcett, 1960.

James, Muriel and John James. *Passion for Life: Psychology and the Human Spirit.* New York: Dutton, 1991.

Kassorla, Irene C. *Go For It! How to Win at Love, Work and Play.* New York: Delacorte Press, 1984.

Kreskin. *Secrets of the Amazing Kreskin.* Buffalo, N.Y.: Prometheus Books, 1991.

Leeds, Dorothy. *Marketing Yourself: The Ultimate Job Seeker's Guide.* New York: HarperCollins, 1991.

Lynch, Jerry. *Living Beyond Limits: The Tao of Self-Empowerment.* Walpole, N.H.: Stillpoint Publishing Co., 1988.

Maguire, Jack. *Care and Feeding of the Brain: A Guide to Your Gray Matter.* New York: Doubleday, 1990.

Peale, Norman Vincent. *The Power of Positive Thinking.* Englewood Cliffs, N.J.: Prentice-Hall, 1952.

Robbins, Anthony. *Awaken the Giant Within.* New York: Summit Books, 1991.

Sher, Barbara and Annie Gottlieb. *Wishcraft: How to Get What You Really Want.* New York: Ballantine Books, 1979.

Winter, Arthur and Ruth Winter. *Build Your Brain Power.* New York: St. Martin's Press, 1986.